"YOU'RE NEXT!"

A MACDUFF BROOKS NOVEL

By

award winning author

M. W. GORDON

"You're Next!"

Published in the United States by Swift Creeks Press
swiftcreekspress@gmail.com
www.swiftcreekspress.com

SWIFT CREEKS PRESS EDITION, JULY 2013

Mill Creek; Paradise Valley; the Madison, the Henry's Fork, the Yellowstone, and the North Platte rivers; and the areas around Livingston, Bozeman, Missoula, Ennis, Emigrant, Island Park, Jackson Hole, Saratoga, St. Augustine, and Gainesville are real places, hopefully described accurately but used fictionally in this novel. This is a work of fiction, and the characters are either the product of the author's imagination or are used fictionally. Any resemblance to actual persons, living or dead, or to actual events or locales is unintentional and coincidental.

Library of Congress Cataloging-in-Publication Data
Gordon, M.W.
"You're Next!"/ M.W. Gordon

ISBN-13 978-0-9848723-3-6
Printed in the United States of America

In memory of my parents who were born more than a century ago when the fish were larger, when there were more of them, and when the streams were less crowded with people seeking them.

And for my grandchildren who when they are my age will find even smaller fish, will find fewer of them, and will find the streams more crowded with people.

ACKNOWLEDGMENTS

This book was written with the encouragement of family, friends, and the many readers of the first two Macduff Brooks novels: *Deadly Drifts* and *Crosses to Bear.*

Particular thanks go to Jeffrey Harrison, Marilyn Henderson, Roy Hunt, Johnnie Irby, and Kevin Schultz.

Very special thanks to my *English for Dummies* teacher, who is also my irreplaceable editor Iris Rose Hart.

In the past two years, three friends have separately given me copies of Chris Santella's *Fifty Places to Fly Fish Before You Die.* I'm not sure what they were trying to tell me. Along with Trout Unlimited's list of *America's 100 Best Trout Streams,* I learned about places I'd like to fish and about exotics such as the Golden Dorado.

Several people have provided quiet places for me to write in Montana, including Joan Watts and Johnnie Hale and Julie and Jason Fleury.

The author certainly knows the ins and outs of fly-fishing and, in addition to bringing the small town to life, Gordon vividly renders the details of Macduff's profession. The story packs in the thrills. . . In a plotline separate from the main murder mystery, Gordon incorporates villains from the first novel, which establishes a sense of continuity and, in effect, leaves open a door for further books in the series. Macduff is an endearing . . . narrator who manages to carry readers through the outlandish plot twists.

A fast-paced, enjoyable . . . thriller that works largely due to its hero's charms.

Kirkus review

PROLOGUE

Elsbeth Brooks was rearranging the antique armoire she used as a storage cabinet next to her small tarnished writing desk that had once served guests in the long vanished hotel on Fort George Island near the mouth of the St. Johns River east of Jacksonville. The main room of her cottage overlooked Pine Island Sound east of Captiva Island, separated from the mainland of Southwest Florida. Her father Macduff's Florida winter home for many years, the cottage once stood on the sandy edge of a salt marsh twenty miles south of St. Augustine. He had transferred the land title to the Nature Conservancy after Elsbeth had the house dismantled, moved two hundred plus miles, and rebuilt at Captiva. Within the house were many nooks and crannies that created fond memories of its decades on the Atlantic side of the peninsula.

She carefully removed the first two manuscripts that her dad had sent her. When she thumbed through the more recent, she found the letter he had written several months previously; he said he was finishing writing more of his life's history, using the word processor Elsbeth had surprised him with at Christmas. She had not received the promised third manuscript; she would ask him about it when they next talked on the phone. She worried about him being so far away, especially when there was ice. He walked better with his knee replacements, but any fall at his age was life-threatening.

Soon after a lunch of grilled snook her neighbor had caught, she walked down her drive to the main road and, to her delight, the mail lady had left a large package that bore her father's name and address. She hurried back to the cottage where she made a cup of English Breakfast tea that she took to the porch with the manuscript. There she snuggled into the cushion of a comfortable swing that had been on their pier in St. Augustine and began to read. As with the first two manuscripts, a letter accompanied the writings.

Ms. Elsbeth Hunt Brooks
14 Seahorse Way
Captiva Island, Florida 33924

Dearest Daughter,

I wanted to send this when I finished it a month ago, but because it involves you, I was worried that you may question my recollections of those years, and which might even affect your acceptance of the two earlier manuscripts.

You have often asked me to move to Florida. I am now ready. The past few months have been hard. I miss Lucinda desperately, and as her death becomes more distant, it has sometimes merged with that of El and made my heartache all the more difficult to bear. You are the end of the line for my family. My only sibling is long deceased and left no children.

Please give this move considerable thought. I do not wish to have you become a care giver. But although I have reached 92, the only sign I show of aging is my doubly broken heart. I will not speak of this again.

Your loving father,
Macduff

Her dad's letters often brought tears to Elsbeth, although this time they were tears of joy and anticipation that he would join her for his final years. She put down the letter, dialed his number, and waited patiently for him to answer so that she could start the process of his move.

"YOU'RE NEXT!"

THE THIRD MANUSCRIPT

1

LUCINDA WAS TRANSFIXED by the stately elegance of mountain pines anchoring the slopes of the Absaroka Range along Mill Creek in Paradise Valley, fifty miles east and south of Bozeman, Montana. Her hands rested on the porch table of the modest log cabin she had come to prefer over her ranch's grand lodge at the side of the same creek a few miles upstream. The third finger of her left hand sported an abstractly twisted setting holding an emerald-cut diamond that acted like a prism projecting rainbow colors flashing against my line of vision as I sat across from her and counted my blessings.

I'm Macduff Brooks, one-time law professor at the University of Florida, College of Law. For twenty years I taught international law as Professor Maxwell W. Hunt. Circumstances that continue to puzzle me resulted in my leaving both academic life and my home in Gainesville, assuming the name I now bear, and substituting teaching fly fishing for law. I'm convinced I did the latter far more competently; I'm an avid fly fisherman, a passable caster, a struggling guide, and I continually contemplate how life might have unfolded if the circumstances of which I speak had not occurred.

I was sipping freshly ground and brewed Antigua, Guatemala coffee made for me by my companion of six years, Lucinda Lang. My elbows rested on the table, my coffee cup held by both hands. I'd been sneaking glances at her over the top of the cup. She had put on a CD of Françoise Hardy singing *Tous Les Garcons Et Les Filles* ("Find me a Boy"), which made me wonder if she was looking.

We were having a breakfast of yogurt, granola, and cut fruit on my cabin porch overlooking Mill Creek. But for Lucinda, who has assumed the role of nutritionist for the two of us, I would be eating a half-dozen pieces of bacon, a couple of eggs fried in the bacon fat, two pieces of sourdough toast—and drinking a Bloody Mary.

Lucinda insists we are engaged. When I ask if that's true, she waves the diamond ring at me and speaks as Falstaff did: "Is not the truth the truth?"

"I guess we're engaged," I uttered when asked was it true, succumbing to surrender if not humiliation, but trying to make my response sound more like a question than a concession.

Two weeks earlier, waiving my .44 magnum, lever-action Henry Big Boy rifle in one hand and the diamond ring on the other, Lucinda had burst into my cabin. Within moments after she shot Park County's Chief Detective Jimbo Shaw, IV, bringing closure to the Shuttle Gals slayings, she had declared without recourse that we *were* engaged. Her close-range shot had hit Shaw's hand that held a pistol pointed at me. At a distance of ten feet, there was little left of Shaw's pistol and even less of his left hand. Shaw was prepared not only to shoot me, but also, if his Glock's magazine would permit, Park County deputies Erin Giffin and Ken Rangley, County Prosecutor Will Collins, and my rescued sheltie, Wuff.

I once offered to put Lucinda's diamond in the wall safe in my bedroom hidden behind a vivid Fechin portrait painting, partly so I wouldn't have to buy a third replacement ring if she lost the current one and partly because I was embarrassed by the twisted setting. She declined, stating the battered ring looked like her.

"It's *my* ring, and now you want it back. Is there someone else?" she asked.

We were both shot by Park Salisbury two years ago while floating in my wooden drift boat *Osprey* on the Snake River in Wyoming. My memory of that day is forever etched where memories are stored, especially because I was going to propose that night over dinner at Moose. A small black velvet box with a diamond ring had been in my possession for two years while I vacillated about whether Lucinda would actually say yes—if I somehow found the courage to ask.

Over the past two years, I don't recall uttering any words that reasonably could be interpreted as a proposal, but apparently I said something *she* assumed to be a proposal, and I guess her wearing the ring expresses her view of the ancient rule that "possession is nine-tenths of the law." After watching her handle my Henry rifle, I don't dare try to take back the ring.

"There is no *one* other," I answered over the top of my coffee cup, without looking her in the eye. "But I can think of a dozen or more other women who vie for my affection."

"All Jackson girls?"

"A few, but also some in Albuquerque, Amsterdam, Andalucía, Athens—I've deleted three from Afghanistan—and that's only the A. I can continue to Zanzibar."

"The truth is that you loved El, and you love Wuff. Do I fit in there somewhere?"

"I'm thinking about it."

"You've already lost one diamond—in the Snake River. Would you like to see this one thrown into Mill Creek?" she asked.

"You mean you want to break our engagement?"

"*No!* I want to break something else, like your neck."

"You're already breaking my spirit by your food choices. Why the yogurt, granola, and fruit? Whatever happened to the American breakfast? Your breakfast menu is not patriotic."

"Consider how healthy you are. Dropped weight you didn't need. Bad cholesterol is down. Your doctor said you're in the best shape in years. A few bullet scars, otherwise. . . ."

"Maybe, but my mental health is in shambles. I don't know whether I'm engaged. I don't know if anyone will drift with me again. Wuff's displaced me with you as her best buddy. And I miss my greasy breakfasts. All this because you invited me to Thanksgiving dinner six years ago."

"Eat your yogurt!"

Lucinda was back. Not a trace of amnesia for weeks. When she has appeared to forget something, it means she *wants* it forgotten. That may be hard to learn to live with. I'm already at a disadvantage. Compared to me, she's smarter, wealthier, cooks better, and is far better looking. The only thing I lead in is the number of bullet wounds from floats gone south.

Five years after we met at Thanksgiving at her lodge, Lucinda and I purportedly began what is called the "engagement period." When she asked a year ago if I was proposing, while we were talking about our future, I apparently answered "probably." I recall I was reading a fly fishing magazine and would have answered "probably" to any question. "Probably" developed to "most likely," again without my full awareness, when she saved my life by shooting Jimbo Shaw, who insisted on being called by his full name: Chief Detective James W. Shaw . . . the Fourth. After the shot, Lucinda held up her diamond-studded finger in front of the relieved but shocked survivors and *announced* our engagement.

The ring she flashed was an emerald-cut diamond in a platinum setting that nearly two years ago had been twisted by a pistol shot. On a fishing float in my drift boat, *Osprey,* on the Snake River in Jackson Hole, a bullet struck a pocket of my fishing jacket and smashed into the black velvet box that held the ring. But it had held a different diamond. I had been shot by a former seriously dissatisfied client, Parkington Salisbury, who also shot Lucinda and Wuff. He was, in turn, put to eternal rest by Lucinda's pistol shots, *maybe* helped by one shot from me, *surely* assisted by several Teton County Sheriff's swat team members' shots, and finished off by being impaled on a sharp branch of a tree lodged in the middle of the river during the spring snowpack runoff.

The shooting parted the diamond from the setting. The diamond fell into the river. The setting was recovered, and I thought it best to replace the diamond in the event I ever actually decided to offer Lucinda the ring. Everyone who knows the two of us repeatedly urged me to propose. Even I realized that all of our friends, as well as Lucinda, would have viewed any proposal with suspicion had I presented the twisted setting alone, missing the diamond.

The new diamond, the original but twisted setting, and the new box usually reside in a safe at Lucinda's lodge. She promised to show me the ring every anniversary of our engagement. I don't know when that is, but I guess I am "probably" engaged.

I'm pretty sure we're not married.

2

ABDUL KHALIQ ISFAHANI was no longer the handsome, swarthy, ramrod-tall Arab he had once been, before I shot him in the head four years ago in an attempted assassination in the highlands of Guatemala. I took the shot from a distance while Isfahani was nearing the finish of his morning run, using my prized Chey-Tac rifle that not only has a scope and suppressor, but also a ballistic computer and rangefinder. Not killing Isfahani has haunted me ever since.

I think of myself not as a professional assassin, but as a responsible citizen responding to a plea from the CIA director of clandestine activities at Langley to kill Isfahani because he was about to lead an attack on two classic buildings in New York City—the Chrysler and Empire State wonders of late 1920s architecture. On a high floor in the Chrysler Building my ladyfriend of two years, Lucinda Lang, had an office where she worked as an investment broker. She earned a huge salary and had bought the prize piece of property along Mill Creek in Paradise Valley, a short way up the mountain road from my log cabin which was built for a confirmed bachelor and is where I live each fly fishing season. It has a small kitchen and a large fly tying table.

Isfahani survived the shooting, but his face was badly disfigured from the .408 caliber bullet. A succession of plastic surgery operations has provided little help in restoring his face so at least passers-by don't stare. While he was pleased to have survived, he carries a hatred for the shooter, whom he believed for three years had been Israel's most dangerous assassin—Mossad agent Ben Roth. Now Isfahani is convinced it was Maxwell W. Hunt, the name bestowed on me at birth and which lasted until eight years ago.

As Maxwell W. Hunt, I was a professor of law at the University of Florida for ten years when El, my much adored wife and best friend, was killed in a tragic accident on the Snake River in Jackson Hole, Wyoming. I taught for another ten years, drinking more and sleeping less, and accepting increasingly invidious assignments for the CIA when traveling abroad giving law lectures.

My last planned lectures as Professor Hunt were never given. They were to be in Guatemala, where I was helping the local CIA mission learn more about a Guatemalan who was a close friend to Isfahani. His name is Juan Pablo Herzog. Almost a decade earlier Isfahani and he were students at UF and enrolled in one of my courses. Lonely from El's death, I became friends with them; they occasionally dined at my home near the law college. Since those university days, Herzog has become the most powerful man in Guatemala. And equally the most ruthless. He rules organized crime by day and with the help of excessive rum dreams of becoming Guatemala's president by night—a Latino version of Dr. Jekyll and Mr. Hyde.

Herzog turned against me when he learned I was undertaking work for the CIA that he believed harmed his aspirational ascent. On my last trip to Guatemala as Hunt—seven years ago—Herzog beat me severely and left me for dead. Isfahani had stood by watching his friend Herzog and not intervening to save the man whom he once believed had been his best mentor. Herzog left the scene with a promise to kill me if he discovered I was indeed linked to the CIA. That discovery has been confirmed.

Saved by persons from the U.S. embassy, I was flown by private jet to D.C. and placed in a form of protection program for compromised agents. The death of Professor Hunt from a massive stroke was announced to protect me from Herzog. My name was changed to Macduff Brooks, and I was relocated to Montana and became a fly fishing guide, following a passion that began in my youth, but which I abandoned when El was killed.

Life over the past seven years has not been what I expected as Macduff Brooks—the summers spent living an idyllic existence fly fishing in the visually stunning Paradise Valley, and the winters spent relaxing and reading on the edge of a salt water marsh south of St. Augustine, Florida.

In my second year of guiding, while floating on the Snake River in Jackson Hole, a client in my wooden drift boat, *Osprey*, was shot from the shore and killed. The following year someone rigged my cabin with explosives in an aborted attempt to kill me, and one year later a shootout occurred on *Osprey* that left me with new scars, Lucinda in a coma from which she emerged with amnesia, and my rescued sheltie Wuff with a limp. Then, three years ago there began a series of murders of women who shuttled my SUV and boat trailer along the Yellowstone River in Paradise Valley. Those killings brought me to the brink of giving up guiding.

I assumed that Herzog and Isfahani were behind all these killings after discovering my new identity and location. I thought that they were merely toying with me by not killing me directly. The truth was they had not discovered my name and location and were not involved with the killings; I simply seem to attract bad people in my new life.

Herzog and Isfahani had not given up and were actually closing in on me. But a killing on the University of Florida campus of a man named Richard Potter—announced to have been a reclusive, retired Professor Maxwell Hunt—seemed to satisfy Herzog that, despite losing his niece and nephew in the search for Hunt, the professor was dead.

That thinking was premature. And it was beginning to trouble Herzog. Isfahani had flown from his home in Khartoum in the Sudan to see his friend, not aware he would be drawn once more into the search for Hunt's successor—who happens to be me.

Isfahani was staying with Herzog in the latter's luxurious penthouse apartment on top of Guatemala City's tallest building. Herzog was drinking Ron Zacapa Centenario, Guatemala's most famous export after coffee. Isfahani was drinking American Southern Comfort, which he never did in Khartoum or anywhere else he was with Muslim friends.

"Juan Pablo, it's been some eight years since Maxwell Hunt was announced to have died of a massive stroke in D.C. when he returned from here. You must be much relieved that he's now dead."

"I should be. But I should have finished him off in Guatemala; I would have if U.S. embassy people—surely CIA—hadn't arrived. We've spent years trying to find him. And we've not been successful. We don't know much about him. Even his name."

"We know it now—Richard Potter," said Isfahani.

"I was elated, Abdul, when I first heard that Richard Potter was really Maxwell Hunt. Strangely, my nephew Martín Paz *thought* he was shooting Maxwell Hunt, and he actually was! . . . I'm much saddened by the loss of Martín and also my niece María-Martina. But knowing Hunt was gone assuaged that loss . . . until recently."

"What do you mean by 'until recently'? When Potter was killed by Martín, we weren't even certain that Professor Hunt hadn't died of a stroke. But we were close to knowing last year that he might have survived. With Potter's death, however, we know the truth—Professor Maxwell Hunt, later hiding as Richard Potter, *is* dead. . . . Did you make any investigation after the killings of Richard Potter and your nephew that suggests otherwise?"

"Briefly. I was troubled that Richard Potter was cremated within hours of his death. No one claimed his ashes. That's not surprising because we know Maxwell Hunt had no heirs. If someone had claimed the ashes, I would want to know more about *that* person.

"I thought there might be DNA from Potter. But about the time he was cremated, his house was cleaned. That might seem odd, but I did learn that he had a maid who cleaned every week and took it upon herself to thoroughly scrub down the house after Potter was killed. She assumed the house would be sold. Potter had left her some money, and she was devoted to him. . . . Even if we had found DNA, what would we have matched it with? Professor Hunt's house and belongings have long been sold. I wonder if any of his DNA was in the house in Golf View when I owned it and where Martín lived as a law student until he was killed.

"Richard Potter should be difficult to trace, Abdul, because he was a made-up person to hide his true identity as Professor Hunt."

"I'm confused about Potter, Juan Pablo. The Gainesville newspaper said that Martín killed a former law professor and then identified and described Professor Hunt's life in Gainesville for eight years living as Richard Potter. Why would Potter have returned to Gainesville where he couldn't safely mix with old friends or go to places where he might be recognized? He had to live very secretly and chose a small nearby town a few miles west of Gainesville. He allegedly was an author of historical fiction set in early Florida. Little more appeared in the papers in the days after the killing, yet Professor Hunt's activities would seem to have been of substantial interest, at least to the university community."

"Abdul, it's been a considerable time since Potter lived in Gainesville. The law school and the community have changed. . . . More troubling is Potter's alleged authorship. I went online and could not find anything written by a Richard Potter. Can you explain that?"

"He might have written using a pen name. Did you search for a series about a family that arrived with the Spanish in St. Augustine in 1565?"

"Yes, but I found nothing," answered Juan Pablo.

"That doesn't make sense," added Isfahani. "We must search further. It could have been made up by the Gainesville newspaper. But why? . . . Juan Pablo, I don't believe Richard Potter was Professor Hunt. I think the university and the CIA were trying to stop our search for Hunt. If Potter *was* Hunt, I can't believe someone wouldn't have recognized him. He went to many sports events on the campus."

"Abdul, perhaps he had some facial surgery to alter his identity."

"But you told me that Martín recognized him at the soccer game because he looked so much like Hunt in the one photograph we have," replied Isfahani.

"Not exactly like Hunt, but enough that Martín identified him using the composite we put together. It's not as though his face was altered very much."

"Juan Pablo, next week I will have evaluations about doing more plastic surgery to my face. I'm flying to Zurich. I'll be back here in two weeks. Then, I can either help you search more for Hunt, or I will have to postpone helping until after surgery."

"Do well, amigo. I need your friendship and advice. Don't worry; *I* will start a further search tomorrow. And talk to you in two weeks."

3

WHILE LUCINDA FLEW to Manhattan the following week to meet with several long-time clients, who welcomed the idea she might return to work full-time, I accepted guiding a few floats on the Madison River west of Bozeman. The Yellowstone River wasn't clear yet of the silt that contributes a rusty opaqueness to the annual snow melt, and in any event the current surged too rapidly to float with clients safely. I missed Lucinda during her absence, but I got to have bacon and eggs and a Bloody Mary for three consecutive mornings.

My initial float of the season was June 21st, the day of the summer solstice—the longest day of the year. The sun would be at its highest and would appear momentarily to stop its northerly journey and reverse its course. Although it's an optical illusion, the closest full moon would look larger than normal. Of all the year's full moons, it travels in its lowest path across the sky. Ancient cites such as Stonehenge are filled with Druid worshippers on the summer solstice. I hope today's client isn't a Druid.

Andy Gonzalez, from Alexandria, Virginia, was booked to float with me alone. Most of my floats are with two people, more often two friends or family. Two clients in the boat lower the cost to each for the float, which is running this year at $475 to $500 for a full day. Add to that a tip and each client pays about $300. But taking one client is easier because he, or increasingly she, sits in front where the guide faces. I prefer taking two when they know each other, especially a parent-child duo or two happy spouses. Two may double the work, but it may triple the enjoyment. I don't like to think about guiding two *unhappy* spouses because it brings back memories of Kath and Park Salisbury, which ultimately ended in her death in Maine by a rifle bullet Park fired, and soon thereafter his death on my drift boat, but not until he wounded Lucinda, Wuff, and me.

Promptly at 8:00 a.m. Andy Gonzalez arrived at the Orvis store—the seventy-five-year-old Tackle Shop in Ennis. It's a quintessential fly fishing town; at the northern entrance stands a larger than life bronze fly fisherman sculpture. A sign to those approaching Ennis reports a population of 840 people and 11,000,000 trout. The town is serious about fly fishing.

I launched my plastic drift boat—my wooden *Osprey* is reserved for repeat clients and friends—at Varney Bridge in a chilly and windy steady drizzle. I might have put in further south at McAtee or even Lyons, but the wind suggested seeking protection of the cottonwoods near Ennis. Plus, there are some side channels past Varney Bridge I like to fish.

We were happy the weather left the river almost exclusively to ourselves. That wouldn't be the case on a normal June weekday, but today started with a heavy rain that discouraged most expectant floaters and drove them into Ennis's restaurants and shops.

Andy was apparently well-off: He showed up in a Cadillac Escalade with the back full of exquisite bamboo rods, several hand-made reels, and the best of miscellaneous gear. The day soon proved he was a cordial and an interesting companion, outgoing and experienced at fly fishing. He looked too young to be retired. He told me he'd worked two decades at the Pentagon.

"Macduff," he asked soon after we were afloat and settled, his tippet ending with a #12 Green Drake, drifting two feet off the bank after a perfect reach cast, "have you ever heard of Corrientes?"

"No. A bar in Mexico City? A beach at Cancun? Or more exotic?

"More exotic. It's in Northeast Argentina. Not Patagonia in the south, where there are also great places to fish for big trout. Corrientes is in the subtropical marshlands of Estero Ibera. The home of the 'tiger of the river.' Shaped like a salmon, jaws of a gator, and color you wouldn't believe. It'll bite through forty-pound weight wire and then try to do the same on your arm or fingers. Kind of a cross between a mean barracuda and a hungry piranha."

"I believe it. It sounds like the Golden Dorado. A fish on every avid fly fisherman's bucket list. I gather they can reach a hundred pounds."

"The ones at Estero Ibera are smaller, but ten to fifteen pounds is pretty good on a fly rod. . . . It's interesting you mention a bucket list. I look pretty good physically, Macduff, but it's deceiving. My doctors have given me at most a year. What I have is too long to pronounce. I don't have a spouse or kids, only a couple of siblings who can't wait for my departure. I'm working on exhausting my assets so there's nothing left when I die; my last couple of hundred dollars will be a generous tip to some guide on my final fishing trip.

"I'm using the time I have left to finish fishing my last dozen places on Trout Unlimited's list of *America's 100 Best*

Trout Streams and about five of Chris Santella's more widespread *Fifty Places to Fly Fish Before You Die*. The Golden Dorado at Estero Ibera is on the *Fifty Places* list; the Madison we're on today is on Trout Unlimited's 100 streams."

"Will you complete the lists in a year?"

"I'll do my best."

I learned during the next couple of hours that completing the fifty places would be the harder challenge. He hasn't done England, Norway, Mongolia, or where there is a tiger fish that is called the Tiger Fish—Zambia's Zambezi River. Montana has twelve of Trout Unlimited's listings and Wyoming six more. That will fill his bucket. He seems determined, even in the face of traveling to Mongolia and Zambia, where there are far more fish than physicians. Neither is a place where one wants to be in need of emergency medical help.

"So, Macduff, tell me about this Madison River."

"The Madison belongs on *everyone's* bucket list. *Both* the Madison and the Yellowstone are listed on Trout Unlimited's 100 best trout waters and different parts of each river are included in the Wyoming and the Montana lists. Both flow northward out of Yellowstone Park.

"The Yellowstone flows almost directly north, exits the park, and meanders through the middle of Paradise Valley in Montana. At Livingston it bends east and heads about 170 miles across Montana and then in South Dakota disappears into the Missouri River. The Madison starts in the park where the Gibbon and the Firehole rivers meet. Usually when that happens, one of the rivers keeps the name, like the Missouri when it adds the Yellowstone's waters or the Columbia when the Snake River joins. But when the Gibbon and the Firehole meet in the park, they're joining to flow on as a newly named river—it's the birthing of the Madison.

"The first ten or so miles of the Madison are in the park as the river heads west until it departs the park, turns north, and enters Montana. That part's called the 'Upper Madison.' Only wade fishing is allowed, mainly because it's in the park. I think you said you're fishing that part in a couple of days."

"Actually tomorrow, with a guide from West Yellowstone who works for Bud Lilly's fly shop."

"You told me you fished with Jack Dennis in Jackson on the Snake, with Mike Lawson of Island Park on the Henry's Fork, and with Dan Bailey's son John in Livingston on the Yellowstone. With Bud Lilly's guide tomorrow, you'll have floated on four great sections of these rivers with guides from some legendary outfitters."

"Should I expect anything today I won't see tomorrow on the Upper Section?"

"Yes. To begin, we're in a drift boat. That's the most popular way to fish the Madison after it leaves Quake Lake—maybe thirty miles upriver south of here—to where it meets the Missouri about the same distance downriver north of here. I personally think the fishing is better around Ennis and diminishes as we near the Missouri. From Quake Lake north to Ennis Lake, the Madison's a pretty consistent stretch of water, often called the 'Fifty-Mile Riffle.'"

"Sounds boring," replied Andy, almost as a question wanting to know why these fifty miles are so popular to fish.

"Catchable rainbows and browns," I answered, "plus easy wading. Good public access. Mountain scenery. No real worries for a new guide rowing first-time clients in a drift boat."

"I take it this isn't your first time guiding on this river?"

"For about seven years I've been towing my boat to this part of the Madison, fifty or more miles from Paradise Valley. The Madison's clear to fish mostly all year, including after the snowpack in the mountains starts to melt. The fishing here is terrific long before the Yellowstone is suitable for a drift boat. But the Madison starts to warm up by July, and we compete with loads of people in inner tubes . . . and most anything that floats."

By lunch time Andy had landed seven trout from twelve to eighteen inches . . . all catch and release and using barbless hooks. . . . I changed his fly only once, from the #12 Green Drake copy of a *drunella grandis* mayfly to a #10 yellow stimulator that imitates nothing known in the world of entomology.

When I'm using a drift boat with a client, I don't fish. I'm not ambidextrous, I don't want to anger or embarrass my client if I out-fish him or her, and I prefer to concentrate on either fishing or rowing—not both at the same time. When I'm rowing, I want to understand the river and it dangers—which are few on this part of the Madison—and watch for other boats, emerging hatches, eagles surveying potential meals, and occasional jet contrails in the clear blue sky that today remind me Lucinda will be flying into Bozeman tomorrow evening where I'll pick her up at 5:37 and again be subjected to her eclectic notions of nutrition.

I should have been ecstatic about the day. Good company and a bunch of fish. Plus the weather improved hour by hour. But I wasn't ecstatic; I was worried that the lure of big-city life would embrace Lucinda as she resumed some of her investment counseling in Manhattan.

Pulling away from the shore after our first stop to wade, which failed to produce even a rise, I noticed over my shoulder the only other drift boat of the day approaching in the far distant south. Our stopping to wade had allowed it to close part of the gap. I didn't give it another thought—the bow of a drift boat and the guide rowing both faced downstream—out of sight of boats approaching from the rear until they ultimately pass. I tend to slow our drift to fish a lot of promising locations, especially along the banks looking for browns.

Forty minutes later I turned to the rear to pick up a fly box I had dropped. I noticed the boat behind us again. Something didn't appear right. The person in the middle seat appeared to be alone. And strangely dressed–wearing a large, heavily padded tan coat one would use in much colder weather.

Being alone isn't unusual; people often fish by themselves in their drift boat to get them to water not otherwise accessible. But they often stop and drop the anchor for a few minutes–it's not easy to fish while rowing. The boat behind us obviously hadn't been stopping. Maybe it was a guide new to this river and checking it out. But it's an easy river to float, unlike parts of the Snake in Wyoming such as the Deadman's Bar to Moose section north of Jackson.

I glanced behind us again. The rower didn't appear to be moving. He, or maybe she, was sitting straight up in the center seat. Then I realized something was very wrong; the oars weren't in the water. And the great coat wasn't fabric; it seemed to be made up of lots of woven twigs, almost like a wicker basket upside down. It looked more like a strait jacket than a fishing jacket. It was a bit too far to notice details, but a head protruded from whatever it was and seemed to be grimacing. Also wearing some kind of head wreath like the Romans were known for.

The boat was truly drifting out of control. It moved downriver with the current, occasionally turning to one side but then straightening out. Once it hit some eddies that spun it around. I guessed the rower was attending to something other than rowing. I've done that many times, trying to find a fly or checking a reel or attending to one of a dozen other distractions from rowing that are nevertheless part of good guiding. But not in this case—the wicker was confining.

"I shouldn't criticize someone else doing a 360 degree turn that I've executed embarrassingly all too often," I thought. Maybe the person did fish and only used the oars when the boat was headed toward the shore or some mid-river hazard such as closing on a "pillow"—that lump of moving water that rises above and often covers the rock its flowing past. The person could be selecting a different fly, trying to run a #6 tippet through the eye of a #20 hook, or repairing a reel. But inside a basket? Well, it takes all kinds. I should mind my own business and attend to my own client.

Twenty minutes later I couldn't help but look back again; the other boat had closed enough to attract my attention. There *was* only one person: a "she," not a "he." She was not selecting or tying on a fly or repairing a reel. She was sitting stiffly upright, *encased* in what on closer view looked like a wicker basket. The wreath on her head was a cluster of small leaves and white berries that reminded me of mistletoe.

As our boats closed further, I saw that the basket was strapped to the guide's seat. The woman's mouth was taped. Terrified eyes stared at me as I rowed hard toward her to help. Ten yards off, I recognized her: Paula Pajioli, the CIA agent located in Bozeman who is my area contact in time of need. Paula wasn't fishing.

When I closed within fifteen feet of the boat, I read horror in her eyes and saw why. Strapped to the front of the strange wicker were several rows of plastic explosives. On top was a timer that was passing the four minutes numbers and ticking down. I used up one of those minutes unable to figure out what I could do to save her. Then another minute reading the large letters of a crudely written sign taped across the top explosives: "YOU'RE NEXT, LUCINDA."

I knew I couldn't disarm the explosives, and I had a client in the front seat who had not seen the other boat until we were within twenty feet. I back rowed as hard as I could to get away from Paula's boat. I couldn't save her, but I might save my client. I screamed at Andy to get down in the boat.

We were no more than fifty feet from Paula when the last second ticked off and she and the boat disintegrated in front of my eyes in a blaze of fire and debris. We were engulfed in smoke and scorching fire. Andy looked unconscious. I could feel the burns on every exposed part of me, fortunately only my hands, lower arms, and face. My eyes hurt most—hot and painful. As the debris settled and the noise of the explosion ended its echoing along the riverbank, I opened my eyes to survey the damage.

"I can't see!" I yelled and collapsed over the oars.

4

A DAY LATER I lay heavily sedated in a room in the Bozman Deaconess Hospital, surrounded by Lucinda, Erin Giffin, Ken Rangley, and various medical staff whose rank apparently was evidenced by the color of their pajama-like scrubs. Ken had been promoted to former Park County Chief Deputy Jimbo Shaw's position, and Erin had moved into Ken's as his chief assistant. Shaw went directly into a county jail cell and is facing a murder trial for killing Pam Snyder, one of the Shuttle Gals.

Erin has become a close friend of Lucinda and a constant irritant to me because she calls me Macduffy, and every time I see her, she whispers in my ear "*Marry her.*" Considering how I must look wrapped in bandages, I'm not exactly one of the most eligible bachelors of Paradise Valley.

Pushing my client Andy Gonzalez onto the floor of my drift boat immediately before the explosion meant he suffered few injuries. I took the full force of the blast and was severely injured, especially some painful, scaring burns. My head remains wrapped in bandages that cover my eyes but leave a breathing slit across my nostrils and mouth. The doctors couldn't assure Lucinda that when the bandages are removed

I'll have full vision . . . if any. The bandages come off in three days.

The sedation had mostly worn off by mid-afternoon yesterday. Lucinda, who managed to book an earlier flight when Erin called her soon after the explosion was reported, quietly entered my room while I was sleeping, hugged Erin, settled into a chair, and remained all night by my bedside. Erin returned at 6 a.m. and chased Lucinda off to get some rest on a couch in a waiting room. Only Erin remained.

"Macduffy, can you hear me? It's Erin?" she whispered when she saw me stirring.

"Your voice is smaller than you are, but I can hear you, *Kendoka*," I answered with a struggle, using a nickname I started because she's an expert in the Japanese martial art of sword fighting known as *kendo*. It hurt to talk; moving my mouth pulled on the burns.

"Andy Gonzalez has gone home; he was in the hospital for a few hours for observation. He says you saved his life."

"*I* put him at risk, Erin," I mumbled. "Had it been any other guide, Andy would not have been hurt. . . . I can't understand how the explosion happened when we neared the boat. No one could have set it for that specific time."

"About all we know," began Erin, "is that there was a huge explosion. A few scraps were found that might be parts of an explosive device. The boat Paula was in was destroyed beyond recognition; your boat was damaged but didn't sink. Apparently when your boat got close to Paula's, a timer started. Maybe a kind of motion detector. Or maybe someone along the river was keeping pace with the boat by car and had a device to start the timer. You were fortunate to row as far away as you did. Andy said you threw your jacket over him—the Simms jacket with the Kevlar lining. It may have saved him from some severe injuries."

"And Paula?"

"No luck. Killed instantly. They're still searching for pieces of her floating along the river. Parts the fish and buzzards haven't gotten. . . . " After Erin regained her composure, she asked, in a rare moment of using my correct name, "Macduff, what on earth was Paula sitting in? You've mumbled something about a wicker man and mistletoe. Mistletoe? Most everything on the boat was either blown into small fragments or incinerated."

Erin's question diverted my attention from my own pain. I answered slowly. "Paula was sitting . . . in a wicker-like jacket or enclosure. . . . On her head . . . were leaves, like a circular crown, . . . maybe held on with a hairpin. I . . . wasn't close enough . . . to tell. . . . There were explosives . . . on the front of the wicker. . . . And the sign."

"Sign! What sign?" Erin asked with surprise.

"A sign . . . on Paula. I'll tell you . . . about it . . . later."

"What this?" asked Lucinda, who couldn't sleep and had walked into the room when I mentioned the sign. "Are you delirious? You have some imagination, Macduff."

Before Erin or Lucinda could follow up, a six and a half-foot male nurse who must have played tight end somewhere entered with a platter of unpleasantries and said, "Enough! He needs rest. He should be dizzy from medications, and he certainly will be when I finish with him. . . . " Turning to Erin, he looked down at her pixie-size figure and said, as though talking to one of Gulliver's Lilliputians, "I think you'd best wait a few days for more questions, until his pain from the burns moderates."

"And," Erin commented, "until his speech makes sense."

The three days waiting for the bandages to be removed served to exchange decreasing physical pain for increasing emotional trauma. I stayed in bed, grumpy. Erin returned to some "emergencies" in Livingston, which proved to be DUIs, domestic scrapes, and the variety of improprieties that occur in every town in America. Lucinda remained with me, at night staying with friends who own and operate Trout Chasers, a comfortable lodging and fly fishing outfitters shop on the Gallatin, a stone's throw north of the deserted Gallatin Gateway Inn.

Lucinda rarely asked me a question during the wait. She guarded the door, keeping the Ennis police and Madison County sheriff's deputies at bay, and sat next to my bed and occasionally read to me anything but news of Paula's murder. The murder was front-page news in Bozeman.

After I fell asleep each evening, Lucinda drove to Trout Chasers and walked the couple of hundred yards from her room down to the Gallatin. At the river's edge, she sat on the porch of a cozy warming house, staring at the deceptively shallow Gallatin River. She had often pulled trout from various parts of the Gallatin, but trout were not on her mind. Her friend Paula Pajioli was dead; I was badly burned and blinded. When the evening chill and exhaustion forced her to move, she used a flashlight to find her way back to her room, and fell sound asleep for an hour or two.

On the day I was certain I would regain my sight, a physician's assistant began unpeeling my bandages. They came off slowly, layer by layer, while perspiration from anxiety flowed off in rivulets. The room was brightly lighted but none of it became apparent to me as each layer was discarded. Everything remained a monochromatic blackness. I didn't want to believe it. With the last bandage off, I waved my hand in front of my eyes. Nothing.

A few minutes later a doctor entered. "Mr. Brooks, my name is Dr. Boonmee Niratpattaramian. I go by Dr. Boon; my last name is a cultural tongue-twister. I'm an ophthalmologist; my specialty is dealing with eye trauma."

"I have only one question for you, doctor. Will I see again?"

"Probably."

"Probably! Anything more specific, like a fifty-fifty chance?"

"'Probably' is the exact word *you* used when I asked you whether you were proposing," Lucinda interjected. "It ended up being a yes. *So will this.* I'm certain."

"Any time schedule, doctor?" I asked, ignoring her raising the proposal debate again.

"My sense is that you've had a significant abrasion which will be slow to heal," said Dr. Boon. Tomorrow morning we'll look inside your eyes more thoroughly and see if there's any internal injury. There are chemicals in explosives; we're hoping you were far enough away not to have chemically induced injury accompanying your burns. Fortunately, you had no apparent blunt force trauma from debris.

"A blunt force could cause a *hyphema*—bleeding of the anterior chamber of the eye. That's the space between the iris and the cornea. You may be out of action for a few months. I know you're a guide and this is the beginning of the season. That's unfortunate. But you're alive. If you hadn't rowed away, you'd be dead. . . . I'm being paged—another putative crisis. Excuse me—I'll be back."

"Lucinda? Are you here?" I said quietly as Dr. Boon quickly departed. I knew the answer. I breathed deeply to inhale her fragrance.

"I'm here, Mac," she said, using "Mac" as she did when she was worried. "We're alone."

"What happened, Lucinda? Have the police arrested anyone? Did anyone see the explosion? Can you tell me. . . . "

"*Mac!* It happened only four days ago," she interrupted. Her voice spoke exhaustion.

"The drift boat that held Paula was totally destroyed; there were enough explosives to topple a building. You were subjected to the concussion from the blast and whatever struck you."

"What do I look like?"

"Mostly burns around your face and neck. There are ointments covering them. You must have been wearing a long-sleeved shirt. No one will notice any damage when you've healed. So the focus is on your eyes. . . . By the way, I talked with my mother in Indiana last night. She wants to come out and help. *And sends her love!*"

"She's never been here. But it's only been in the past year that she hasn't referred to me as 'that wretched person.' Please tell her to come."

"She's a smart lady, Macduff. She had a rough couple of years. You remember her lawyer, Leonard Jackson; he committed suicide last month. He apparently couldn't face trial. My mother owes you. She knows that. It's hard for her to admit it."

"What happened to Lucifer Henry?"

"Mother said the 'former' Doctor Henry disappeared. His license was revoked, and he was indicted. Bail was $50,000. He paid it and probably fled the country. He certainly wasn't happy with you."

"Your voice is soothing," I murmured. "A link to our past. I'll be OK. . . . I wonder where Henry is. And if he holds a grudge strong enough to have come after us by first killing Paula?"

"You have to rest. We'll be going home to your cabin in a few days. Dr. Boon said he'll release you in the middle of the night and have you taken to the cabin in an ambulance. He doesn't want the police waiting for you downstairs. They can come to the cabin when you feel up to it. . . . You shouldn't feel as though you have a problem in the world. Given some time, your eyes will be fine."

"You haven't mentioned the sign on Paula's chest, Lucinda. Do you know about it?"

"I do, but not much, Mac. There was nothing left of Paula or the boat. . . . You told Erin there was a sign on Paula. I overheard you. But I didn't want to ask about it."

I realized I'm the only one who saw the sign.

"I had my client Andy Gonzalez down in the boat before the sign was readable. I don't think he saw anything, including the wicker and leaves. There was a sign on Paula. It said 'YOU'RE NEXT' . . ." I paused, not wanting to say the last word.

"They're after you, too, Mac? That has to mean Herzog and maybe Isfahani."

"No."

"Why 'no'?"

"There was more on the sign after the 'YOU'RE NEXT.'"

"What?"

"It said . . . 'LUCINDA'!" From her speech I sensed a tremble in her lower lip. I heard her get up and move away from my bed.

"That means if it were Herzog and Isfahani, they know more than your identity and location. Why would they come after me, Mac? They want *you*."

"Herzog is ruthless. He likes to taunt his victims. He must believe I was involved with his niece's and nephew's deaths. He may want to kill you before he targets me. To warn me he's coming after me next. He'd have no qualms about killing Paula. The only thing she did wrong was to be part of my life. . . . I think you need to leave Montana. Go stay with a friend who Herzog and Isfahani don't know about. Maybe your friend in Connecticut. The one in Farmington you went to be with the day Isfahani was to pilot his plane into the Chrysler Building."

"Not a chance. I'm not leaving. And I'm calling Dan in D.C. *Right now*."

5

DAN ANSWERED his cell phone immediately. "Lucinda?"

"Where are you, Dan?"

"In Montana. Just landed at Bozeman. About twenty minutes away from you. Paula was one of ours. We don't take killing another agent lightly. Especially the brutality of the way she was killed."

"They nearly killed Macduff as well. Does he count?"

"Yes, but he's different."

"Different? You mean he's not an agent, so he doesn't get special treatment?"

"That's not what I mean. Paula is . . . *was* an agent who wasn't in any protection program. She worked in a specific geographical region and a lot of people knew who she was, where she was, and some knew who she worked for. Macduff is different. He's not widely known . . . we hope. We don't want to jeopardize him. We want to keep Paula and Macduff separate."

"Meaning?"

"As far as we're concerned—for public consumption—Macduff was merely a local guide who tried to rescue someone he didn't know."

"But there are people who know Macduff is dependent on Paula. Erin Giffin, for instance. Plus Ken Rangley. Maybe Wanda Groves, Macduff's attorney."

"We'll talk to them. But there's no reason to think that someone was after Macduff. Period."

"Not true, Dan."

"What do you mean?"

"Mac's told me in the last half-hour that there was a sign on the front of the wicker covering Paula that read 'YOU'RE NEXT.'"

"What does that mean?"

"There was more. After the 'YOU'RE NEXT' was a name: 'LUCINDA.' That's *my* name, Dan."

"Jeeze! . . . I'll be at the hospital in a few minutes. This isn't a good subject to talk about while driving."

Dan arrived, took one look at me dozing and grabbed Lucinda's arm and directed her into the hall.

"He looks crappy," said Dan. "How bad is he?"

"We don't know. The bandages came off this morning. We prayed that he would see when they were removed. But he still can't. . . . I'll be talking to the doctor in another hour."

"Does he sleep much?"

"So, so. Short naps. He should wake any time."

"I'll be staying over. Can you put me up?"

"I'll write directions and give you a key to my ranch guest house. I'm not sure how safe Mac's cabin is. I'm staying here."

"I'm not sure how safe *you* are. It was *your* name that was on the sign. . . . Who might be after you?"

"I haven't thought about it. Macduff only told me about my being targeted a half-hour ago. I thought first about Herzog and Isfahani. But if they know that Macduff was Maxwell Hunt, wouldn't they have gone right after Mac? And not after me?"

"They're sadistic enough to want to play games. But not this kind. It gives you too much time to move on. We could run you both through the protection program and put you somewhere they'd never find you. Spain or the U.K. Maybe Scotland."

"Don't promise 'never,' Dan."

"Figure of speech."

"Poor choice. Do you know where Herzog and Isfahani are?"

"Not exactly. It's part of why I flew here. I want to talk to you and Macduff when he's awake. . . . But we can wait until after Paula's funeral tomorrow . . . Are there any others who might want you both out of the way? Or just you?"

"Dan, it's been only a month since Jimbo Shaw killed Pam Synder. Can't we have a little breathing room?"

"Not you two. I asked if anyone else might be after you."

"I can't think of even one person other than Herzog and Isfahani who would want to kill either of us. *Not one!*"

6

AS LUCINDA CONSIDERED Dan's question, a twenty-year-old, battered, right-hand-drive Jeep Cherokee pulled up to the mailbox at Lucinda's ranch on Mill Creek. Martha Roberts, the postal delivery woman for as many years as the Jeep had weathered, dropped a lone envelope into Lucinda's mailbox and headed up the road to the few remaining cabins before the national forest closed in on both sides.

Lucinda's housekeeper Mavis, who Lucinda shares with me, drove up as the Jeep was leaving. Mavis honked and waved at Martha, got out of her car, and took the letter from the box. It was addressed to Lucinda. Martha didn't know Lucinda was spending most of her time at my cabin. That was best, for had Martha known, she wouldn't have approved. On the other hand, Mavis knew exactly what was going on and strongly approved.

The address on the letter was unusually bold and appeared to have been written pressing a ball-point pen hard against the paper, suggesting, perhaps, anger or stress on the part of the writer: "Lucinda Lang Ellsworth-Kent." Mavis was surprised—she had never seen the name Ellsworth-Kent" used along with "Lucinda Lang." The envelope was from a hotel and postmarked "New Orleans."

A man named Robert Ellsworth-Kent had given twenty dollars to the New Orleans hotel desk clerk to hold the letter for several weeks and mail it on June 21st. Mavis set the letter beside her on the seat. Lucinda had called an hour ago and asked Mavis to leave the gate open and prepare the guest room for someone identified only as "Dan," who would arrive a little after dusk and stay at least the one night.

Lucinda had never mentioned Dan to Mavis. But I had; Mavis knew Dan was from "Back East" and did some work for me. She had no idea that he did far more work for me than he ever imagined would be required when he led me—as Maxwell Hunt—through the protection program that ultimately "created" Macduff Brooks. Mavis had never heard of Maxwell Hunt. Dan's told me he's devoted more time keeping me out of trouble than he's spent on any ten other people in the program.

Mavis opened the guest cabin, made certain it was ready for Dan, and left the letter on the kitchen table. She would drop by the next morning and make sure Dan had found the letter before he headed back to the hospital.

When Dan arrived at the open gate, he drove in and, as Lucinda told him, crossed Mill Creek on her private bridge, turned left, and drove slowly up a slope to where there were several buildings. It was nearly sundown and the late evening light tumbling down the Absaroka Range ahead reflected off Mill Creek. A fiftyish woman was walking down the road and waved to him. He stopped and rolled down his window.

"You must be Mr. Dan?" Mavis asked.

"I am. And you must be Miss Mavis?"

"That I am. But really Mrs., not Miss. I live near here and have a husband and daughter. I work for Miss Lucinda. And I work for Macduff. You passed by his cabin a short way down the road. But you can't see it from Mill Creek Road. Macduff's cabin is on the south side of Mill Creek and entered from another road. His cabin's much smaller than this ranch. But Miss Lucinda spends a lot of time at Macduff's place. I'd wager you know that."

"I do."

"Sometimes I wonder why. You know what she's been through over the past few years. Being shot, her amnesia, and probably a lot more I don't know about."

"You sound as though you disapprove of her being with Mac?"

"No. I don't. But if he's sensible, he'll make an honest woman of her and *marry* her. They are engaged, you know?"

"I do. It seems Macduff is the only one who has some doubts about that."

"Well, I don't. If Miss Lucinda says he proposed and she accepted, that's good enough for me. Macduff will never find anyone like Miss Lucinda. Sometimes I think he treats his dog Wuff better. After all, he adopted Wuff. So he should marry Miss Lucinda."

"I don't disagree one bit. We'll work on him."

"You do that. Miss Lucinda needs her friends to talk some sense into Macduff."

Mavis directed Dan to the guest cabin, told him where the letter was, and left for home, closing the high wrought-iron ranch gate behind her. She hoped Dan would remember the letter because he seemed so preoccupied.

Dan was overwhelmed by the stunning elegance of Lucinda's ranch. Further up the slope beyond the guest cabin was the main house—an architectural jewel. Not large, but merged within the surrounding landscape. Dan settled in, worked on some problems with other protection program people, and turned in at ten, which was midnight back in D.C. He had placed the letter to Lucinda in his briefcase, perplexed with the addition of "Ellsworth-Kent" to Lucinda's name.

When Dan arrived at the Bozeman hospital the following morning, I was awake; a nurse was checking my blood pressure and pulse. Both were normal. I turned my head toward the door, but my eyes weren't focused on Dan. Mostly, they looked down, seeing only darkness.

"Feeling better, Mac?"

"I feel pretty good. A few burns hurt. Lucinda told you about my sight. *It* hasn't changed."

"It will, given time," said Dan, without having any basis for making such a prediction.

"Yeah, I guess so," I replied . . . "Here for Paula's funeral?"

"Partly. Some other agents are here investigating, but the FBI and local police have taken over. We're trying to stay a step ahead of them, although the chief FBI investigator said in no uncertain terms to stay off their turf. We see it differently."

Dan turned to Lucinda, who looked exhausted and in need of some of her own time in bed. She hardly said a word after a mumbled, "Hello." He handed her the letter, giving her a gentle hug. It was obvious there had been tears during the night. Lucinda walked around Mac's bed to a corner by the window and opened the letter without looking at the address. There were three handwritten sheets and when she began to read, her face grimaced, and her hand shook. Finishing, she dropped the letter to the floor and put her hands to cover her eyes. "No," she cried, gasping for breath, "this can't be true," and ran from the room.

Dan picked up the letter and read it to himself:

Lucinda,

It's time I wrote to you. Thanks to you I spent the past fifteen years in prison on this Godforsaken island. I'm sick of hearing screaming sea-gulls. But no longer; my years behind bars ended last summer. I am free to join you.

Much of my prison time was spent reading. You know that when I was a boy, my parents took me for two weeks each June to the Orkney Islands. I liked best reading about the Vikings. As you know, my father was English, but my mother was Danish.

We rented the same small cottage every year at Skara Brae, a village that pre-dates both Stonehenge and the pyramids. My favorite places to visit were the Stone Age tomb at Maes Howe and the Standing Stones of Stenness. I went there often by bus. Especially on June 21st—the summer solstice. On that longest day of the year, the sun is at its maximum power.

Near the Standing Stones was the Barnhouse Settlement, more than a dozen ancient ruins of buildings. The entrance to the largest faces north-west, and on the summer solstice the setting sun shines down the passage-way into the building. It had to be a place of ceremonies. Maybe ones of sacrifice, which I dreamed of seeing, especially when they put the person in a wicker-like basket, with his head sticking out and crowned by a wreath of mistletoe. Not far from the Standing Stones is Watchstone, from which on the shortest day of the year, the December 21st winter solstice, the suns sets into a notch in the nearby Hoy Hills. I yearn to go back. During my time in prison I studied to become a Druid priest, completed the Bardic course, and was ordained a priest in the High Order of Druidry. When you come back to me, we will go to the Orkneys on the next summer and winter solstices.

I want you back. You know I never accepted the divorce; it could have no effect on me in a far distant land without my right of response when you served the papers. You are my wife, and I will see that you return to me.

I know where you live. And I know you are living with someone named Brooks. That makes no difference. You are mine. I want you to think very carefully about this because sometime in the months ahead I will come for you. If your friend Brooks gets in my way, he will suffer. I will have you again.

Robert

"Dan! What happened?" I asked.

"Lucinda's upset over a letter she received. . . . She walked down the hall. I'll get her," he said, handing me the letter in an act of obvious futility.

Lucinda was still trembling when Dan walked her back. She didn't say a word until she entered the room, stood looking out the window, and quietly said, "I was wrong when I said there wasn't a person in the world who would want to kill me other than Herzog and Isfahani. There is another."

7

ROBERT ELLSWORTH-KENT KNEW exactly where he was and what he was going to do. Three months earlier as spring was unveiling, he arrived in New Orleans by bus from New York City, after landing at Kennedy International on an overcrowded and delayed flight from London's Heathrow. He found a modest, downtown New Orleans hotel, paid a month's lodging, and bought a five-year-old rusting, cherry-red Ford 150 pickup. He used cash for the transaction, which was done in the name Robert Smith as stated on a UK passport that had been forged by his prison cellmate who was serving time for—who would guess?—forgery. Ellsworth-Kent paid for the truck using dollars he'd converted at Barclays in London from a pounds sterling account he had long maintained, but little needed, while serving a fifteen-year term at the prison on the Isle of Wight.

On the bus ride south from New York, Ellsworth-Kent had begun to give thought to how he would deal with Lucinda and her companion, whatever his full name was. Once settled in New Orleans, Ellsworth-Kent frequented singles bars and met a different woman each night. Passing off his claims as a consequence of too much gin, none of them were impressed by his calling himself a Druid high priest. But then he met Hannah Markel. She had been in New Orleans for a year, working as a waitress and saving as much as her conditions permitted. They discovered that each was deeply attracted to cults, especially the Druids.

Hannah initially was especially impressed with Ellsworth-Kent's ordainment. "What should I call you," Hannah asked the night they met.

"When we are alone together, like this, call me 'Robert.' But when others are present, I should be addressed as 'High Priest Einar of Kirkwall.' Einar was a Viking Earl of Orkney."

"I have been to Kirkwall!" exclaimed Hannah.

"When? And why did you go there?"

"When I was at Dartmouth College in New Hampshire, I spent a year abroad at the University of Aberdeen. My family's roots rest deeply in the Scottish highlands."

"But how do you know Kirkwall?"

"My roommate was a local girl from the fishing village of Stonehaven near Aberdeen. She convinced me to go with her over the Christmas holiday to the far north of mainland Scotland and then to the Orkney Islands. In Kirkwall we stayed at a hostel and visited the usual sights—St. Magnus Cathedral and the two ruined Earl's and Bishop's palaces. Then my roommate—her name was Heather—suggested we hire a taxi and visit something called the Standing Stones, near Stennes. We visited on December 21st, which was the winter solstice, when the sun stops at its lowest point in its travels, and then starts to come north again. I saw the sun settle in a notch in the hills to the west. It was inspiring."

"I can't believe this," said Robert. "I spent many childhood summers in that area, and each June saw the summer solstice pass, but never the winter solstice at the Stones. It was too cold, and we were back in England. I remember Kirkwall well. I want to go back to the Orkneys."

"So do I," Hannah surmised, "I think I could live there."

"How do a Midwest American girl who went to Dartmouth and a Brit who went to Sandhurst—and both love the Orkneys—meet in, of all places, a bar in New Orleans?" asked Robert.

"Some meetings are planned by the ancients and are meant to occur," opined Hannah.

By the second night they were sleeping together and spending the days hand-in-hand walking the streets of New Orleans.

Four days after they met, Markel joined Ellsworth-Kent to begin a journey west in his truck. Driving north to Baton Rouge, they crossed the tan, opaque Mississippi River. From the high bridge Markel could see the river's legendary powerful currents, and she knew that deep within its waters unseen forces were at work. They stopped for lunch in Lafayette and relished the local Cajun Crawfish Étouffée, but less so a full bottle of a dusky red French wine that was not memorable.

"Hannah, why had you planned to head west?" Robert asked after lunch.

"There is a man living in Montana who I shall kill," she answered, with no show of emotion.

"Kill! Why? You don't want to live out your life in prison," responded Robert, without adding that his statement was founded on his own experience.

"It's difficult for me to discuss. But I'll tell you more as we travel. I promise. The man lives somewhere near Livingston, Montana."

"Did he hurt you?"

"He didn't touch me. I've never met him. But he has hurt me very much."

"What does he do?"

"I don't know. I think he's a fishing guide. But he won't be doing it for long."

Diverting northwest only to confront gridlock in Dallas and Fort Worth, they abandoned the interstates and used obscure county and state roads that took them northwest through rural Texas. Ellsworth-Kent thought Lubbock was a cowboy imitation of England's Blackpool, both ideal sets for a movie about life after a nuclear attack.

The long drive through Texas behind them, they crossed into New Mexico and spent the night at a modest motel on the outskirts of Taiban. Markel thought the name curiously similar to "Taliban," but doubted that terrorism had ever visited the dreary town. She looked at brochures she had picked up at the state welcome center and learned that they were close to Stinking Springs, where the state's most famous historic figure, William Bonney—better known as Billy the Kid—escaped from Sheriff Pat Garrett, who seven months later shot and killed the Kid. Perhaps most New Mexicans would prefer to promote Lew Wallace as New Mexico's most prominent historic figure: general in the Union Army during the Civil War, the future state's territorial governor, and author of *Ben Hur*. But Hannah and Ellsworth-Kent agreed that the Kid was more colorful and more deserving of their admiration.

Shortly before Albuquerque, again avoiding traffic, they turned north on a road called the "Turquoise Trail." The American West has always drawn attention from British visitors. Ellsworth-Kent had read about Taos as the place of both the famous Indian fighter, Kit Carson, and the notable "Taos Eight" artists, who settled there a century ago. Using false names, the couple stayed at a small motel just a few doors away from the Carson home, which had been the target of some American Indian tribes who were not pleased with honoring an "Indian fighter." Ellsworth-Kent wondered why.

"Robert," Hannah tried to explain, "American Indians, or as some people call them to be politically correct, 'Native Americans,' had much reason to distrust the whites' expansion westward, promoting and signing treaty after treaty with promises the U.S. never intended to fulfill. Kit Carson was a scout for the soldiers; the West was full of Indian fighters."

"I guess the difference between Carson and the others was that he shot straighter and lived longer. But he wasn't killing *native* Americans; the Vikings were settled in America earlier."

"Robert, you keep avoiding telling me *where* you're going in the West. To California? Alaska? And *why* you're going. Do you plan to kill someone?" she said, finishing with a smile.

"Yes. . . . I will tell you why."

Ellsworth-Kent told Markel about his short marriage to Lucinda and his intention to see her again. He wasn't clear in stating that he intended to renew their lives together, but Hannah later deduced that from their various conversations.

"Do you love Lucinda?" Hannah asked.

"I thought I did. But no longer. I've met you, and I realize Lucinda will never want me in her life again."

"Do you plan to hurt her?"

"I plan to sacrifice her. And also the man who has stolen her from me. But only after I have sacrificed some of their friends."

Markel and Ellsworth-Kent used their time both while driving and having drinks in their motel rooms to talk about how they would deal with Lucinda and Macduff. Ellsworth-

Kent never mentioned that Lucinda was living with someone. Markel never mentioned that Macduff was living with someone. To Ellsworth-Kent the name Brooks meant the man who was living with the person he would kill; to Markel the name Brooks meant the person she would kill. But the name had not arisen in their conversations.

As the days passed, their mutual hatred for their separate prey became magnified and led them to talk of brutal revenge. Two days after they left Taos for Jackson Hole, they had outlined a plan of retribution, yet unaware that those separate targets lived under the same roof. They would soon learn.

When Markel asked Ellsworth-Kent how the killings should be done, he replied, "The sacrifices must be done in the old way—wicker man and mistletoe!"

8

IT TOOK LUCINDA fifteen minutes after she dropped Ellsworth-Kent's letter before she was ready to tell Dan and me anything more.

"Lucinda, is this letter related to whatever you were going to tell me in March at the St. Augustine cottage?" I asked quietly.

"Yes," she said in a whisper, while moisture controlled her eyes.

That Florida spring day, she had grabbed my elbow while I was working in the yard and walked me down the twenty yards from the slight rise that is the pedestal for my cottage. The rise protects the cottage from the kind of high water that accompanies hurricanes. They don't come often, but when they do, the marshes are flooded, and water reaches my mound. I might lose vehicle access for a few days, but the building will be there. And it won't be flooded.

The bench-swing that Jimmy, the husband of my caretaker Jen, made for me holds only two. Before Lucinda came into my life, the swing seemed large; now it fits two people perfectly if they wish to be close and touching. Somehow on that March morning Lucinda managed to wedge herself against the side of the swing away from me. I felt alone again. Her move hinted at the seriousness of what she wanted to talk about.

"I know when something's troubling you," I said softly.

"More than you can imagine," she responded. After a long pause, she added, "I need some time. I don't think I'm ready to talk about it now."

"Then don't. You'll tell me when the time is best."

I've often thought about that day, but have never asked Lucinda what she intended to say. Apparently now was the time—not because she wanted to talk about Ellsworth-Kent, but because she wanted to share what had come back into her life so abruptly and shockingly.

After what seemed long enough for her to change her mind, I sensed that Lucinda turned from the window of my hospital room and looked at me. I imagined her beautiful green eyes, from which I knew streams of tears cascaded to dampen the front of her blouse.

"I don't know where to start, Macduff. . . . Maybe with the letter." She started to read it but stopped in the middle of the first sentence and said to Dan, "You do it, please."

"Mac, I'm going to read you the letter that came yesterday to Lucinda's ranch. I brought it to her this morning. It's postmarked New Orleans. The writer's address was written in the corner in bold letters: "Robert Ellsworth-Kent, DSO, Spinnaker House, Freshwater, Isle of Wight, England." He must have brought it from England and mailed it in Louisiana.

Dan read the letter once more, this time aloud.

"Lucinda," Dan asked, looking up in search of answers, "What *is* this? A crank? . . . 'You are my wife'?"

"Please read the rest," she whispered.

"*Again?*" I asked when Dan finished. "What did he mean by 'I will have you again'?"

There was a deafening silence throughout the room before Lucinda responded. "Mac, there's one part of my life I've never told you about. . . . I was married for two months to Robert."

"Married? When?"

"Long before I met you. When I was working in London."

"You were married for two months?"

"I should have left him after two weeks. Mac, it's all too awful to talk about. I'm afraid it may mean the end of us."

"You mean you're going back to him?"

A momentary silence suggested she wasn't convinced whether to say "yes" or "no." I was worried the trauma would bring back the amnesia she suffered from for months after the shootings on the Snake River three years ago.

"Hardly," she finally whispered, "Robert Ellsworth-Kent is my Juan Pablo Herzog. A man who surely will kill me when he finds me."

"But he knows where you live in Montana."

"Yes. Arrogate Ranch is guarded 'round the clock because we've lost some cattle. I can add a couple of more men. Or we could go to your cottage in St. Augustine."

"It wouldn't take him long to find out about that. He said he would come for you in the next months."

"He's devious and calculating. He'll take his time. First he'll scare me and then strike suddenly."

"He may have scared you already. He's scared me already. Could he have killed Paula? . . . Why did you marry him? And divorce after two month? Why was he in jail? . . . Did he hurt you?"

"Mac! One question at a time. . . . Let me go back to nearly ten years before you and I met. There is an irony in that. You lost your wife El at about the time Robert lost me. At least I thought he did. And Dan, you should hear this."

Her story began.

"Robert Ellsworth-Kent was a graduate of England's prestigious Sandhurst, the equivalent of our West Point. He was decorated for valor during the 1982 Falklands conflict with Argentina. What I didn't know was he came away from that brief conflict with brain damage, which caused him to have severe depressions.

"I met him at a reunion of veterans of the Falklands conflict. He was utterly charming. Oxbridge accent. Exceptionally handsome in dress uniform with his Distinguished Service Order medal. That's the DSO on his address. I fell for Robert immediately. I didn't know about his hospitalization or his problem with depressions. We married two months later.

"On our honeymoon to France he lapsed into a serious depression. He couldn't sleep, and when he did doze off, he had violent nightmares that he was back on the battlefield in the Falklands. He blamed me for his problems and knocked me down in our hotel room. The problem reoccurred two weeks later. I was sent to the hospital with broken ribs. The marriage was annulled two months after the wedding on grounds of misrepresentation and fraud. Robert was institutionalized after our split. I didn't visit him, but he tried to contact me several times, wanting me to visit. I never answered him.

"I left London and moved to New York. Six months later Robert was released and soon went into such a depressed state that he got into a fight with some Argentine citizens residing in London who were protesting England's presence in the islands Argentina calls the Malvinas. The protesters were demanding a return of the islands to Argentina. More protestors joined each day. It was near where Robert was renting a small flat. He first argued with some of the protestors. But one day, after drinking on top of taking medication, he got into a shouting match with protesters. He was beating three of them pretty badly when the police tackled him. He grabbed a policeman's gun and shot the protester and one policeman before he was finally subdued. . . . An old girlfriend of mine in London sent me newspaper clippings.

"Robert was imprisoned and placed in a psychiatric ward. I lost track and did my best to forget him. I wanted to put him completely out of my life. About a year ago, my London friend sent me news about Robert, but little more than that he'd been released from prison. Now the letter."

"Do you think he's a threat? Or just wants to scare you?"

"He's a threat."

"What about us?" I asked, after a pause.

"I never told you about Robert. You're entitled to change your mind about our engagement."

"Are we engaged?"

"You're damn right we are, regardless of what you remember about the night you proposed."

"Did I really ask you to marry me?"

"In so many words," she answered.

"I think I need a drink."

"I think *I* need a drink. I just happen to have a bottle of Gentleman Jack here in my bag. I bought it for you, Mac. I thought we might celebrate our engagement . . . again."

"Better drink to our *survival*. . . . As to being engaged, I'm more concerned with losing you."

9

FIRST THING the following morning I called Dan at Lucinda's ranch before he left to come to the hospital.

"Got a minute?"

"Sure. How are you this morning?" Dan inquired without mentioning he was, in fact, asking about my sight.

"The same as yesterday morning and each morning since the killing. . . . I'm blind, damn it! Can't you tell?"

"Give it time, Mac. . . . I'm worried about Lucinda."

"What do you think?"

"What I truly think is we should have let you walk seven years ago in D.C., when you threatened to drop out of the program. Now we have to deal also with the Pajioli murder *and* Lucinda's issue with her ex. Maybe you and Lucinda should go back to Spain, using the passports we gave you last year: Mr. and Mrs. Christopher Collins. Stay away for a year or more."

"I'll have enough trouble getting around here in Montana and in Florida, where I'm familiar with things. I'd be useless in Europe. A blind fishing guide who doesn't speak the language. . . . There's been no suggestion that the sign about Lucinda being next was anything but a scare to divert the police. I think Pajioli *was* the target. Not Lucinda."

"I think you're wrong, Mac. That idea might have been credible two days ago, but not when we add Ellsworth-Kent's ambitions to the mix. Lucinda's not free from harm or something much worse."

"Maybe. . . . Update me on Pajioli."

"They haven't found anything helpful. Nothing! No DNA. No prints. No idea who or how many were after her and maybe after you and Lucinda. Remember, Pajioli was *our* agent. My responsibility! Despite the FBI and the Madison County Sheriff's Office in Virginia City, we're looking. . . . Even the Ennis town police are investigating. Nothing! . . . I don't know whether truthfully there aren't any clues or the investigators are screwing up. Now we have to add Ellsworth-Kent. That doesn't help us."

"Maybe he solves it. . . . What about the wicker man and mistletoe?"

"Must be the killer's signature. Tempting us, and doing a good job."

"What's next?"

"I'll call our office in London and have it do a background check on Ellsworth-Kent. I expect the British Army will cooperate. We should be able to find Ellsworth-Kent; his bouts with depression cause him to seek medications. Without antidepressants, he gets into trouble with the police. He can't stay hidden long. And he must have a disability pension and receive a monthly check. I'll let you know when I learn anything. Talk to you later."

Lucinda had been listening on the cell phone's speaker.

"What do *you* think?" I asked her.

"That I'm safe with you." She walked to my bed and sat on the edge. She felt much better than Percoset.

"Then I feel safe with you," I whispered.

"And we'll probably both be shot!"

Dan flew back to D.C. We talked again five days later.

"I have some information, Mac. Robert Ellsworth-Kent got out of jail last spring. His medical records were screwed up and he was never provided psychiatric help. He just walked out into the fresh air of England's Isle of Wight."

"That's where he wrote to Lucinda from?"

"That's right. He didn't stay in England long. He seems to have enough money to survive without taking a job. Probably service related disability payments. . . . He flew to the U.S. Landed at Kennedy in New York. Took a bus to New Orleans—where we lose him. That was three months ago."

"I would have worried more if you'd said Bozeman or St. Augustine. Anything else?"

"A few things too unexplored to mention. Budget cuts have left us shorthanded."

"I hope that doesn't mean we'll be short *lived!*"

"I can't be of any more help than saying 'Be careful.' . . . Sorry."

"No complaints. I'm glad you know about this."

"It's a pleasure to help Lucinda. She's a hell of a lot better looking than you."

10

TWO WEEKS AFTER the day I was brought to the hospital unconscious on a stretcher, I was discharged conscious in a wheelchair. I left it at the hospital door in exchange for a cane. Not a long white pole painted red at the bottom. Just a plain cane with a curved handle. My lack of sight hadn't changed, but I was vain enough not to want that fact advertised.

Sitting in the passenger seat on the way home to my Mill Creek cabin, I was in danger of losing more than my sight—the way Lucinda drove. Being unable to look out as the world flashed by helped. I didn't dare say a word and sulked most of the way home.

"I'm taking you into your cabin," Lucinda said, without showing any emotion as she turned off the engine.

"Dumping me?"

"I'd like to. You weren't good company on the ride home. I know you hurt, but your burns are healing nicely."

"To hell with the burns. I'd like to see."

"It's a gloomy day, drizzling. No sun. I look awful. Not good viewing today, Macduff."

"I'll take you awful or not."

Lucinda stood with her arms crossed, leaning back against the SUV and watching what I'd do. I got out and walked in short steps toward where I vaguely thought the house might be. I was embarrassed enough in front of Lucinda, even without knowing I had an additional audience—two of Dan's men sent to guard the cabin until my sight returned. I hope they don't view their assignment to be permanent.

"You're heading for the garage," Lucinda called, now walking closely behind, the way she drives. "Turn ninety degrees to the right."

I tried, estimating ninety degrees but really trying to walk toward where I heard Wuff bark from inside the house."

Lucinda caught up with me, locked her arm in mine, gave my hand a squeeze and my butt a little pat, and stopped us at the foot of the stairs.

She let me go and asked, "Remember how many steps on your front porch?"

"I should know. I made them. Three steps up to the porch and nine feet of porch to the door."

"Sounds right. Go ahead. I'm next to you."

"I'd like to sit outside for a bit. The drizzle has stopped, and the smells are fresh and woodsy."

"Want a cushion?"

"A glass of Gentleman Jack would be softer. . . . And please let Wuff out."

"Do you think she'll stay inside with us on the porch?"

Settled on a soft cushion with a double Gentleman Jack in my hand, I was savoring a sip when my cell phone rang.

Lucinda answered. "Macduff," she said, muffling the phone. "Sounds like Dan Wilson's secretary. He usually calls himself." She handed me the phone.

"This is Macduff."

"It's Dan," he said. His secretary apparently went on to other work. "How's your progress?"

"Everything is perfect except for my sight. Nothing has changed since we talked a few days ago. Maybe that's not entirely true. Every few hours I think I'm seeing a trace of light, a slight arrival of some images and a welcome change from the intense darkness. But maybe it's my imagination."

"I want to bring you up to date on Herzog and Isfahani."

"Trouble?"

"With them it's always trouble. We're having discussions with the publishing house that threatens to publish Whitman's book. . . . Mac, let me get back to you. A colleague just dropped a report on my desk that updates Herzog's and Isfahani's activities."

"I'll be here. I can't go far. But it's refreshing to be home."

Over the next couple of days I developed a feel for where things were in my cabin, at the cost of some bruises and scrapes. Some were to my body, others to my soul. I was itching to get out and try a little casting. I might learn something that would help when I'm teaching a blind vet to cast in the Project Healing Waters program. There may be no better way to get the feel of a rod and where the line is on a cast than trying it blind.

At breakfast one morning, Lucinda's aura was mesmerizing. Even better than the smell of bacon, which, since she took over as our nutritionist, I haven't experienced in two months except the three mornings while she was in New York.

I must have looked like a burned-out light-bulb. Lucinda is sleeping soundly for the first time since the incident. I'm not. I wake up, but don't dare get up.

"We need some exercise; take me fishing."

"You're kidding."

"No, I'll behave," she promised.

"Fat chance!"

"Try me. You said I had to do more therapy so my amnesia doesn't return. Fishing's therapeutic."

"But with a blind man? . . . Where do you want to fish? Run the rapids through Yankee Jim Canyon?"

"Are you trying to get rid of me?" she asked.

"I've thought about it."

"Think about taking me fishing . . . while I think about what to cook for dinner this evening."

"Should I ask?"

"Sure. How about Bay Scallops with broccoli and almonds?"

"I like my almonds crushed and fermented, in a glass of Amaretto."

"But you'll be having a glass of Gentleman Jack; you don't need Amaretto."

"And I certainly don't need broccoli. President Bush's most famous words as president were 'I don't have to follow Mother's dictum to eat that damn broccoli anymore.'"

"President Bush is not your nutritionist; I am."

"Broccoli gave President Bush an irregular heartbeat."

"That was a false diagnosis. And you're already irregular—all over."

"Thanks. What about the Bay Scallops? We don't have any."

"I can buy them."

"On eBay?"

"I wish the explosion had taken out your voice box instead of your sight," she suggested. "Let's go fishing. I'll take a camera. It's time I did some more photography. The menu can wait."

We sat on the porch watching the moon rise over the Absaroka Range and planning our day fishing.

"Macduff, we never made it to the top of Passage Falls last year. Remember? A couple of days before we started east? Are you up to that hike?"

"I hope it's a round-trip hike. I'll go if you let me walk behind you with my hand on your shoulder. That way if I fall I'll land on something soft and warm."

"If you fall, I'll leave you for the bears and big cats. . . . You used to hike there often before we met?" she said as a question.

"When I wanted to hike alone, that trail was my address."

"Why?"

"The trail first follows Passage Creek. You know that part. And you know I like moving water—creeks, streams, pools filled with eddies at the bottom of waterfalls, rivers that aren't wide, tidal flats, and the coastal ocean. I have no interest in ponds and lakes. I like being in a forest near moving water. It's always changing. As a Greek philosopher centuries ago observed, 'You cannot step into the same river twice, for other waters are ever flowing on.' Good observation. . . . I also like the absence of man-made noise. There's music to the forest, and the solo is the sound of flowing water."

"You're a private person."

"Yes," I answered quietly and carefully. "More so after El's death. And compounded by the uncertainties of the protection program."

Lucinda packed some food in a small backpack after breakfast, while I fumbled around to find her seven-foot bamboo rod and a fly box. The nine-footer she uses floating the Yellowstone and other rivers isn't needed on Mill Creek and its tributaries and would get in the way fishing close to the bank among fallen trees and dense brush.

Not a word was exchanged while she drove uphill along well-graded Mill Creek Road to the trailhead for Passage Creek Falls. Wuff wasn't welcome—the trails are off limits to pets. They're reserved for the permanent residents—big cats, larger bears, and increasingly an occasional roving wolf pack.

The aroma of conifers eclipsed the morning air. I could enjoy that, but not the wildflowers that were beginning to show their seasonally ostentatious colors, exhumed from the concealment of a monochromatic winter.

Downstream from the falls, the creek conceals colonies of small native cutthroats. We stopped at a pool a few steps from the trail, crafted by arbitrary circumstances of nature—a lightning-fractured pine fallen across the creek had formed a promising pool for the new season.

On the bamboo rod I'd made for Lucinda for a Christmas that seemed long ago, the line guides wrapped in bold raspberry silk thread—a color she often chooses for sweaters and scarfs—I tied on a diminutive #18 Yellow Humpy dry fly that she handed me, setting the reel drag so she wouldn't snap the lean 8x tippet. Tying a clinch knot that I had done hundreds of times was easy; I'd often said I could do so blindly. I showed Lucinda how to dapple the fly, holding the rod tip out over the pool and twitching the tip, urging a little line out to drop the fly gently onto the surface of a calm, upstream corner of the pool. Often I can't see the fish. But sometimes I can see a shadow on the bottom.

"I'll do it, Macduff. Shake out a bit of line, drop the fly lightly onto the surface, and give it a little twitch. . . . I got one! I never saw the fish take the fly from the surface!"

"It must have been hanging deep," I ventured. "If there's a hatch and bugs on the surface, the trout is likely to be moving along a little under the surface and sucking bugs in. This fish came up from the bottom."

"My fish is headed downstream."

"Downstream can't be far. Don't let it go into any brush that's in the water."

"Now it's coming back instead of heading for the swifter water below the pool. I need the net!"

"I was carrying it clipped to the back collar of my vest. I pulled it free and handed it to her. It's all yours."

"I can't hold the net and the fish!"

"You have two hands. Keep holding the rod with your right hand, without any slack in the line. Rod tip up and slowly bring the tip back toward you and the fish will follow."

"OK. I've got it in the net. Now what?"

"Set your rod down on the bank. Reach in the net and slip the hook out. It's barbless and will come out easily. Then enjoy the beauty of a fish you caught and landed with no help."

"I'm taking a picture, or you'll soon deny I caught it."

I imagined that the cutthroat—quivering in her hands—showed her more color than was fair to lesser species. She was so entranced with its beauty that I had to tell her it was time to return the fish to its own world.

"Slip it into the pool facing upstream and letting water flow through its gills. It will swim right out of your hand when it's ready."

"It's gone, Macduff. . . . That was fun."

"Try for another."

She did and quickly caught two more before the fishing went completely flat.

"Where have all the fish gone?"

"You've fished out the pool. It's attributable to your having an exceptional guide."

"And a blind one at that! Let's go to another pool and fish that out, too," she said. I knew that famous grin was there, but I couldn't fully enjoy it.

An hour later, at the very top of the falls where the water commenced its hundred-foot drop to a frothing pool below, we rested together on a huge boulder that each spring was moving in small increments toward the falls. The rock was certain to ultimately fall off the edge, settle in the creek, and form new trout habitat. Lucinda sat a little higher, her head down on my shoulder. She made the forest bouquet even better.

"Why do you fish?" Lucinda asked in a whisper so as not to disturb the forest sounds. "I know it's important to you, but you're not consumed by it. We've landed a half-dozen small trout, and even without your sight you seem as happy as I've ever seen you. We could be floating on the Yellowstone—I can row us on an easy stretch—a river that draws people from around the world. Or we could go to Labrador or Patagonia or New Zealand and catch the monsters that embellish fly fishing magazine covers. But you chose to bring me *here*?"

"I did."

"Should I link that to your being such a private person?"

"Yes."

"Would you rather be here alone?"

"Yes," I answered. She pulled away a little; I could feel her stiffen. "*We are* alone," I murmured. "Being alone doesn't mean being by myself. I'm less fulfilled being here alone than with someone who shares my feelings about this place. Maybe that's the teacher part of me. I loved being in the law school classroom with gifted young people. As a guide, I try to teach more than casting and catching fish. Some history, some geology and geography, some biology and botany. Anything that comes with 'being here.' Maybe you were asking 'Would you rather be here *without me*?'. . . Not for a moment. . . . Today's the best time I've ever been here. I like being alone . . . *with you*."

She tucked her head tighter against my neck. "Would *you* like to fish?" she whispered. "You can use my rod. I'll help. I see fish rising in the next part of the creek above the falls."

"Let's leave it for another day."

Lunch was fresh fruit, assorted roasted vegetables, and a Montecino Tuscan red wine. "What's for desert?" I asked.

"Nothing! Did you expect baked Alaska?"

"No. Maybe tiramisu to go with the Italian wine."

We leaned back against a pine that had for the season halted the boulder's progression to the creek. I drifted and dozed, waking to find my head in her lap. I felt her face and hair. Her hair was moving slightly in the soft mountain air, the eddies of her burnished strands ignited by the high noon sun. For a moment I thought I could see light.

The back of Lucinda's hand was on my cheek. She leaned over and brought her lips to brush mine. Hardly touching, but enough to feel different warmth and a pulse that wasn't mine. We were both slow to come to days like this.

"Do that again—please," I said.

"It comes at a price," she answered.

"Can I afford it?"

"If you apply for some federal stimulation," she said.

"I'm already stimulated," I responded.

"The federal plan doesn't cover that."

11

WHILE I REMAINED at my cabin over the next few days, with no sign of my vision returning, twelve-hundred miles south, in an exquisite convent in Antigua, Guatemala, restored as the luxurious Hotel Casa Santo Domingo, Juan Pablo Herzog and Abdul Khaliq Isfahani were in the outside part of the main bar, talking over drinks.

"Abdul, so your surgery in Zurich is scheduled for next month?"

"Yes, the doctors told me last week that they can make changes that will result in fewer people staring at me. It will restore my confidence. And my determination. . . . Your Guatemalan rum is delicious, Juan Pablo."

"What irony!" remarked Herzog. "Here I am in what was once an active Catholic place of prayer having a glass of rum with a Muslim. It's a strange and changing world."

"I want to change it more. I want the head of Maxwell Hunt. After what he did to my head."

"So you now believe me when I tell you Maxwell Hunt posed as the Israeli Mossad agent, Ben Roth, and shot you here in Guatemala."

"Yes, I now believe you."

"You want his head. Like Perseus with the head of Medusa? Cellini at his best? What would you do with Hunt's head?"

"Adopt its Christian symbolism. Brought to life again with John the Baptist. I'd be a modern-day Knights Templar. Hunt's head would grace my wall. I would sit in front of it every evening and applaud my revenge for his causing me to look this way. And I would. . . ."

"You can't be a Knights Templar. You're a Muslim. Muslims killed Knights Templars."

"I'll pretend. . . ."

Herzog's cell phone rang, interrupting Isfahani's psychotic ranting. Herzog put the phone to his ear.

"Yes."

"Am I speaking to Señor Herzog?"

"I am Señor Herzog."

"My name is Allan Whitman. I must see you. It's about Professor Maxwell Hunt."

"How do you know Hunt?"

"I was an agent for the CIA when he was brought back from Guatemala and placed in a protection program. I was part of the group that met to decide on a new name and new location for Hunt."

"So it's . . . it's true," Herzog stuttered, looking toward Isfahani and turning on the speaker so he could hear. Herzog whispered, "Abdul, we finally have a confirmation that Hunt did not die of a stroke. And that he's in a protection program." Again speaking into the phone, Herzog said, "I am elated you called, Mr. Whitman."

"Hunt's death was announced by us as a cover-up. He was very much alive, though beaten badly. He received emergency treatment from our doctor in Guatemala City."

"But, Mr. Whitman, there was another announcement last year that he was killed in Gainesville—shot by my nephew Martín Paz, who was then killed by an agent of the CIA."

"That was another CIA diversion from the truth."

"How do you know this? Were you involved with the killing of my nephew?"

"The CIA wasn't involved in that killing. I still have friends at Langley. They truthfully don't know who did the shooting. I suspect that Hunt believes it was CIA."

"Why do you use the name Hunt, if your group gave him a new name and location? What is the name he goes by now? And where does he live?"

"His name and whereabouts have value to me. I know both. But there is a price for them—if you are interested."

"Tell me more."

"Where can we meet?"

"Here in Guatemala would be best. I will have you flown here in my private plane. Can you come next week? Where are you now?"

"I'm in D.C. I can come anytime next week. Call me with the arrangements."

Whitman hung up and looked at the manuscript he had written about his time in the CIA, including placing Florida law professor Maxwell Hunt in the protection program with a new name and location. The book would disclose both. But the CIA had insisted it approve the manuscript. Whitman had signed the usual agency statement when he joined the CIA, agreeing not to publish anything about his work without having the manuscript reviewed and approved. He had tried unsuccessfully to obtain approval and now considered publication in England an option. A decision that would make him hide abroad for the rest of his life. A life the CIA thinks should best be shortened if Whitman followed through with publication.

He had decided he would be better off selling the name and location of Maxwell Hunt to Herzog or Isfahani instead of publishing the book. He thought $4 million a fair amount. Herzog was a very rich man. After all, he had offered that amount to the law college at Florida to fund a chair honoring Hunt. Herzog offered the donation only to obtain the information he so coveted. It shouldn't matter if he paid the $4 million to Whitman in exchange for even more accurate information. And Herzog would not have to honor a man he hated.

Whitman had read and secretly photographed the Hunt/Brooks file just before he left the agency. The file included detailed information about Brooks. And about his lady friend, Lucinda Lang.

Pouring a Negra Modelo beer, Whitman sat back on the sofa in his sparsely furnished apartment and smiled. In the background was the music from Puccini's *Tosca,* another tale of intrigue and deception. The renowned tenor Luciano Pavarotti was playing the role of Cavaradossi and singing *E lucevan le stele* before he jumped to his death. He thought that Macduff Brooks would much prefer to jump to his death than face Herzog and Isfahani. But Whitman didn't understand that by dealing with Herzog and Isfahani *he* might be the one jumping.

12

AT SEVEN A.M. the following day, while I watched Lucinda preparing something in the kitchen that looked unpleasantly healthy, Dan called.

"Macduff, sorry to interrupt, but I talked with people at our mission in Guatemala last evening."

"Good or bad news? Is Herzog dead?"

"No, and it's not anything we can't handle. But it may mean a sanction."

"So Herzog will be dead soon?"

"Not Herzog. One of our former agents."

"Jeeze! Dan. What caused this?" Lucinda tapped "speaker" on my phone to listen.

"You remember a few months ago I told you about Allan Whitman, an agent with us here in D.C. who retired under pressure and then wrote a book about his experiences at the CIA?"

"Don't remind me. But I thought his tentative publisher had withdrawn and the matter was over."

"That's still our belief. At least with regard to publishing in the U.S. We're more worried about his attempt to publish it in England."

"Will you kill him if he goes ahead? That's water over the dam for me. The book gets published. Whitman dies, and the public, including Herzog and Isfahani, get to read the book. After that, I won't be hard to find."

"*Listen* to me, Mac. We've kept a trace on Whitman. He went to Guatemala five days ago by private plane registered in the name of a Panamanian corporation we know is indirectly owned by Herzog through a Cayman Islands entity. Our agents in Guatemala followed Whitman when he landed. A car met him at the Guatemala City airport and took him directly to Antigua where he met with Herzog and Isfahani for three hours. He must be discussing a deal with them. We don't know whether he contacted Herzog first or Herzog contacted him."

"Do you think Whitman would sell my name and location?"

"If he can get away with it and extort a lot of money, absolutely. We don't know specifically what they talked about, but we have a good idea."

"Why else would they get together except for Herzog's attempt to find me?"

"Whitman was unhappy with us when we threatened court action if he went ahead with publishing his book. I told him our objection was only to the chapter describing the protection program, and especially where it named you and said you lived near Emigrant in Paradise Valley. Whitman said that he stood to be paid an advance of a half-million and making that kind of disclosure was essential to arouse readers' interest. If he's lost the U.S. contract, there's still Europe.

"I suspect he believes the information about you has value to Herzog and Isfahani. Herzog has plenty of money. But he'll drive a hard bargain with Whitman and might play dirty."

"Meaning?"

“Hold Whitman hostage and ‘persuade’ him to disclose your identity without any payment. I know Whitman; he’s squeamish. He’ll talk.”

“Is Whitman still in Guatemala?”

“We don’t know. We do know they parted after their meeting, and Whitman went back to Guatemala City. We lost track of him; he slipped out of his hotel late last night.”

“Any flights to the U.S. last night?”

“No. We’re watching both commercial and general aviation departures. It’s about sunrise in Guatemala, and there’s no sign of pre-flight activity around Herzog’s plane. Whitman may be flying later. Possibly a private plane from another city. Or he might have been ‘visited’ at his hotel room by Herzog and Isfahani last night, the same way you were nearly a decade ago. If that’s the case, we don’t have any idea whether Whitman talked. . . .

“One other matter. Our London mission heard that a major British publisher is considering an agreement with Whitman to publish the book, with almost a million-pound advance. That’s about a million-and-a-half in dollars. We’re meeting with the publisher in London tomorrow to ‘discuss’ the matter. ‘Discuss’ includes threatening to file a complaint in the English High Court requesting an injunction.”

“I thought ‘discuss’ also might include harsher measures.”

“Really? Is that what you think about us?”

When Dan hung up, Lucinda turned and asked, “What’s Whitman like?”

“I’ve seen him only once, on my first day with the CIA in D.C. when Dan led me through the process of getting a new name and location. Whitman was introduced as Allan Jones, if my memory is functioning. He’s short and overweight. Stomach bulging and hairline receding. Wore the usual dark suit;

white shirt; red, white, and blue tie; and a little American flag pin. Light complexion. I remember he said he was from Oklahoma. When I commented that I'd be willing to re-locate anywhere except the Great Plains states, he took offense. . . . But he was mostly involved with discussing a new name for me, not a new location. He was present the whole time."

"He must be an afflicted man. But he should at the very least understand the danger he's putting you in. I don't think he knows about Lucinda."

"Yeah, I guess," I replied, my attention distracted by the thought of what Herzog might do to Lucinda.

"Macduff, you look troubled," commented Lucinda. "You've been rubbing your eyes. Do they hurt?"

"No. It's that Dan's not encouraging. Whitman's in Guatemala with Herzog and Isfahani. No good will come from that. . . . I'd like to think I'm about to do some guiding on the Yellowstone. It's that time of the year; the river's slowed down and regained its clarity. I've talked to the guys at Angler's West in Emigrant. They have as much work for me as I want to take on."

"Your eyes could clear any moment, and you'll be ready to guide," she said.

"I'm more concerned with *you*," I replied. "We have no idea who was behind the bombing on the Madison. Especially whether Ellsworth-Kent's responsible, and if he isn't, how he plans to get you back. Add to that Herzog and Isfahani closing in on who I am and where I live, and I wonder if we shouldn't give up the idea of my guiding this season and drive to Florida."

"Would we be any safer there?" she asked. "Does Whitman know about your Florida cottage? If—God forbid—Herzog and Isfahani learned your name and location, couldn't they find out about you having a place in Florida by asking around Paradise Valley?"

"Probably. Remember that Whitman knows where I live."

"Let's stay put," Lucinda suggested. "We're guarded by some of Dan's people. You have an arsenal here in the cabin."

"I'd feel better if I had an assault weapon. The Chey-Tac isn't helpful at close range. My lever action rifles are more for display or hunting game. That leaves a few pistols. Not much defense against a psychotic attacker. . . . And I'm not exactly in shape to do any shooting."

"I am. My Glock's in my purse. . . . If you'd feel safer, we could stay at my ranch."

"I don't think so. Ellsworth-Kent's after you. He must know about your ranch."

"But Herzog and Isfahani, with Whitman's help, want *you*. They're more determined than Robert."

"You're usually right. Let's talk to Dan about leaving the two men here at my cabin as though they're guarding us, while we stay at your ranch."

"We can use one of my small cabins I use to house guests and help. One's available, and it's in between others currently occupied by my ranch foreman and his helper. We can move any time. . . . One thing I must ask. You're vulnerable because of your sight. Where would *you* feel safer?"

"I can't answer that because I don't know who killed Paula Pajioli, or why. I don't know Ellsworth-Kent, especially why he expects you to go back with him. *If* he really does. . . . I don't know what Whitman's up to and how much he's told or plans to tell Herzog and Isfahani. . . . But your suggestion makes sense. Let move into your guest cabin—today."

By evening my cabin was occupied by two of Dan's men. Lucinda and I were where we really didn't want to be, but her guest cabin was best for the moment.

Generally, the first one up in the morning grinds the beans as part of our coffee-making ritual. Life with Lucinda hasn't altered my drinking coffee, but she has altered *wha*t I drink. Only beans organically grown. Preferably shade-grown at a high altitude. According to her, the higher the bean is grown, the milder it should be. She insists the best coffee is from Antigua, Guatemala. Hopefully, it's not grown on a *finca* owned by Juan Pablo Herzog. With over nine hundred coffee producers in Antigua, there's little chance of drinking his coffee. But I know he's been buying out the small producers, offering little money and gratuitously adding a lot of coercion. The day may come when the Antigua Coffee Growers Association is an "association" of one.

The bean grinding process isn't work for us, but a welcome release of the first aromas of the new day. A Tuscan coffee shop owner told me years ago that I should always make my coffee from beans ground immediately before brewing. It's not that Lucinda and I are bourgeoisie baristas, but we do prefer to start the morning with the best, before the day collapses around us.

"This cabin's a little sparse, Macduff. Are you OK with it?"

"I don't know. I can't see it. You made coffee; the bed's comfortable. Wuff's not whining to go out to pee. Neither are you."

"I woke up about three this morning and sat in the chair by the window that looks out across the deck and beyond to the mountain. I had an idea, and I want your yes or no."

"I'd like to know what it is before I answer."

"I should go back to Robert. . . ."

"Are you serious? You *want* to go back? And leave me and Wuff?"

"No, but it would be fairer to you. . . ." For several minutes not a word was spoken between us. Then Lucinda's mood changed and she said, Mac, what I *really* think is that I should hire you to sanction him. First, shoot Ellsworth-Kent. Second, do the same to Whitman. And finally, take out Herzog and Isfahani."

"That sounds like a vigilante duo. A modern Bonnie and Clyde. Brooks and Lang sounds good. . . . More like a country music duo. Couldn't we just capture them?" I asked, and then added, "I didn't do too well shooting Isfahani."

"And if we capture them, what do we do with them? They're all a danger as long as they're alive."

"We'll make them disappear."

"How, Mr. Houdini?"

"Don't ask. But Dan will help. . . . Maybe you'd like a shot at Isfahani. He was trying to crash his plane into *your* building."

"Yes. Give me just one shot."

"I think of my errant shot that only disfigured him. We know enough about him to do a sanction. He's surely involved in some activities that sooner or later are going to hurt, if not kill, a lot of people. He's mad about the aborted attack on Manhattan, and every time he looks in the mirror, he must be furious at my playing the role of Ben Roth, assuming he belives by now the shooter was Maxwell Hunt and not Ben Roth. The Israelis have done an effective job denying Roth was involved.

"But Isfahani's always on the move. According to Dan, one day he's in Guatemala with Herzog. The next he turns up in Khartoum meeting with al-Qaeda cells. Then he's at UF for the dedication. Dan said he's flown to Zurich. Likely depositing some ill-gotten funds. He's hard to pin down."

"He could be having more surgery in Switzerland. . . . Do *you* think he's certain you're not dead?" she asked.

"No question. I avoided that possibility for several years. The meeting with Whitman in Guatemala must have confirmed I'm alive. What else would Whitman have talked about other than telling Herzog and Isfahani facts Whitman knows about me. That's a lot, but it doesn't have to be much more than my name and location here in Montana. There's no denying I agreed to be Macduff Brooks and relocate here."

"Montana's a big state."

"Yes, but he'll also know I was going to become a fishing guide. Most of the fly fishing is in this southwestern part of the state. If he has my name, how many fly fishing outfitter stores would he have to walk into before he meets someone I know who gives him my cabin's Mill Creek location? I haven't exactly kept a low profile. Remember that I'm part of the Simms Pro Guide bunch, and we gather every April in Bozeman for their *Ice Out* program. Guides are there from every corner of Montana, as well as in a lot of other states."

"If we did take out Isfahani, Mac, how would Juan Pablo react?"

"With vengeance. They're best friends. Herzog would assume we'll go after him next and would try to get to us first."

"Is it a risk we want to take?"

"Probably," I replied.

"Is that 'probably no' or 'probably OK'—like your proposal two years ago?"

"I've caught some of your amnesia. It includes the day I 'probably' proposed."

"I'll decide that, Macduff. . . . Should we take on an easier target first, Ellsworth-Kent or Whitman?"

"If we could get to Whitman before he tells Herzog and Isfahani about me, I think 'yes' and 'Whitman' are the answers."

"Then let's do it. Go get your Chey-Tac and start practicing."

"After I finish my coffee."

13

ALLAN WHITMAN had not heard from Herzog and became increasingly furious over his unwillingness to pay Whitman's extortionate demand of $4 million in exchange for the new name and location of Professor Maxwell Hunt. But Whitman had little doubt he was fortunate to have made it back safely to D.C. by traveling by bus to Belize where he flew to Washington. Herzog had a short fuse, and Isfahani never intervened when Herzog took out his frustrations on others. Isfahani had heard of Herzog's using a chainsaw on one adversary years ago on a tennis court in Guatemala.

Whitman's judgment was clouded by his inability to come to grips with his rejection for promotion at the CIA. His manuscript exposing agency secrets evidenced his anger. While there, he never received promisingly high annual evaluations, but he was certain he was qualified and deserving of the coveted position he was denied. Whitman sought solace in drink, and on an evening brimming with mist, he left his apartment and walked to the nearby bar—a seedy, smelly and, despite the ban, smoke-filled place—called simply "Joe's."

He sat slumped at the far end of the whiskey-bleached bar and ordered the first of what soon became several single malts, not speaking a word except to the bartender, and then only to mumble "refill."

At first Whitman didn't notice the stranger who without a word sat down on the barstool next to him. But it wasn't long before the scotch, mixed with Whitman's desire for vengeance, caused him to tilt his head partly toward the man and murmur, "I hope your day was better than mine."

"Depends on how bad yours was."

"Let me tell you about it. . . ."

And Whitman did, without a break. For the next half-hour he poured out his emotions and hatred for both the CIA and the publishers who had rejected his book proposal.

"That's a sad tale," said the man. "The next drink's on me."

And the next and two more after that. Whitman was tumbling off the edge of coherency.

"All I did was write the damn truth!" he spurted, single malt dribbling down his chin.

"But you told me that when you were hired you promised not to write anything about your work without approval," the stranger said. "If you do, won't you lose your pension?"

The thought bothered Whitman and brought his full attention to regaining composure.

"That's why I'm thinking of doing something different. A book would be obvious. But I can sell part of the information for cash. Like the new name of this Professor Hunt we placed in a protection program and his address in Montana."

"From what you've told me, Hunt might be killed if you sell his name to this Guatemalan guy."

"I don't much care about what happens to that bastard Macduff Brooks—that's the name we gave Hunt."

"I suggest you think more about this. . . . Gotta go. Wife at home expected me two hours ago."

The man slid off the bar stool and walked toward the door. Whitman watched him and noticed he was limping slightly. He muttered to himself, "maybe one of his legs had gone to sleep from sitting on one of these goddamn, lousy, hard-edged bar stools." Whitman was not a happy man.

Whitman also left after a few minutes, swallowing the last drop of his "one for the road."

The next morning a call came to his apartment, waking Whitman at 10:30. He had an intense headache that worsened when he rose and walked to the kitchen counter where he'd left the cell phone charging.

"Yeah," he uttered.

"Mr. Whitman. Juan Pablo Herzog in Guatemala. How are you?"

"A little under the weather; I think a front's moved in. Or it's my sinus." He was embarrassed by his conduct the previous night, but enthused by hearing from Herzog. "Have you thought any more about my offer, Señor Herzog?"

"I have. I think we can agree on a price. Can we meet?"

"Yes, but this time here in D.C."

"I'll fly up and stay at the Hay-Adams. . . . There's a small bar a block west of the hotel called 'Lounge Suite 14.' It has a few private rooms. I'll arrange for one, under the name of Maxwell Hunt. Shall we say next Monday evening . . . at seven?"

"I'll be there." Whitman was overjoyed and began to think that he would soon be living at some quiet Florida retirement community and playing golf.

The following Monday was a grim, gray day of intermittent drizzle in D.C. The ordinarily reflective white stone of the government buildings appeared a sanded gray. The streets were wet as Whitman came out of the Farragut West metro station and, for the first time in his life, dropped a five-dollar bill in the hat of a homeless man who was partly blocking the exit. Whitman easily located the bar: Lounge Suite 14. The room Herzog had reserved was on the second floor in the rear, overlooking empty ground-floor outside tables and bleak office buildings beyond.

Fifteen minutes later Juan Pablo Herzog walked into the room, carrying both a briefcase and, from what Whitman could discern, a pistol not carefully hidden under his left arm. He looked at the briefcase hopefully, more so when Herzog opened the top and exposed stacks of engravings of Ben Franklin. He knew that meant $100 bills. Whitman thought the payoff would be sweet.

If Herzog paid Whitman $1,000,000, it would mean there were 10,000 such bills. He thought how much easier large transactions would be if the government hadn't stopped issuing bills larger than $100. Were the engraving to be of Salmon P. Chase rather than Franklin, it would only take a single envelope filled with a hundred bills to total $1,000,000. One modest package that would slip into a jacket pocket rather than a briefcase obvious to all. But the large bills were retired decades ago and were now collectors' items worth even more than their face value.

"How are you, Allan?" asked Herzog, causing Whitman to focus on the offeror and not the offering. Whitman was surprised at Herzog's concern and cordiality. But also impatient that Herzog didn't immediately address Whitman's demand.

"I'm doing very well, Señor Herzog. Are you prepared to meet my price? It is, after all, no more than what you would have given the law school had they agreed to accept your gift in exchange for information about Hunt. There was no certainty that such information would have included the name and location of Hunt, and you would have honored a person you despise. I will give you his new name, his exact location, and other information about him from his file. You'll receive everything in the CIA file on Hunt as of the date I retired."

"Mr. Whitman, I am prepared to pay you, but not $4 million. Unlike the law college, where I offered to endow a chair, you have no alternative. I am the only person interested in purchasing the information about Hunt. And I have other sources."

"That's not so. I have a publisher ready to sign a lucrative agreement for the manuscript which I will give you or destroy, as you wish, but only when you've met my price."

"I've checked on your ability to have the manuscript published. I believe your two prospective publishers, one in New York City and one in London, have decided not to publish your book even though they might profit from doing so. They are both under threats of judicial actions by the CIA if they go forward.

"You must be realistic in what you ask. I'm prepared to give you the $100,000 in this briefcase, but nothing more. I don't have any assurance that what you will tell me is accurate. I have no way of knowing other than your awareness that if the information is not true you would forfeit your life—at a painfully slow pace you would not enjoy."

"When you confront the new Hunt, you will know I have not lied," Whitman said, guardedly. "Hunt appears little different from his earlier days. He wears clear-lens glasses and has a moustache. We made a couple of minor facial touch-ups, but there is no doubt that, when you stand face-to-face with Hunt in his new role, you will be convinced and pleased."

"I would expect nothing less. If the information proves to be inaccurate, you will pay a very dear price. What we plan for Hunt, we would do to you."

Whitman was perspiring. He knew he was no match for Herzog, who appeared to be armed. Plus, the $100,000 was something, especially when his poor bargaining position was considered. But perhaps he could bargain for more.

"Mr. Herzog, to show my good faith I'll tell you a few things about Hunt. He lives a long way from here. You know he lost his wife nearly twenty years ago. He has been living with a woman who is quite wealthy. The woman's name is Lu. . . ."

Whitman never finished his sentence. A nearly silent .357 magnum bullet, which had passed effortlessly through the thin glass window, shattered both the window and the rear of Whitman's head. His blood splattered on the front of the aghast Herzog, who grabbed the briefcase and walked quickly out of the room, wiping his face free of Whitman's blood with his drink napkin. Herzog was glad he had made the reservation for the room in another name. After all, he had thought *he* might have had to kill Whitman.

Herzog walked to the metro, rode one stop to Foggy Bottom, exited, and hailed a cab to drive him to the general aviation section at Dulles airfield, where he had landed his jet less than three hours earlier.

In another four hours Herzog was back in the comfort of his condo in Guatemala City, sipping a glass of his favorite Ron Zacapa Centenario, made by a company he was considering "acquiring." He held up an old photograph of Professor Hunt taken at a Thanksgiving dinner years ago at his Gainesville home, and thought "Glasses and a moustache?" He lighted a Cohiba cigar he had bought on a recent trip to Havana and reserved for special occasions. "And he lives with a wealthy woman whose name begins with 'Lu'?" he pondered. "Something like 'Lucy' perhaps?" He would go on line in the morning and search for names beginning with "Lu." One matter continued to perplex him: "Who killed Whitman?"

14

ON THE PHONE the following morning, Dan Wilson sounded relieved. "Mac, we've solved the Allan Whitman problem. . . . No, that's not fully accurate. The Allan Whitman problem has been solved. But not by us."

"What do you mean?"

"Last night Whitman was killed, shot while talking to someone in a back room of a bar here in D.C."

"Shot by the person he was talking to?"

"No, by a single bullet from a nearby building. A .357 magnum rifle. Whitman was sitting with his back to the window. The bullet went through it and hit Whitman in the back of his head."

"Who was he talking to? Who did the shooting?"

"The first is easier to answer. It had to be Herzog. From the descriptions given us by the bartender, Whitman entered alone, ordered a drink, and took it to a private room upstairs at the back of the bar. The room had been reserved in the name of Maxwell Hunt! Whitman was joined a half-hour later by a late-forties to early-fifties white male who was almost certainly Herzog. He was wearing a dark suit, white shirt, and a tie a waitress in the bar said was green and white with some kind of foreign flag in the middle. She said the man stopped her when he came in and asked where the restrooms were.

"The bartender said the man left in a hurry an hour later, probably right after the shooting. The room's on the second floor, so the window shattering wasn't heard. The rifle must have had a noise suppressor. No one was seated in the outdoor area and apparently no one heard the glass break. When the bartender went into the room to get the drink glasses, he found Whitman on the floor in a pool of blood, embellished by glass shards, and called the police."

"How did you find out about it?"

"We've been tailing Whitman," Dan admitted.

"Did you have a man there?"

"In the bar. He saw them both come in—separately—but saw only one man leave. He didn't know what Herzog looked like, but according to his description, confirmed by the bartender and waitress, it must have been Herzog. After he left quickly and wasn't followed by Whitman, our man went looking. The bartender was so busy he didn't notice our man slip upstairs where he entered the room and found a body face down on the floor, checked to make sure it was Whitman, confirmed he was dead, and quietly left."

"Did one of your people shoot Whitman?"

"No. That's the truth, Mac. And we don't know who it was."

"Dan, Whitman may be dead, but the police will search his place and find his manuscript."

"We have it."

"How?"

"Our man called me as soon as he left the bar. I went with two other agents to Whitman's condo. We found a manuscript in a three-ring black binder, opened his word processor, and found the master manuscript on the hard drive. We took the hard drive. We also searched Whitman's car and garage for any more copies. We've formally intervened in the case because a foreigner was involved. The D.C. police and the FBI, as usual, are upset with our presence. We told them the killing involved an important foreign official, which made the death international and gave us jurisdiction."

"Did Herzog have Whitman shot?"

"Unlikely, Whitman apparently was sitting with his back to the window at a small table. Herzog was facing Whitman. If the bullet had missed, it likely would have hit Herzog. He wouldn't have taken that kind of chance. I think he was surprised by the shot. According to our man, Herzog looked shocked when he left."

"You said your people didn't shoot Whitman. Do you expect me to believe that? We've been through this before when Herzog's nephew Martín Paz was shot in Gainesville."

"No. You probably won't believe me. But it's true. It wasn't our *modus operandi.* We were prepared to take him out, but by other means. Most likely an *induced* heart attack."

"How do we know if Whitman gave Herzog the information he wanted? . . . My name and location."

"We don't. But we assume that since it all happened so quickly, and Herzog must have left before he planned, that Herzog didn't leave with the info he sought. At least he didn't leave any money; there was none on Whitman's body."

"That sounds like a lot of speculation and little fact."

"The best we can do right now."

"While you're on the line, Dan, is there any reason to believe that Whitman or Herzog were involved with killing Paula Pajioli?"

"Whitman—no. As far as Herzog or Isfahani is concerned, I don't think so. If Herzog and Isfahani knew about Lucinda and you, they didn't need Whitman any more. They already would have the information they needed. I don't think they would have wasted time playing games by killing Pajioli. If they did kill her, the sign would have said 'You're next, *Macduff*.' Herzog has no quarrel with Lucinda."

"So who killed Pajioli?"

"*Definitely* not Whitman. *Probably* not Herzog or Isfahani. *Maybe* Ellsworth-Kent. And maybe someone else who dislikes you or Lucinda. . . . By the way, how are your eyes? And how's Lucinda bearing up over Ellsworth-Kent's appearance?"

"Don't know about my eyes. I'll meet with the doctor this week. Sometimes I think I'm seeing some light. But that proves to be wishful thinking. . . . Lucinda's been great; she's not saying much about Ellsworth-Kent."

"Remember that I want an invitation to the wedding."

"Wedding? I'm still trying to figure out if we're engaged."

"Trust me. You are. And you're the lucky one."

Dan hung up. Lucinda had heard most of our conversation. She was making a meal from ingredients I've never seen before, much less heard of.

"What on earth are you making?"

"I'm getting things ready for dinner. I overheard that Whitman is dead. We need to celebrate. That must mean Herzog and Isfahani are not an immediate problem. But I wonder how much Whitman told them?"

"What are we going to have in celebration?"

"Braised duck in Italian red wine with olive gremolata. I'm making the olive gremolata to start."

"*Gremolata?* Can you translate that into what it's made from? It doesn't sound digestible."

"Parsley, capers, garlic, orange and lemon zest, and olives."

"Does it go into a blender with some coconut rum and become an exotic drink?"

"*No.* It's a sauce that goes on the duck."

"Isn't there a more humane way to kill the duck than to smother it with gremolata?"

"The duck is already dead."

"Did it drown in the wine?"

"No. It was shot. Like Whitman. And you if you keep complaining."

"I'm not complaining. Just curious about your culinary talents."

"I know what you'd like. For me to hold everything."

"No, hold the duck and everything else except the red wine. That way, you don't either kill an innocent duck or waste a perfectly good bottle of Italian wine."

"Would you prefer that we stop on the way to town and have a hotdog?"

"Only if it comes with fries."

"Let's go fishing. I need some fresh air."

"Shall we float the Madison?" I asked.

"And get me killed?"

"We've never fished the Madison together."

"But you can't see yet."

"There's very little to hit on that river."

"Maybe, instead, we could take a few days, tow the boat to Jackson, and have John Kirby float with us on the Snake?"

"Sounds good. We haven't seen John since he was here and we floated the Yellowstone down to Carter Bridge the day

Marge Atwood and Pam Snyder were attacked at Marge's place."

Two of the Shuttle Gals, the group of five women who do shuttles of drift boats on the Yellowstone, were attacked by five Mexican youth-gang members who were bent on raping and killing them. But the tables were turned; Marge and Pam killed them all, three at short range with a shotgun. The women became immediate Montana celebrities. Unfortunately, Pam was killed a short time later. I never know when I'm floating with a client and one of this group is doing my shuttle, whether the client has come to fish or be photographed with one of the surviving gals.

15

IT WAS STRANGE to be driven through the Yellowstone and Grand Teton parks on the way to Jackson and be unable to see. It must have been my lack of sight that made receptions from other senses more conspicuous and compelling. Sights were replaced with sounds and smells. Sounds of waterfalls and bubbling mud pots and venting steam, occasionally interrupted by calls from animals and birds. But it was the smell that drew the same question from me that thousands of sighted visitors ask: *What is that smell?*

The soothing fragrance of Lucinda as we entered the park, enhanced by the scents of sagebrush, balsam, cedar, and pine, was soon overwhelmed by the rotten eggs odor of hydrogen sulfide gas from the mud pots. Yellowstone sits on top of one of the largest volcanos on earth. It's called a supervolcano—meaning more than I like to imagine in volume and violence. No supervolcano has erupted in recorded history. When Yellowstone does explode—not if—it will reconfigure part of our Mountain West. This supervolcano is a caldera, deviously resting like a Coke bottle sitting in front of a mischievous kid you know will pick it up and shake it until it bursts.

Speed limits, migrating RVs, and lunch at the Lake Hotel all set back our Jackson Hole arrival until nearly sunset. But we reached Dornan's cabins in Moose in time to unpack, pour a drink, and relax on our porch. Lucinda photographed the final sliver of sun disappearing beyond the Tetons and gave me a minute-by-minute account of what I was missing.

I'd called ahead to Juan Santander, who was staying with his aunt Cassie Eckstrum. He would meet us at the Pizza Pasta Company for dinner. I wasn't sure what information I could get from Juan about his recent actions, but I intended to press him to talk about them.

Lucinda went into the Mangy Moose to find a fleece jacket. I was standing next to her when someone tapped me on the shoulder. I turned instinctively 'though doing so didn't mean I could see anything. I was wearing sunglasses and trying not to show my blindness.

"It's Juan, Mac. Aunt Cassie told me about your injury. Any change? Have the police learned anything about who rigged the bomb that killed the woman?"

Juan Santander and I first met when I agreed to take someone fly fishing on the Snake River as part of Project Healing Waters. That someone turned out to be Juan, who the organizer of the floats labeled as the most contentious member of the dozen combat-wounded disabled vets who had been flown to Wyoming from Walter Reed Hospital in D.C. I met Juan at the Gun Barrel Restaurant in Jackson as he came flying out the door with a strangle lock on the head of my Teton County deputy friend Huntly Byng. I separated them and thus started off the following day uncertain if there would be another killing on my drift boat—me!

Notre Dame, Rhodes Scholar at Oxford, and Team Six of the Navy Seals are a few things Juan has in his favor. But like many of our troops in places where our successive presidents have engaged in their favorite little undeclared wars, Juan was seriously injured and suffered brain damage in Afghanistan.

When he slipped overboard from my drift boat to save a small child who'd fallen off the bow of a passing canoe, Juan didn't give a thought to the fact he was doing so without a right eye, hand, or leg. He was so tense when he got the kid into my drift boat that I thought he'd kill the child's irresponsible, drunken father. He didn't, and our time together that day developed into a friendship that has grown as we've fished together.

A year ago, on the University of Florida campus, after Herzog's nephew Martín Paz had shot Richard Potter, believing him to be Professor Maxwell Hunt, someone, in turn, shot and killed Paz. Lucinda was immediately and absolutely certain that the person who saved us by shooting Paz—who claimed he had to kill us because we had watched him shoot Potter—was Juan Santander.

More recently, in D.C., when someone shot Alan Whitman while he was preparing to disclose to Herzog my name and location, in exchange for an undisclosed sum, once again Lucinda was certain the shooter was Juan.

Though Whitman and Paz are out of our lives, Lucinda and I believe the glass remains half full. Herzog and Isfahani are very much alive and pursuing me, while Lucinda's ex, Ellsworth-Kent, is on his way to Montana to reconnect with Lucinda.

I'm happy to have Juan around. It was good to relax with him over dinner at Moose. A couple of drinks loosened me enough to ask him questions perhaps better left unaddressed. I waited until we had cappuccino and dessert before I dared to begin.

"Juan, Lucinda's convinced me you were the one who shot Martín Paz by the tennis courts at UF last year."

"Let's not go into that," he responded. "The matter's over. Paz didn't shoot you. He's out of the picture. We should focus on Herzog and Isfahani."

"If you say so. . . . But first, did you shoot Whitman last week in D.C.?"

"Mac, there's nothing to be gained by asking these kinds of questions. Dan Wil. . . I mean . . . damn! You're putting me on the spot."

"So you've been working for Dan Wilson?"

"I've talked to him off-and-on."

"Not another question. I think you've told me all I wanted you to."

"Mac, I owe you. Big time. You and Cassie have put me back on my feet. I would do *anything* for either one of you."

"Just don't add *yourself* to the people Herzog and Isfahani are after. They know nothing about you. My best bet is that they think some unidentified CIA agent shot Paz and Whitman."

"That sounds fine with me," Juan replied.

John Kirby and I launched *Osprey* in the morning a few yards upstream from the bridge at Moose on the west side of a narrow stretch of the Snake River.

"How many times have we floated the Deadman's Bar to Moose section?" I asked.

"Lots. It's your favorite. It starts off with that spectacular stretch Ansel Adams made famous in one of his photographs."

"How many times have we floated this Moose to Wilson part?"

"Never, until today. I know . . . your next question is 'why'? You should have been a professor; you ask so many questions."

"I thought about it. But my question *is* 'Why *this* section today?'"

"It has its good and bad features. Some of the fishing is excellent. But the levees we'll see after we exit the park aren't exactly attractive to view or very practical from most any perspective, other than that of homeowners who've built along the river and then begin to worry about flooding. The same problem is true of Paradise Valley along parts of the Yellowstone River. And probably throughout the country wherever people build on a floodplain. The homes we'll pass are known more for their square-footage than any memorable architecture. Maybe that's a benefit of your not being able to see. Just relax and enjoy the smells and sounds."

"Do the levees go all the way to our takeout at Wilson?"

"And beyond. They extend twenty-four miles. We've got a long float today, about fourteen miles. There's no place to take out before Wilson. The part where we are now, still within Grand Teton National Park, retains its natural features: channels and braiding, bends, and vistas along the sides. But that ends where the levees begin. Quite obviously, the impact of the levees is debated aggressively. They've restricted the river's flow to a narrow channel. And they've prevented flooding, which is good for the homeowners and ranchers. But flooding is a natural characteristic of rivers.

"The levees initially hurt the cutthroat population, encouraging silting, which, in turn, diminishes cutthroat habitat. But as they say 'Cutthroats have a dumb gene.' They've adapted rather than departed.

"This section was once heavily braided with multiple channels. There were many spring creeks that were important spawning areas. Much of that has been lost."

"So, if it's all bad, why are we here?"

"To catch fish. They've survived. And to some extent adapted. The numbers are pretty good. . . . Plus, you've been asking to fish this section for five years. I'm doing it to let you make your own decisions on how good it is compared to the sections from Jackson Lake south to Moose."

"There's no getting away from the fact that the upper sections have the better views of the Grand Teton," I responded. "But I'm glad we're running this section, *especially* since I can't see the levees."

"Speaking of fish, Macduff, while I've been talking, you've had four or five rises to your Adams fly that you've totally ignored. I appreciate your attentiveness to my soliloquy, but you're here to fish. Having trouble feeling movement in the line?"

"I can talk blind, but it's hard to fish blind. Look at it this way: Those fish I missed will live to be caught another day." I focused on feeling the line with the fingers of my left hand and, sure enough, I soon felt something different—a momentary halt in the fly floating. I didn't know it was a cutthroat that sucked my #16 Adams under and set off in search of some way to relieve itself of the uncomfortable pull on its mouth. A few minutes later John netted my first Moose-to-Wilson trout. He described it as a ten-inch cutthroat, sporting the iridescence of the crimson throat that gives it the name "cutthroat."

"John," I asked, while we ate lunch by a levee, "I haven't heard another boat go by. Maybe I just missed them, but usually there's some talking. Why so few boats on this section?"

"Another of the benefits; only one scenic rafting outfit has permission to do this section. Two rafts have passed us. Likely, there won't be another raft or drift boat all day."

In mid-afternoon, I asked, "How far have we floated?" without making it sound like "How soon do we get there?"

"We're about ten miles past Moose, four from the takeout at Wilson. We're almost where the Gros Ventre River joins the Snake."

"Reasonable place to fish?"

"It's a good place for rainbows as well as cutthroats. Just upstream of the confluence, the area even produces a special strain of cutthroat. It grows fast and is a fighter. . . . We'll do a little wading in a few minutes."

I had doubts about wading. But John insisted I get out and led me to what he said was a good spot. A hand on his shoulder proved to be better than using a wading stick. My tippet crowned with an Elk Hair Caddis, within ten minutes I hooked up with a twenty-one inch rainbow. . . . It was the biggest fish I never saw!

Wilson Bridge essentially divides the northern portion of the Snake upriver to Jackson Lake and the southern portion downriver to the Palisades Reservoir. The first three sections, starting at the Jackson Lake Dam and including the section we floated today, are at least mostly in the park. From Wilson down to the canyon—meaning South Park Bridge—the land is privately owned with several public accesses. The canyon beyond, leading west to Palisades, has some famous Class III and IV rapids, including the "Kahuna" and "Lunch Counter." Pretty good fishing—fewer but bigger fish—plus spectacular scenery, especially in the fall when the cottonwoods are a variation on a theme of solid gold.

Arriving at Wilson, like reaching any takeout after a day with a friend, was a downer. I know it had to be unduly tiring for John. He made me sit in the front seat, which as a single passenger I would have done anyway. He could keep an eye on me while I couldn't keep an eye on anything. I owe him; it's time he came and stayed at my Florida cottage and spent some time with me fishing the flats.

16

LUCINDA HAD PLANNED to float with us but she'd been asked by her Manhattan investment firm to meet with several clients. A fair number of clients from various parts of the U.S. had retired and moved to Jackson Hole and often needed advice as they shifted their focus from growth to income.

John dropped me off at the Wort Hotel where Lucinda was waiting by the curb. When we settled into our chairs in the Silver Dollar Grill, I ordered the Rocky Mountain Basil-Encrusted Free Range Lamb, with house-made jalapeño mint and Granny Smith apple jam. Lucinda combined a Tuna Tartare with the Wort's classic Hickory-Smoked Pheasant Soup.

"Macduff," she demanded after I ordered, staring at me for an adequate answer, "You ordered something you'd never eat if I prepared it. Explain that!"

"I like lamb, especially when it's free. Basil's pretty good and you know I love Granny Smith apples."

"And the jalapeño?"

"I'm hoping the mint trumps the jalapeño. If not, I'll scrape it off. You should be pleased with my venture into the delicacies of fine dining."

"You don't know the meaning of 'fine dining.'"

"I can call the server over and change my order to fries and a bison burger."

"Just sit and be quiet. . . . May I taste your lamb?"

"I was afraid of that. Leave me a bite. . . . Do you want to stay in Jackson another day? There are enticing shops lining the downtown streets."

"I don't need another day," she said. "This valley's such a visual delight; I know how much you want to see it, especially the Grand Tetons. Let's come back as soon as your sight does the same."

"Thanks. When we sat last evening on the deck at Dornan's, knowing you were thrilled watching the sunset, I could hear only the wind. I so wanted to see those mountains. Maybe we could stop at the lodge at Old Faithful; I can at least listen to the geysers."

"Sure. After breakfast I'll call and reserve a room," she said.

On the way north through the park, we stayed a night at the restored Old Faithful Lodge, resplendent in its freshness. Lucinda and I walked past what was my new world, the bubbling sounds and acrid smells of the geysers and mud pots. It was surreal and at times disconcerting; I was glad she was close to me.

Arriving back at Mill Creek the next day as the sun set, Wuff met us at the cabin door. Mavis had kept her and dropped her off when I called ahead as we left the park at Gardiner. Wuff grabbed my pants and led me to the kitchen, sat by the cabinet door where her treats are stored, and whimpered. When I gave her one, she consumed it in a gulp, ran into my bedroom, jumped on the bed, lay down on my pillow, and was sound asleep in five minutes. Lucinda and I had to lift her off when we went to bed.

Erin called in the morning. She chatted with Lucinda for a half-hour and then asked to talk to me.

"Any improvement, Macduffy?"

"Not yet. I guess I'm destined never to see your smiling face. . . . I *hate* this. . . . What's up?"

"Talked to a Madison County deputy who's working on the Pajioli case. They have no fresh ideas about who rigged the boat that killed Paula. They're baffled by the wicker man and mistletoe. I mentioned that I didn't think the fact that the killing occurred on the summer solstice had any relevance. He asked, 'What's the summer solstice?' I dropped it. He doesn't think much of the FBI people who are there. They haven't shared any useful information, and the deputy seems a little jealous about protecting his turf. . . . You have any new ideas?"

"The only person who comes to mind is Lucinda's short-term husband, Robert Ellsworth-Kent."

I'm certain Erin knows I have a past to which she isn't fully privy. It's that past where my real threats lie—with Herzog and Isfahani. But when I start to think about them, I run into a wall: Why wouldn't they have come after me *directly*? Juan Pablo Herzog doesn't play around. If he wants me out of the way, he'll do it and then maybe go after Lucinda. In any event, I can't open this discussion with Erin.

"Where's Ellsworth-Kent, Macduffy? Does Lucinda have any idea?"

"We don't know where they are," I answered, "I wish the hell I could see," I added, showing my lack of concentration.

After Erin hung up, Lucinda looked at me with her get-your-act-together face, and said, "You're going to learn to live without sight, not whimper about it. Look at Juan. No right hand, no right leg, no right eye. Thousands of sightless people lead successful lives. Marry. Have children."

"Children? Wow! You're talking as though my blindness is permanent."

"Well, what if it is? We'll deal with that if it happens. Don't be such a grouch!"

"Next you'll want to use a defibrillator on me—and shock my sight back."

"Not a bad idea."

17

I WAS GETTING AROUND the cabin without crashing into tables and chairs. Lucinda had felt comfortable flying to New York for three days to meet with clients. She arrived back tired and frustrated. I was waiting in the rustic lobby of the Bozeman Airport, below the staircase that sweeps down to the lower floor. Wearing my dark glasses, I stood alone in the middle.

There was a long hug.

"Macduff, who brought you? Someone waiting for us in their car?"

"No."

"Did you come in a cab? That's expensive, and we'll have to take another cab back to Mill Creek."

"No."

"What's going on?"

"You look so gorgeous."

"How can you te. . . ."

I took off my sunglasses and stared at her green eyes. Vision is indeed better than smells and sounds. "I tried the defibrillator idea. It worked!"

"You can see?"

"Every bit of you."

There was a longer hug.

"When did this happen?"

"When I woke this morning I could see. Erin was going to drive me. I called her and said I had another ride. I wanted you to be the first to know. . . . How was Manhattan?"

"It wasn't pleasant. But that can wait. How should we celebrate? Go to Yellowstone? Go to Manhattan where I can play the seductive ghost role once more? Fly to London?"

"None of the above. I want to go back to the cabin, sit on the porch, and look at you."

"Just look?"

"Maybe touch. And smell, like we did with the mud pots in the park."

"Are you comparing me to a mud pot?" she asked. She had been back only ten minutes and she's exasperated with me.

"This isn't going well."

"I could get a cab," she offered.

"Back to the cabin?"

"Back to Manhattan!"

By this time we were at the car. I put her bags in the trunk and before she got in grabbed her and hugged her again. She smelled delicious.

"Macduff, someone's going to walk by and think you're ravaging me!"

"You asked how I'd like to celebrate. Ravaging sounds perfect."

It was good to be together, and we didn't say much on the drive home. When we arrived, she pulled a bottle of *Pouilly Fuissé* from the wine cooler, I took two wine glasses from the rack, and we sat outside on the porch. For the next ten minutes, I sat staring at her mesmerizing green eyes and grin. Then I realized she had said that Manhattan wasn't pleasant.

"Tell me about Manhattan."

"I mentioned some time ago a broker named Frank Wu. He joined our firm a week before I was shot and took leave time. He transferred to New York from our Beijing office. Wu has covered for me off-and-on over the past two years. But now he's pushing me to turn over all my clients to him, telling me I've lost too much time to return full time and be effective. Without exception, my clients have told me they want no part of him and will take their business to another brokerage unless someone they trust takes over. That is, of course, if I want out.

"I've decided I do want out . . . of Manhattan. But I like working. My boss has talked about opening a small office in Bozeman. Working there and living here in Paradise Valley would cover two areas where there's considerable wealth. Since I started coming out here, I've signed up sufficient local clients to cover about half my day. Now I have contacts in Jackson Hole. I think I'd fill up my time in three to five years, *if* I want to become full time again."

"You look exhausted," I commented. "And troubled. Is there anything else to talk about? I don't believe you're threatened on the basis of lack of expertise and success with clients. If you do want to work out of Bozeman, we can always have a small condo there in the event of bad weather. And we can make some space for you in my Florida cottage so you can work with clients from there during the winter. It's your decision."

"There is something else. Wu cornered me two evenings ago at the office. In the coffee room. It was about 6:30. We were the only two left working. He'd been drinking since lunch time; I suspect he's becoming an alcoholic. I was stirring my coffee when he came up against me from behind, reached around, and grabbed my breasts. Wu's strong; he spends a lot of time in a local gym. When I tried to get away, he pressed me against the counter and was reaching under my skirt when the night cleaning crew walked into the office.

"Wu backed off, and I left immediately. One of the night crew thought I could use some help and walked me out. Wu tried to follow, but we closed the elevator doors on him, and when we got to the lobby, I ran out and flagged down a cab before he could catch up. I think Wu would have tried to rape me given the chance.

"I put my S&W .32 in my purse as soon as I reached my apartment and carried it with me to the office yesterday. I was surely violating city or state gun laws, but they haven't helped reduce violent crime much, if at all. Burglaries are way up because the burglars assume Manhattan homeowners don't have any guns."

"Yesterday morning Wu passed my office, stuck his head in, smiled, and said, if I stayed past five, he would take it to mean my wanting to pick up where we left off the previous night. Where *we* left off! I slipped out of the office at three and came back here today.

"I'm not sure how to deal with this. I know he'll argue 'consent' if I say anything to Jake Bridger, our manager, who will say, 'If you complain, it'll be the old he said—she said.' Bridger said I should ignore Wu and go back to work; he'd speak with Wu."

"Do you feel safe going back?"

"No. And Bridger likely won't say anything to Wu. I'm staying here for a month or two. I brought work I can do with the help of the Internet."

“Have you thought of filing a complaint with the New York City police? If Wu has any kind of record of sexual harassment, they should be able to track it down.”

“I’m afraid of him, Mac,” Lucinda commented, reverting to my nickname when she’s troubled. I feel a lot better carrying my pistol, but I’d hate to have to use it in New York City.”

“I’d like to fly to New York with you and have a talk with Wu.”

“I told you, Mac, that he’s a tough character. I don’t think you’d want to take him on.”

“There are other ways, Lucinda—lots of other ways to be persuasive. . . . But if he’s nothing more than an office Lothario, it wouldn’t take an accident to cure him. If you pulled a gun on him, you’d best be prepared to use it. If you use it, it’s a crap shoot about what would happen with the New York City police and prosecutors. Much less keeping your job. And perhaps even working for anyone else in investments.”

“We need to talk to Dan. He’s more experienced than we are at looking at these events.”

“Let’s refill our glasses and try to sleep.”

“Refilling will be easy. Sleeping is less certain.”

18

DAN WILSON RAN A CHECK on Wu. Neither of us expected Dan would find anything significant, but at least we could tell Lucinda we tried. Unexpectedly, the CIA files proved to be an appropriate place to start. The following morning Dan called with the results and asked that Lucinda join us on the line.

"Our mission in Beijing has a file on Wu," Dan began. "He's from a politically connected family of one-time die-hard communists who lived lavishly under Mao. They made the conversion to capitalism without missing a beat, largely by paying off government officials. Wu's father has become a billionaire, with much of his money transferred to Singapore, Panama, and Swiss banks. We believe he set up a fund for Wu in a Liechtenstein foundation that's sufficiently large so that he never has to return to China.

"Wu's on a short leash because he's been in trouble that's embarrassed his parents. He's in the U.S. because of frequent difficulties with the Triad in both Hong Kong and Guangzhou. Guangzhou is the former Canton; the Triad is the collective name for the underground branches of Chinese organized crime.

"There may have been a contract out on Wu in China. He worked for the Beijing office of Lucinda's New York based investment firm. They wanted to fire him in China, but we suspect his father paid off some people—including your top officers in Manhattan, Lucinda—so Wu wouldn't be fired. He's working in the New York office only as long as they agree to keep him. That may not be for long—despite the bribes.

"I checked with friends over in Foggy Bottom; Wu carries a Chinese diplomatic passport. That means we all need to be especially careful of him. He could rape or even kill Lucinda with nothing more in the way of punishment than being kicked out of the country. Mac, you remember the problems with Victoria and Roberto Montoya; Roberto carried a diplomatic passport."

"I remember the Montoya woman and her brother all too well," I responded. . . . "Is Wu accident prone?"

"In our view *everyone* is accident prone. Depends on what kind of accident. But there's a better way. If something happened to Wu, his father would be over here in a minute, calling in all his chips in Congress. It could be embarrassing to us. And to Lucinda. If they went into her background, that would bring you in, Mac. You don't need that. . . . We can have him declared *persona non grata* and kicked out of the country."

"Could he come back as a tourist?"

"No. *Persona non grata* is what we say it is. We decide if and when it's over. If Wu tried to return, he'd be rejected whether or not he presented his diplomatic passport."

"Dan," Lucinda asked, "is there any chance Wu was involved with the Pajioli murder?"

"That's longer than a long-shot. He couldn't have killed Pajioli without help. He's been in the country long enough, but he had no quarrel with Lucinda until *after* Paula was murdered.

Of course, he could be involved with Herzog or Isfahani. But our records don't show Wu's ever been in Guatemala. And until Whitman was killed, Herzog and Isfahani didn't need any help, or so they thought."

"Any links between Wu and anyone in or from the Sudan?"

"No. . . . So, I see no link to Herzog or Isfahani. There are better people to focus on."

"Who are you tracking now?"

"Always Herzog and Isfahani—for your protection. Plus, Ellsworth-Kent. Your ex, Lucinda."

"Don't remind me," she commented. "Where are they all?" Lucinda inquired, expecting her main worry had to be Ellsworth-Kent. But a murderer? She found that hard to accept, not thinking about his having killed the police officer in London.

"Herzog's in Guatemala," Dan continued. "He hasn't been very active since Whitman was shot. Herzog may still be mending his psychological wounds from the loss of his niece and nephew. And he may feel the loss of Whitman, *if* he died before telling Herzog anything about you two. . . ."

"Do you think Whitman told Herzog before he died?" Lucinda asked.

"Impossible to know. But it's been four-to-five weeks since Whitman was killed. I think Herzog would have acted very quickly after he received the information about Mac. Probably immediately, while he was in the U.S."

"And Isfahani?" I asked.

"He was in Khartoum in the Sudan, but he's gone to Switzerland. Our missions in each country are tracking him. He's linked to Sudanese al-Qaeda terrorists; he's on and then off our list of wanted terrorists. Truthfully, Isfahani's the one we'd like to see have an accident. . . . His face still looks awful, thanks to you, Mac. His operations thus far have made it worse, like an actress who rejects aging and has had far too many sessions with her plastic surgeon.

"Lucinda, Ellsworth-Kent has gone completely off our radar screen. Last thing we knew he was in New Orleans in March and April. Then, he abruptly left. He may be anywhere, including Paradise Valley."

"That not comforting, Dan," said Lucinda.

"What he may be planning for you isn't comforting either."

19

AUGUST PASSED QUICKLY. Having become accustomed to being sighted for a half-century, I'd lost full appreciation of what sight means. I won't lose that appreciation now that my sight has been restored. Many hours passed while I was blind by listening to music, especially the oboe concertos that I once played alone in my music room beneath my cabin. I haven't scraped an oboe reed in six months.

During those sightless weeks, I tried once or twice to play when Lucinda wasn't with me at the cabin. The results were fine for pieces I'd memorized, such as Marcello's D minor concerto. But when I wanted to try a new piece, I couldn't read the music. Then I split my only good reed, put down the oboe, and haven't touched it since. I'll get back to it. Music was such a part of my life that I sometimes said I would rather lose my sight than my hearing. Now I'm not so sure.

Hearing Vivaldi's *Four Seasons* or the sound of Lucinda's voice is a spiritual blessing, but blindness imposes a dependency on others that I found distressing. Since my sight's returned, I'm more aware of the variations of all the senses, whether it's sight, sound, smell, taste, or, especially with regard to Lucinda, touch.

The hopper season on the Montana and Wyoming rivers began in late July. Favorite hopper waters for me are the Snake north of Moose, the Firehole in Yellowstone Park, and, of course, my own Yellowstone River through Paradise Valley. When grasshoppers begin to launch themselves among swaying blades of grass along the banks, they sometimes abruptly realize that their playful energy, aided by wind, has randomly cast them over a bank and onto the surface of the water. Unless they escape quickly, they become a meal for an aggressive brown trout lurking below the surface.

When I think of my experience with hoppers and browns, few combinations bring a more rapid or aggressive response to a fly landing on the water. A hungry brown looks like a nuclear sub blasting up through the ocean's surface.

I may be in the minority, but I rarely add a dropper when I fish hoppers. I'm trying to draw browns to the surface to hit the hopper, not have a tailing nymph draw a trout's attention in the depths. But at times when I'm fishing from a drift boat and I'm not trying to place my fly *under* an overhanging bank, but rather have my hopper drift *along* the bank, I may add something behind the hopper like either a proven, old-standard nymph, maybe a #16 or 18 Pheasant Tail, or a relatively new kid on the block, a similar size Copper John. Currently, I'm experimenting with a Prince that has a fluorescent pink head in front of a tungsten bead, adding of little of the brilliant color I use in my saltwater flies in Florida.

The truth is that I usually don't add nymphs behind anything and *never* when I'm fishing with my friend and guide, John Kirby. I like to focus on one fly, and when I start adding more, I feel like long-line fisherman after tuna off Newfoundland. I'm not especially fond of the Scottish practice of having as many as four flies on hooks dropped into lakes for trout, just as I'm never pleased to see an artificial plug with two three-gang barbed hooks. I like one hook that's barbless, despite a lower number of fish in the net.

Sometimes I'll play around with a single nymph, such as when there's been no surface activity for a long time and none appears likely to occur before my fishing time is up. Always lurking in my memory is John Kirby, whether or not he's fishing with me. He's a Georgia Bulldog who lists nymphs alongside Florida Gators as cellar dwellers. He's been known to bite off my nymph and toss it into the river.

As soon as I'd regained my sight, I began tying hopper fly patterns, especially stocking up on Dave's Hopper, the version I've had most success with over the years. I have a couple of boxes filled with hoppers, ranging from the works of art represented by Dave's to the ugly foam and rubber of so many others. The latter floats like a piece of—well—a piece of foam and rubber. I like mine with some substance *beneath* the surface film. Not as much as an iceberg, but enough to simulate a real hopper and doesn't look like a foam indicator with rubber legs, which browns must consider to be a smear on their intelligence, however limited that may be.

Dave's Hopper is a great fly of the even greater icon of fly fishing—Dave Whitlock. I'd be embarrassed to tie one in front of him, unless he had an hour to spare while I fumbled tying the hopper's legs. I can do a pretty good job of tying his hopper with two left or two right legs or two on top or two on the bottom. When I do tie, I use a photo I took of a real hopper on its back. Every fly tying book I have has all the flies viewed from the side, like the works of art they often are. But I've never seen a trout break the surface, look at the side-view of the hopper, and then attack.

I'm partial to a hopper fly that looks like a hopper, but not to the extent that I'll use what is nothing more than a small, molded plastic lure. There's a line between flies and lures that isn't easily drawn. I'll tie some rubber legs on some hoppers, but I draw the line well before I'm tempted to fish with a molded, plastic, nearly exact copy of a grasshopper body. If I want exactness and imitation, I'll net some hoppers alongside the river, take them home, strap on a hook below, and immerse them in resin. Does that make them bait? I saw a plastic *hellgrammite* fly that was so realistic it was little more than a plastic *hellgrammite* lure. But I keep one for entomology lessons with clients.

Just a week ago a small #16 Dave's Hopper brought me a brown that matched the hook size in inches on a sun-drenched day in Yellowstone Park when the browns had mostly moved up the Little Firehole to escape the warmth of the geysers. The hopper was a little ragged from use, but I tied it on anyway.

My first cast, forty-five feet across to the far bank, flipped the hopper fly on top of some tall grass. Before it snagged, I gave it a little jerk. It tumbled back into the water. The hopper hadn't started its float before a brown went at it like a tarpon. After a couple of long runs of desperation, first downstream and then a haphazard, energy-draining reverse upstream, the fish was dormant and breathing laboriously in my net, the barbless hook on the fly easily slipping out of the corner of its mouth. Another few seconds and it was back under the bank, waiting for however long its brain said to stay put or until it couldn't reason with its own hunger.

After tying flies for a couple of hours, I burn out. My first fly, maybe a small Adams Trude, usually takes me twenty minutes to tie, the second one takes six or seven minutes, and then I get into a pattern of about four to five minutes each. If I could maintain that pace for three or four hours, I'd have a good supply. But after tying the same pattern for an hour, I get bored and shift to another pattern, maybe an Elk Hair Caddis. Trying to tie a Dave's Hopper usually brings me to my knees. I scribble a note on the pad on my table that says "Buy two-dozen Dave's Hoppers." To add to the one that I tied which Dave would reject as the work of a blind drunk.

By mid-September, I had actually tied a few Dave's Hoppers and was ready to hit the riverbanks. Fortuitously, Lucinda walked over to my tying table and asked, "Can we take a few days and go fishing?"

"Where?"

"Let's wade and leave *Osprey* here," she replied.

I thought she wanted to leave the boat at the cabin and wade because I wasn't ready to float again. My first float of the season on June 21st, the summer solstice, didn't turn out well. I nearly lost my plastic drift boat. And I did lose my sight for a few weeks.

After Lucinda answered some e-mail, we tossed Wuff in the back of my SUV and headed to the Box Canyon on the Henry's Fork, a little south of West Yellowstone, near Island Park and a long cast to Last Chance. We'd slanted through the northwest corner of Yellowstone Park after entering at Gardiner, were tempted by Mammoth's liquid terraces, wowed by the black onyx along the high road to Norris Junction, and welcomed partnering with the Gibbon River as it dropped to fuse with the Firehole and create the Madison, where we admired the migrant trumpeter swans visiting from Alberta. We stopped twice to wade at some small creeks that on every passage pull on our attention.

I watched Lucinda patiently work her way upstream on a creek three rod lengths broad, throwing fine short reach casts that laid the #18 caddis imitation gently at the top of successive pools, bringing a rise if not a fish on half her casts. She's at the point where learning new casts brings her a lot of satisfaction. The reach cast is new to her. There's not much to it, other than adding to a normal straight cast a movement of the rod tip off to the right or left just before the end of the forward part of the cast. She started with very slight moves to the right or left, which didn't produce the results she planned. When she fully extended her arm right or left, she produced a nice mend in the line *before* the fly landed. The result should be that the line lands with a mend on the upstream side of the fly.

After all, a reach cast is essentially a straight cast followed by a mend. Doing the mend in the air makes sense because the fly isn't jerked about after it has landed on the surface. Any form of mend in the air keeps the fly from being pulled by the current as soon as it would if it landed in a straight line from the rod to the fly. The reach cast has helped Lucinda have a lot of days where she out-fishes me. But she knows it doesn't take a reach cast to do that.

"Your exquisite casts are graceful," I said, toned with praise, and after a pause added, "That's not surprising; it's the result of having a highly skilled teacher and guide."

"You mean John? He'd enjoy hearing that nice compliment, Macduff."

I guess I've become little more than her driver and rower. Maybe I should offer to take over the cooking, but there are limits to asking others for help.

As we passed where the Gibbon and the Firehole form the headwaters of the Madison, I wondered how I would feel going back to the Madison near Ennis. The thought renews memories of the explosion that killed Paula Pajioli and temporarily blinded me.

To shift my focus from that day, I turned to Lucinda and said, "We might not catch anything, but where we're heading on the Henry's Fork is on Trout Unlimited's *America's 100 Best Streams*, and therefore we *have* to fish it."

"We *have* to do it? It's absolutely required?" she asked, with doubt.

"Yes. That's called logic."

"Do you have any more logic for me to learn?"

"Yes, lots. I'm full of logic."

"Isn't your logic an attempt to convince me not to argue with you?"

"No. It's not an attempt to convince you *not* to argue. Not arguing with me is simply part two of the first logic principle."

"Have you been sipping the Gentleman Jack I packed for you?"

"Drinking Gentleman Jack is not related to logic. It's more a health food *requirement.* Like drinking a brimful glass of red wine every day. . . . But thank you for thinking about my health."

"If I hang around you anymore, am I going to end up thinking like you?"

"I hope so."

Settling in at the cabin in Island Park where I lodged during guide school close to a decade ago, Lucinda and I soon hiked down to the Box Canyon. It was approaching dusk, diminished by the obstructing mountains to the west. She wanted to use the bamboo rod I made for her, which not long ago hung over her mantle in Manhattan. I think she once thought of it as that quaint thing a strange Montana guide made for her.

The rod expresses the beauty of varnished bamboo, but it's only seven feet long. The Box isn't seven-foot rod country. I loaned her one of my Sharpe's rods. A decade-and-a-half ago lecturing at Aberdeen, Scotland, I received from my hosts an unexpected honorarium of several hundred pounds in Bank of Scotland fifty-pound notes. I convinced myself it wasn't real money. Since I didn't expect to be back in the UK for several years, I went into a local fly fishing shop and came out with two Scottish rods. They're 8-foot, 6-inch, 5-weights—"The Gordon" model. My mother's maiden name was Gordon and she was from Scotland. There's a sense of family using them, especially after having been exorcised of all the old family names when I adopted my new surname of Brooks.

My guide friends like these Scottish rods. I could give scientific reasons about how and where they bend, the stiffness, the way they load, how they adjust to one's casting style, and the balance—like I hear a lot of guides and rod manufacturers talk about. But the truth is that I don't understand most of that talk. Or maybe I understand that ninety percent of it is pure market-speak, like they do with golf clubs and tennis racquets. And probably Frisbees and marbles. To me these rods *feel* good, and they're effective, like my Glock pistol. I think I cast as efficiently with one of them as with a couple of *very* expensive rods in which I've overindulged. I know Mel Krieger, Lefty Kreh, or Joan Wulff could put a #2 pencil into the mouth of my Glock, attach a fly line to the tip of the pencil, and outcast most people I've seen fly fishing with $800 rods.

When Lucinda and I reached the Box and planted our feet enough to maintain balance, she roll-cast a black rubber-legs into the river. I started to explain to her that the rubber-legs is used generally in late June about the time of the salmon fly season and that she might want to copy me and use an old-faithful Adams. But as I got the first words out, her rod bent. She turned, grinned, and said, "Good luck with that little-bitty Adams," and was off wading downstream, following what had to be a good fish.

But I was absolved—a cutthroat rose and hit my Adams within seconds of my dropping it upstream below a large rock near the far bank. Water rushed by the rock so fast it swirled back forming an eddy and leaving a small, smooth-surfaced pool on the downstream side of the rock. My fly had dropped into the middle of the calm water and a cutthroat, pleased with a piece of food floating into its territory that would take little energy to reach and consume, slurped the fly in the same way Wuff starts her dinner.

As I looked up to see how Lucinda was doing, a little curious to know whether she knew I had a fish on, she turned her head toward me abruptly to say something, slipped on a rock, and went in, twisting and splashing butt first. I headed toward her, using my walking stick she ridiculed as being for old men and trying to keep my own fish on the line. Lucinda had gone in over her wader top. I'd let her start without the walking stick, but insisted she wear a wading belt, buckling it up fairly tight while she argued that the waders were high enough to keep out the river.

She popped up dripping, letting out a sentence that included a couple of words that were firsts for her around me. Words that *should* be saved for these moments. She quickly regained her footing and then held up the rod so I could see the fish was still on. Five minutes later she landed a seventeen-inch rainbow.

Mine turned out to be thirteen. We were soon on our way up the hill to get her some dry clothes. She couldn't stop laughing.

"Did you get a picture of me with my big fish, Macduff?"

"No, but I took a good one of you looking like a fish—half submerged. It would look great on the cover of *Fly Fishing.* Your butt was sticking up like a feeding duck."

Our cabin that night faced west, straight into an Idaho sunset that competed with the best of those in Montana, but maybe not with Moose, Wyoming, sunsets beyond the Grand Teton. On the porch, we shared a bottle of fruity, oak aroma Argentine *Malbec* wine, from the Uco Valley in Central Mendoza. *Malbec's* a new thing in the U.S. So are we. It fits. We ended the day tucked under a big blue and white checked quilt; Wuff curled up at the foot of the bed.

20

IDAHO KEPT OUR ATTENTION for three more days; it could have been far more but for the beckoning of work accumulating at Mill Creek. We fished more southerly parts of the Henry's Fork around Ashton, plus sections of the Teton and the Fall rivers.

On the way home north, I made the wrong turn a dozen miles before West Yellowstone and found us heading north on 87 over the Continental Divide and toward Ennis. Maybe it wasn't a totally unintentional turn; I've always liked Ennis. At least before Paula Pajioli was murdered close by.

When Lucinda saw a sign for Ennis, she asked, "Are you comfortable with taking this route?"

"I have to face it sometime. The Madison's a great fishing river, especially early when the Yellowstone is too fast and too cloudy to be attractive."

"Are we going to stay in Ennis?"

"Nope."

"Nope?"

"*Nope.*"

"You're so talkative. And equally articulate."

"Only when I have something worthwhile to say."

"Telling me where I'll be sleeping tonight isn't 'worthwhile to say'?"

"You'll be sleeping with me . . . and Wuff."

"Do I get a choice?"

"No, or I'll be sleeping alone. . . .We're staying at 'The Sac.'"

"That doesn't sound very enticing."

"It's in Three Forks. North of Ennis. It's only a little longer from Ennis to Bozeman than the more direct route through West Yellowstone and along the Gallatin River."

"What's 'The Sac'?"

"It's the Sacajawea Inn. Named after you-know-who. Built in 1910 to serve passengers of the railroad."

"1910? Does it have running water and toilets?"

"We'll find out."

"What else is in Three Forks?"

"Winston's."

"Winston who?"

"Winston Rods. Formally the 'R.L.Winston Rod Co.'"

"Good rod?"

"One of the best. . . .Three Forks is like Ennis as far as fishing is concerned. But while the Madison flows by itself past Ennis, Three Forks is close to where the Madison, the Jefferson, and the Gallatin join and become the Missouri. Lewis and Clark named them. They thought all three were about equal, but none comparable to the grand Missouri. So they named the three after the President—Jefferson, the Secretary of State—Madison, and the Secretary of the Treasury—Gallatin."

"How's the food at The Sac?"

"You'll love it. When I was there a few years ago, about the time we met, I didn't understand a thing on the menu. I do remember they served Thai Chicken Lollypops. I had bison ribs. I knew what bison ribs meant better than Thai Chicken Lollypops."

The following morning we sat at breakfast reading a complimentary copy of the *Bozeman News.* I took the sports, Lucinda the more serious front section.

"Mac, listen to this!"

Yesterday, September 21st, Karl Escher, a St. Augustine, Florida hospital administrator who was building a cabin high on the east side of the Continental Divide in the Sierra Madre Mountains west of Encampment, Wyoming, was murdered on the North Platte River not far from the Saratoga town center. He had been tied to the middle guide seat of his drift boat, inside what looked like a wicker basket. A cluster of mistletoe was in his hair.

A young couple, students from the University of Wyoming at nearby Laramie, was fishing a little ahead of Escher's boat. They noticed it floating downriver and rowed toward it because it seemed out of control. When the students got closer, they saw the wicker, mistletoe, and explosives attached to Escher. They were fairly certain that a sign on the wicker said, 'I'm getting closer.' The couple rowed away before the explosion.

The incident appears to be nearly identical to the murder on the Madison River near Ennis in Western Montana last June, when a federal government employee, thought to be working for the CIA, was the victim. That murder seriously injured a local fly fishing guide who was rowing to offer help. The sign in that case was believed to say, 'You're next, Lucinda.' Lucinda is the name of the guide's lady-friend.

Macduff Brooks, the guide, lives on Mill Creek, a tributary of the Yellowstone River in Paradise Valley. He has been the focus of foul play on several western rivers. A few years ago two persons were killed in his drift boat, and in the last two years, three women who ran a drift boat shuttle service were found at different takeouts along the Yellowstone River, murdered, mutilated, and tied to a cross on Brooks' boat trailer. The mur-

ders were all solved—partly by Brooks and his lady-friend, who is now his fiancée.

The FBI and the Town of Saratoga, Carbon County, and state police are all investigating Escher's murder.

"Mac, what does this mean?"

"I don't know why it occurred near Saratoga. That's a long way from Mill Creek if we're the targets. It doesn't make sense. It could be a copy-cat killer totally unrelated to Paula Pajioli."

"The sign apparently didn't have any name on it, but it sounds as though it was linked to the murder on the Madison near Ennis. That murder was linked to us, Macduff."

"Let's leave as soon as we finish breakfast. We need to talk to Dan Wilson when we reach my cabin. He may not know yet about Escher's murder."

21

WHEN WE REACHED my cabin's driveway, a glistening black Suburban was parked blocking my gate. All the windows of the Suburban were darkened. I couldn't tell whether anyone was in the vehicle. I honked. No response. I wished I had a boot to clamp on a wheel. But I settled by taking my Glock from the glove compartment and putting it in the right pocket of my jacket.

Getting out, I put both hands into the jacket's pockets, my right hand around the grip of the Glock. I've been accused too often of not being ready when someone intended to shoot me. Then I noticed the license plate was U.S. Government. Halfway to the Suburban, both front doors opened, and two men in suits got out, both holding FBI identification at arm's length in front of them.

"Macduff Brooks?" asked the one from the passenger side.

"Yes," I responded, my hand pulling away from the gun and out of the pocket.

"I'm Agent Chester Stern." Nodding toward his colleague, he added, "This is Agent Peter Drain."

"What can I do for you? We're tired from a long drive, so if you'd like to move your SUV, we could . . ."

"We'll move it when we're through. We want to talk to you about the deaths of Paula Pajioli and Karl Escher, the guy who was killed on the North Platte yesterday."

"I've talked to the Madison County Sheriff's Office homicide investigators, Ennis police, and one other FBI agent about Pajioli. As to yesterday's killing, my fiancée and I were in Three Forks last night after driving from Island Park on the Henry's Fork in Idaho. We have no knowledge of the Escher murder yesterday near Saratoga, other than what we read in the Bozeman newspaper at breakfast this morning."

"There are still questions to be answered."

"OK. Move your SUV and follow us in to my cabin. We can talk in a little more comfort."

"We'll follow you. But don't try anything. And keep that gun in your pocket."

"There's only one way in to my cabin. If I'm in front of you, it'd be hard to 'try anything.'"

"Don't be a smart ass," said Drain. Stern turned to Drain and shook his head.

I heard Stern quietly say, "Drain, I'm in charge of this investigation. Back off."

At my cabin Lucinda went inside. Neither agent challenged her.

Drain looked at Stern angrily and said crisply, "This SOB has been nothing but trouble for more than a decade. My first case was when he was guiding on the Snake and his client—a former U.S. ambassador—was killed. Brooks was uncooperative. Since then another guy was killed in his boat, and then the last couple of years three women were raped and crucified in his boat. He's obviously involved with Pajioli's death—he was there. And now Escher's murder yesterday. Brooks belongs behind bars."

"Agent Stern," I interjected, "I'll talk to you on condition you leave your pit bull in your SUV. And, to be accurate, the three shuttle service women were not close to my boat when they were murdered. They were killed and deposited on my trailer."

"Now, Brooks. Drain may be right about some of the murders."

"Such as?"

"People have died around you, Brooks. You're *involved*."

"Such as?"

"The shuttle service women. There were never trials of the killers of the first two."

"Julie Conyers was killed by a Mexican woman named Victoria Montoya. The file shows the information her brother provided about her involvement. As far as we know, she's in Mexico in an institution that she'll likely never leave. Her brother affirmed she killed Conyers. Montoya can't be extradited.

"Olga Smits was killed by Helga Markel. She admitted it in writing before she died in a traffic accident in California. The state doesn't try dead people. It's all in *your* files."

"What about Paula Pajioli? You were there."

"That's right. I was in another boat and was injured when her boat exploded. For several weeks I was blind. Fortunately, it wasn't permanent."

"I told you, Stern," interrupted Drain, "he's evasive. Let's take him in."

"Our conversation is over," I said, my voice a little stronger. "My attorney is Wanda Groves in Bozeman. I'll talk when she's present. . . . Close the gate on your way out."

"Don't leave your cabin, Brooks. That's an order."

"You don't give orders, Stern. Go get an arrest warrant. Bring charges. But be careful, or I'll bring some of my own against you two."

Lucinda came out as the two agents left, spinning the Suburban's wheels and gunning the vehicle down the driveway.

"Are *Sturm und Drang* for real, Mac?"

"They have the power behind their badges. They abuse it, but they are FBI. Dan Wilson has tangled with Stern, who knows that Dan and I have become friends. And the CIA thinks the FBI employs a bunch of arrogant amateurs. Stern will try to take out his frustrations on me since he's no match for Dan Wilson. Don't worry. They know what they can't do, and they came close to overstepping their authority just now. Wanda will file a complaint with their agency. But it won't do much good other than helping build a record of abuse of their positions."

"I worry about them, Mac."

"I do, too, but we can't give in. I suspect they won't return. They haven't a shred of evidence that points to either of us."

"Another thing. You told them I was your fiancée. It's the first time you've said that. Why?"

"Freudian slip? Misunderstanding? Common error?"

"None of the above," she said.

22

THE PHONE ALWAYS seems to ring when we walk out onto the cabin porch to relax. And it's often Dan Wilson. Right on schedule, in mid-afternoon while we were on my porch the phone rang. And it *was* Dan. I sat on the swing; Lucinda leaned against the edge of the railing.

Dan knew only bits and pieces about the murder of Karl Escher on Wyoming's North Platte River. Lydia Parsons, the CIA agent who covers that state and reports to Dan, arrived in Saratoga six hours after the murder, but she had little success in penetrating a cloak of secrecy created by the Town of Saratoga police chief, the Carbon County sheriff, the state police, and the same two FBI agents who tried to intimidate me yesterday. Each organization demanded primary jurisdiction over the investigation. The foursome was no more cooperative among themselves or with Parsons than one would expect among members of the U.S. Congress.

Parsons nevertheless remained in Saratoga and patiently listened, picking up a fragment here and a fragment there from newspaper reporters, local fishing guides and outfitters, and a local Encampment rancher who often rented a cabin to Escher when weather halted his access to his building project in the mountains. But Parsons learned little more than was already in the newspapers.

"I do have one thing to tell you both," said Dan. "Not about Escher in Saratoga. It's about Lucinda's colleague in Manhattan, Frank Wu."

I tapped the speaker phone button so Lucinda could listen.

"You found Wu?" I asked. Lucinda sat down on the swing next to me to listen.

"No. But he's now preoccupied with other problems. Lucinda shouldn't worry."

"I'm listening, too, Dan," said Lucinda.

"I hope all this killing is not going to bring back your amnesia; you've been through enough for a lifetime. You two need to settle down somewhere, have some kids, and become couch potatoes like the rest of us."

"Living with Macduff? I don't think I have ever seen him sitting on a couch. . . . Tell us about Wu. Does he still have the hots for me?"

"Maybe, but if so, they're on the back burner and cooling off quickly. He has other things to worry about. He's being sought by police for aggressively beating a young woman behind a New York night club. Apparently, Wu became worried that his diplomatic immunity didn't impress the woman's father, who threatened to kill Wu. Ironically, the woman was from Korea and her father is Korea's representative at the U.N. in New York. He also has diplomatic immunity. Whatever goes around comes around. Yesterday, Wu's father asked us to send him home. His father is apparently both losing power in China and losing patience with his son. But we can't find Wu. We have an idea that he's fled to Canada rather than return home to China; we think to Vancouver where there are lots of Asians.

We've asked our Canadian sister-agency—the CSIS—to look for him."

"Thanks, Dan. Lucinda and I are going to talk about leaving for Florida."

"Good idea. The Montana and Wyoming authorities may be losing patience with you. Leave before they get a court order requiring you to stay."

When Dan hung up, Lucinda walked to the swing and sat down next to me close enough for me to feel her trembling. She couldn't utter a word.

"Is this getting to be too much for you?" I asked after a few minutes of silence.

"I bought my ranch to have a place of peace and rest from Manhattan," she answered. "It isn't proving to be like that. I haven't slept at the ranch more than a few nights since the killing of Park Salisbury on the Snake three years ago. My amnesia was no sooner cured then you lost your sight on the Madison in June. Now I'm causing the problems—if it isn't Wu after me, it's Ellsworth-Kent."

"And me. I'm after you too. I have the hots for you and it's not on the back burner."

"You've caught me. And this hook isn't barbless. . . . Macduff, it's not whether I can handle all this. It's *how* we're going to handle our problems together. We've got issues we can't run from."

"There is a way out . . . for you."

"Tell me."

"Sell your ranch. There are other great places—Colorado's beautiful. So is Oregon. And Washington. Even north of here in Montana or Idaho. . . . Alberta might be safer. . . . You seem happy to be back working, assuming the Wu problem is over.

You still have your comfortable apartment in Manhattan. You like the city and its culture."

"You want the ring back, Mac?"

"What made you say that?"

Holding back the flood of tears that were about to cascade from those seducing eyes, she murmured, "You're different from everyone I've ever known. Professionally competent, like a lot of our friends. I see some vulnerability when we talk seriously. Vulnerability few men admit. Like Mavis often tells me, 'Wuff's a lucky dog to have found you.' So am I. You don't dance the same steps as most others. You have a rhythm all your own. I've been trying to adapt to that rhythm. . . . *So there!* And you can't have the ring back."

"*You* asked if *I* wanted it back. Now you won't give it back!"

"I just remembered *you* said I was your fiancée. I like that."

"Me, too. Staying?"

"Yeah."

Then the flood of tears broke loose. But tears of fear were soon flooded out by those of joy.

23

WE BARELY MOVED even as evening broke and coolness flooded Paradise Valley. Wrapped with sweaters and under a blanket thrown over our shoulders, Lucinda and I remained on the porch swing, watched the sun vanish between two serrated peaks to the west, and remained until occasional shivers were replaced by a persistent chill from the plummeting temperature.

Lucinda had two glasses of Montana Roughstock Whiskey. I matched her with Gentleman Jack. After the second glass, I understand and worry about the fact that Herzog, Isfahani, and maybe Ellsworth-Kent are chasing me. Finishing a rare third glass, I don't much give a damn.

"Macduff," she said quietly, not wishing to disturb the blackened silence, "can we pack up and head for Florida? I'm not scared, but I'm a little tense being here."

"I'd like to do that. I sense and share your being nervous. But I'm also scared . . . of losing you. And causing that loss. It happened once—with El's death—which I might have avoided. I wouldn't survive it happening to you. . . . We do need a change. I don't like this second killing.

"I know Karl Escher. From my St. Augustine dock I can almost see his house across the mud flats and salt marshes, sitting between the first and second dunes on the coast. We're friends socially. I know about his work at the hospital. He knows I guide in the West during the summer. He's asked me a dozen times to stop at his cabin when I passed through Emigrant on the trip between Montana and Florida. And before you and I met, I'd asked him to come and stay here in Montana and fish with me on the Yellowstone. He's done a little salt water fly fishing. . . . It's hard talking about him in the past tense; I haven't accepted the fact that he's dead.

"I hope it was a one-time copy-cat killer with no link to us or to the Pajioli murder. Perhaps a local disliked him and copied the Pajioli killing to cover it up. But try as I may to believe that, I think it's someone after me, using you. I've had someone trying to kill me from the time before I moved here, starting with the beating by Herzog and compounded by the deaths of his niece and nephew. Now Whitman is dead, not by my act but there's a link between us. If Whitman didn't tell Herzog my name or location before he was shot, Herzog will be even more determined to find me. Apart from Herzog and Isfahani, there's Ellsworth-Kent, and who knows who else."

"You're overreacting," she whispered. "Whitman's dead. That doesn't mean Herzog and Isfahani aren't involved. But I have a hunch they're not. And Ellsworth-Kent's after *me*."

"Do you think Herzog and Isfahani have backed off?" I asked.

"Not for a minute," she said. "I sense that they want you dead and aren't pussy-footing around trying to scare you before they strike. Maybe I'm wrong. I think they'll go after you when Isfahani's finished with his surgery, and they'll strike the minute they know your name and location. Quick. Violent. No quarter.

That means they didn't kill Pajioli or Escher. . . . Macduff, can you imagine what Herzog thinks of you? He blames you for the deaths of his nephew and niece. And Whitman, who may have been a sentence away from naming you. Plus, you tried to kill and succeeded in disfiguring Herzog's best friend."

"If you're trying to panic me you're doing great. What concerns me most is they'll go after you because you're with me."

"As far as my ex goes, Macduff, what worries me is that he'll try to kill you just because you're with me. Your name hasn't been on the signs on the wicker man, but he's using your thing—fly fishing—to get to me." She squeezed my arm and planted a welcome kiss on my cheek.

"You may be too emotional because of your past relationship with Ellsworth-Kent," I commented. "You were closer to him than I ever was to Herzog or Isfahani."

"I'm more mad than emotional. But I believe Ellsworth-Kent's the most logical killer of Pajioli and Escher."

"Why would he kill two people he has no quarrel with?" I asked.

"He wouldn't, normally," she answered, "but I suspect he came to the U.S. thinking I would go back to England with him, but soon realized I wouldn't want any part of him. I don't know what made him change his mind; he may hate me with such a passion that a few bodies along the path to finding me wouldn't trouble him. But he may be as likely as Herzog and Isfahani not to beat around the bush but to come after me directly. If that's true, why hasn't he acted more quickly? And who killed Pajioli and Escher? Why is their killer playing a game? . . . What do you think?"

"I thought the problem with Ellsworth-Kent was that he *loves* you so much he'd take me out to get you back, as distorted as that seems. You believe that now he *hates* you?"

"I think one thing one minute and another thing the next. It's bizarre and hard to be rational. That's part of why I'd like to leave for Florida."

"I don't disagree about Herzog and Isfahani not having backed off," I answered. "I don't know Ellsworth-Kent, so I can't speculate. . . . We're leaving out of the mix your colleague, or former colleague, Wu. Wherever he may be. . . . And, maybe it's someone else doing the killings. Someone we don't know about—yet."

"Whatever, Mac. We can talk about it on the long haul to Florida. I'll feel safer there. Do you want to go by way of Saratoga? We like staying in Encampment."

"I don't want to be even close to Saratoga or Encampment. . . . We could fly you to New York when we get to Atlanta or Jacksonville. Or sooner, from Billings."

"No way! By now we're in this together. Please . . . not another word about my hiding."

24

IT'S HARD TO LET GO of an Elysian fall in Paradise Valley, but we needed to start the journey east before early snowfalls scared us into hibernation. We had delayed a month watching the leaves turn, and it *was* time.

Wuff and I drove to Bozeman where the auto service department prepped my SUV for the road. The rough roads along the upper part of Mill Creek and other fishing destinations took a toll on my tires and their balancing. Fortunately, unlike my drift boats, there have been no bullet holes to plug in my SUV.

Before heading home to Mill Creek, I drove through the older neighborhood around MSU, older more in years of the houses than in years of the occupants. Many of the latter are students at MSU. They were waxing snowboards and skis. Yards were blanketed by leaves that filled the color chart of fall variations of a theme of yellow and red. It was to be a football weekend: Idaho State was coming to town. The Bobcats were hosting the Spuds.

On a Wednesday morning when the leaves of the cottonwood trees along the Yellowstone River were undergoing a final transformation, the three of us left our summer paradise.

We were willing to exchange the last of the autumnal hues for a safer feeling away from the incidents of June and September.

Heading south through the two parks, we remarked with joy that the hordes of summer visitors were gone and both parks were beginning to close their lodgings, restaurants, and stores for the coming winter. Soon most of the roads would be closed as well. Grand Teton National Park and Jackson Hole were also emptying of tourists, but soon a different group would arrive—the skiers, snowboarders, and snowmobilers.

We visited with John Kirby and Juan Santander for a day. John was getting ready to take people on snowmobiles and starting on winter replenishment of his fly fishing gear. Juan was living with his aunt, Ander Eckstrum's widow, Cassie, and thus far staying out of trouble.

Lucinda and I continue to disagree about Juan's role in saving us in Gainesville when Juan Pablo Herzog's nephew, Martín Paz, was about to shoot us after he killed my look-alike, Richard Potter. Juan's been working with John, who is determined to make Juan a successful fishing guide. Cassie told me she had a surprise for him for the forthcoming Christmas—a new Clack-a-Craft drift boat.

We could have stayed in Montana, but a mild and sun-filled Florida winter was beckoning. Early snow was falling in Paradise Valley, having begun the day after we left and printing an image on my mind of my cabin with a mantle of white. A day's drive south of Jackson, first through the sour, natural gas odors of Pinedale, followed a couple of hours later by joining the eighteen-wheelers traveling east on I-80, put us very little east of our starting point, but 300 miles south in more predictable weather.

Once we were out of Wyoming and into Colorado, I felt comfortable calling the sheriff in Saratoga. He told me he knew

Escher and thought townsfolk liked him. The sheriff couldn't imagine anyone having a grudge against Escher. He said that the town was shocked about both the way the killing occurred and that the victim was Escher. Unfortunately, neither the county nor the town has adequate resources to undertake a comprehensive investigation. And they don't like the way the two FBI agents have stepped in and are throwing their weight around. The Saratoga sheriff remarked that neither agent could complete a one-piece puzzle. I disagree. I'm sure it was on the test for joining the FBI.

I understood that we weren't dealing with towns and counties and even states that have deep resources for complex investigations. Especially for murder.

Montana's Madison County has about 7,500 residents. There are four incorporated cities, including Virginia City and Ennis. Ennis has fewer than 1,000 residents.

Wyoming's Carbon County is similar. It's twice the size of Madison County, with some 15,000 residents. Saratoga has roughly 1,600 residents. The county seat's in Rawlings. No location has an adequate tax base.

Concerned about facing multiple town and county investigators, I next called the person I first met when I moved to Montana what seems like a century ago—Ken Rangley in Livingston, Park County's Acting Chief Detective.

Ken used his connections to talk to both the Madison County Sheriff's office in Virginia City, Montana, and the Town of Ennis's police chief. He then talked to both the Carbon County Sheriff in Rawlings, Wyoming, and the police chief in Saratoga. All four were people I'd tried to get information from, with varying success. Not fully unexpected, Ken said the cooperation between the former two in Montana was exactly the opposite of the animosity between the latter two in Wyoming. Furthermore, Ken didn't want any part of the two FBI agents. Lucinda and I share his views.

25

THE DRIVE EAST became painful to the senses. Avoiding dodging traffic on the crowded interstates east of the Mississippi would be worth an extra day on the usual four-day trip. The traffic in the West wasn't yet screaming gridlock; we had traveled I-80 to Cheyenne, then headed south on I-25, passing through Denver and making a hard left in Pueblo to the east. Only then did I realize I'd once before faced the drive across southern Kansas and had vowed never to do it again.

"Lucinda, this isn't going to be a very attractive drive now that we're out of the mountains and heading due east through one big cornfield to Missouri. You'll have to learn to appreciate horizons."

"There must be something worthwhile to see along the way," she replied.

"That may prove a challenge."

"I'm looking at the guidebook, Macduff. We could stop at Mullinville, where a fellow named Liggett decorated land alongside the highway with structures made from wagon wheels, tractor gears, road signs, streetlights, and even bowling balls and toilet seats. . . . I guess they twirl, glint, and rust their way into Kansas art history. What do you think?"

"I think if Liggett were English, he'd have won the Turner prize."

"We could stop in a few miles and see a more natural state cultural treasure—Greensburg's Big Well—one of the Eight Wonders of Kansas. The Big Well is a thirty-two-foot-diameter, 109-foot-deep hole, with a ladder that can be climbed down—for a couple of dollars."

"Wow! Exciting. What do we do when we get to the bottom?"

"Keep going. Don't interrupt, Macduff. The book says that the Big Hole vies with the Kansas Underground Salt Museum at Hutchinson and the huge electric coal shovel at West Mineral for the most visitors. Don't you think that all this *southern* Kansas culture must be embarrassing to the good folk of Cawker City, in the *north* of Kansas? That's where the *major* Kansas tourist attraction is the world's largest ball of twine, 7.98 million feet—making the ball weigh 19,119 pounds."

"That should be enough to gift-wrap the whole state. And send it to Brazil as foreign aid. . . . Maybe not. We need the corn. . . . But not the ethanol, considering what ethanol has done to destroy my St. Augustine flats boat's outboard."

Crossing Arkansas and Mississippi on a Saturday afternoon, we killed three-and-a-half hours listening to a football game between two institutions of something other than higher learning.

"Macduff, actually listening to the game *being played* occupies very little of that time. I'm reading an excerpt from the *Wall Street Journal's* erudite one page a week devoted to sports. It says here that an average pro football game lasts three hours. But the playing time only totals eleven minutes!"

"If they could decrease that to five or six minutes, they could make a lot more money from advertising."

"You're interrupting again. This is important. The article goes on to say that other than advertisements, most of the air time is spent showing replays, players sitting on the bench, players standing with other players who don't get to play, players running on and off the field, players discussing things in the huddle, and players waddling up to the line and waiting for the ball to be snapped."

"At least they don't scratch and spit like baseball players," I ventured. "What the fans would prefer is more time seeing the cheerleaders."

"Maybe that's what *you'd* prefer. . . . According to the *Journal*, it's currently about three seconds. How does a fan explain this game to a foreigner?"

"In a few weeks my favorite football game will be on TV, watched across the country by a national audience that appreciates football the way it once was. It's the Army-Navy game."

"I know, Macduff. I went to that game about five years ago, before I bought my Montana ranch. At the final whistle the two teams first went to the loser's side and, standing before the students, sang the losing team's *alma mater*. Then both teams went to the winner's side and sang their *alma mater*. The reward for winning was to 'sing second.' Can you imagine this being done in the SEC, the Big Ten, or the Pac Ten?"

"I suspect there are more instances of good sportsmanship in that one game each year than most of the whole fall Division I college schedule, where cheap blocks, helmet spearing, celebrating, and taunting are either accepted or ignored, and one of the assistant coaches needs a license as a bail bondsman."

"True, but he can double up and also cover parole and probation."

After the long drive to St. Augustine, with no detour to Gainesville, we welcomed the safe refuge of my piney woods cottage. We vowed not to leave the cottage, deeply hidden among towering oaks and pines, except for food and drink at the supermarket a few miles south.

Lucinda doesn't yet know what her future holds in New York City; I've been hoping she's ready to exchange life in the fast lane in the Big Apple as a highly paid investment broker for life in the much slower lanes of Montana and Florida as a promising but poorly paid photographer. The compromise may be opening a Bozeman branch for her investment firm. It's her call.

After being together in my Florida cottage for two months . . . without a single trip to Gainesville . . . along with our rescued sheltie Wuff, fully recuperated from being shot on my drift boat two years ago, we ventured no further than the nation's first permanent European settled city, St. Augustine. Others contest this fact, mainly modern-day pilgrims in Plymouth, Massachusetts, who annually re-enact stepping from a *Mayflower* replica to "Plymouth Rock."

When voyagers landed at what became Plymouth in 1620, our St. Augustine was ready for its first rehab. No one debates that St. Augustine was settled in 1565, but when I was in grade school in Connecticut, something over a half-century ago, only one teacher even mentioned the city, and she said, "But St. Augustine doesn't count—it's Spanish." If she's still alive, she would understand that being Spanish does count. A long-time friend in Mexico City during my teaching years often reminded me that although we took a lot of territory from Mexico in 1847, it is getting the land back bit by bit, and it's all fully developed!

26

FOR THE FIRST TIME, Lucinda and I went all-out decorating my Florida cottage for Christmas. We lighted porch railings and hand rails and even the dock. We would be the only ones to see the lights, other than my caretaker Jen and her family, but the decorating made us feel good.

Jen's husband Jimmy, who does odd jobs for me, helped me extend the dock to store two kayaks I rigged for fly fishing. Together we built a fish cleaning table, adapting an ad in *Florida Sportsman,* the magazine that has as many covers showing smiling, half-naked girls holding seldom looked at fish, as *Fly Fishing* has covers of smiling, fully-clothed guys holding photographically distorted but greatly admired fish.

I've sometimes thought of adding a bikini-clad girl to my drift boat crew in Montana, taking only one client at a time and reserving the front seat for an MSU coed serving ribs, chips, beer, and salsa. I would have a Hooter's-on-the-River and could double my rate. She could stay at my cabin during the season. I suggested the idea to Lucinda. . . . She thought it was a bad idea! *Very bad.*

The fish table *was* a good idea and used frequently. We grilled what we caught—enough flounder, sea trout, blues, reds, and a few snook—to exceed our daily protein requirements. Plus, fish taste better than rattlesnake. Jimmy agrees with me, but we don't tell that to Jen.

We kept the radio and TV off, except for occasionally checking The Weather Channel for approaching cold fronts. Lucinda did miracles in the small kitchen. I didn't help when I couldn't catch fish on demand for our dinners.

The cold set in around mid-November and drove most of the fish out of the marshes and further south, or, if they stayed in our marsh into deep holes. But I know the location of a couple of those holes, where usually I can catch a redfish or sea trout for dinner.

Christmas morning we were opening presents to each other when Dan Wilson called from D.C. I thought it kind of him to call and wish us a Merry Christmas. But that wasn't only why he called. After brief holiday greetings, his tone turned rigid.

"How many times have you been to Gainesville?" he asked.

"Not once. The Gator women's soccer team had an off season—didn't make the playoffs. When I heard myself say that, I realized how much I missed going to Gainesville for a game or two soon after we arrived from Montana."

"I hope they keep losing next fall," said Dan, "if that's what it will take to keep you away from Gainesville. . . . Mac, it's not about Gainesville, but there is some bad news. Another explosion on a drift boat. In Montana."

"This time of the year? Are you certain? The float season is long over. I'm looking at my phone's weather and it says Bozeman two degrees above zero, Livingston seven, and Missoula a stratospheric nine. . . . We haven't had much news. Haven't bought a paper, gone on-line or watched TV for a week. When did this happen?"

"Four days before Christmas. Not during a usual fishing float, but it involved a drift boat. The killing happened on the Clark River at Missoula. In fact, almost downtown in Missoula, a little downstream of the mouth of Rattlesnake Creek."

"Who on earth was floating in December?"

"It's something new involving some of the fraternities and sororities at UM. They float to raise money for a kids' hospital in Missoula. It's becoming a tradition . . . starts at the end of fall term exams just before the Christmas holiday and is repeated for three nights. Each night they do a candlelight drift on the portion of the river that goes through the town. They're determined; they drift with their candles lit even when snow is falling."

"What happened?"

"On the second day—the 21st—somehow a drift boat was set afloat and caught up with the others that were being slowed down by their rowers to reduce their speed alongside the town where all the spectators were lining the banks. Tied to the seat of the boat inside a wicker encasement was a fiftyish law professor at UM. He had mistletoe is his hair. Some students recognized him."

"Do you know his name?"

"Fred Tansley. Is that important?"

"Yes. I know Fred. He taught tax law as a visitor at UF. We tried to get him to move permanently, but he loved the West and Missoula. . . .That means Herzog and Isfahani could be involved. Tansley was at UF when Herzog and Isfahani were students. I had him to a Thanksgiving dinner that both Herzog and Isfahani attended."

"That's not good, Mac. Herzog and Isfahani could reach you through the link with Tansley—a friend of Hunt also connected to you as Brooks, as all three wicker man and Mistletoe murders have been. I'll have someone in Missoula tomorrow. . . . I would have thought that a drift boat with a single person tied to the guide seat would draw some attention while it floated."

"I suspect the students were drinking to keep warm. Not coffee, more likely Montana Roughstock Whiskey. Or a favored beer made in Missoula—'Moose Drool.' Whichever, when the boat was adjacent to the old part of town, where UM's located, the explosion occurred."

"The Pajioli and Escher murders occurred on a river when a single boat exploded—set off by a timer. How did it happen in Missoula?"

"There was a crowd lined along the river to see the candlelight. Someone in that crowd could have started the timer, or directly set off the explosion."

"Was there any kind of sign on Tansley?"

"Yes—attached to the wicker man—but what it said is a subject of debate among people who say they saw the sign from the shore."

"Any consensus?"

"The snow that stuck to the lettering had covered and partly melted the cardboard sign. All we can tell is that one word had a 'DUF' in it. And there might have been 'NEXT,' but some say that word or part of a word was 'TEXT' or 'TENT' or 'MEX.'"

"I don't like the 'DUF,' which could be part of 'MACDUFF.'"

"We'll never know. The explosion destroyed the sign. The final night of the floats was canceled."

"Anyone else killed or seriously injured?"

"Fortunately not. It was cold enough that the intense heat of the explosion dissipated and was cooled as it expanded outward from the boat."

"What's next, Dan?"

Lucinda had set down the present she was unwrapping. The cheer of Christmas had quickly vanished.

"Dan, this is Lucinda. Mac and I plan to return to Montana early—in March. There's a celebration on the Ides of March—the 15th—each year at Big Sky. We've been invited to stay with friends. It means an earlier departure from Florida than usual and puts us in Montana on the spring equinox, a week after the Ides celebration. Would you prefer that we stay here?"

"Let us do some more investigation before I answer that. But for now stay where you are."

"Thanks for letting us know about Missoula. Merry Christmas and Happy New Year." I meant it, but it was hard to think of this Christmas as being "Merry." Certainly not for Professor Tansley's family.

When Dan hung up, I refilled our eggnog with an extra splash of rum. The mood in the cottage was glum. Lucinda looked confused and displaced. I couldn't have looked any better.

"Three murders, Mac! When will it end?"

"Depends on who the killer is and his or her intentions."

"You don't seem to believe now that Herzog and Isfahani are behind the three killings?"

"That assumes one person is responsible for all three. Or in Herzog's case working with a friend other than Isfahani—he's still in Switzerland. But it could be that each of the three was an entirely separate murder, with Pajioli's murder being copied by one or more others in killing Escher and now Tansley."

"If it's only one person, I'm scared because of the 'You're Next, Lucinda' sign on Pajioli."

"There's probably more than one, Lucinda. And we don't know how to interpret the second sign or even read the third."

"Lucinda isn't a particularly common name. How many Lucindas do you suppose there are in this area who have some link to fly fishing? Me! Period! Plus the second sign on Escher which read 'I'm getting closer,' suggests a repeat killer or killers, who could be Herzog and Isfahani or my former husband. The third sign has a 'DUF' in it and maybe the word 'NEXT.' That doesn't sound encouraging."

"Is there anything common to all three?" I asked.

"I haven't thought about that. But there have been three murders, starting in June and followed in September and now in December. . . . There is something that might link them. They were three months apart."

"Does that mean that if there's a fourth it will be in March?" I asked.

"That's a possibility. Not just in March. On the 21st of March."

"Spring equinox?"

"Yes. Each of the three was on the 21st of the month. You know what that means, Mac. They were on the summer solstice, the autumnal equinox, and the winter solstice. That means the next could be on the spring equinox. We've talked about being at Big Sky on the 15th."

"I don't like to arrive until the middle of April, when the snow begins to melt. Earlier it's too cold and frustrating. Maybe Big Sky isn't a good idea. It's a temptation of habitability followed by inevitable regressions to sub-freezing and snow."

"Is there anything else that links the three murders?" she asked. "The first was not far from our cabins. The second a long way off in Saratoga. Now the third was somewhat closer in Missoula."

"All were on blue ribbon trout rivers," I responded. "All are on Trout Unlimited's list of the 100 best streams in America. Well, almost. The Missoula killing on the Clark was close to Rock Creek, which empties into the Clark just outside Missoula. Rock Creek's on the list; the Clark isn't."

"The killer might have used the Clark because it was common knowledge that the UM students would be floating just before Christmas. This is the first time there was an audience."

"We need to talk to Dan again soon. He's more experienced than we are at looking at these events."

"Let's have a nightcap and then try to sleep."

27

THE REMAINING DAYS of winter passed excruciatingly slowly. Filled with anticipation that morphed into trepidation, we counted the days to the spring equinox on March 21st. Perhaps spring would be a time of rebirth; summer, fall, and winter had certainly been seasons of finality.

I was restless. Nothing about the killings was uncovered in Montana or Wyoming, at least nothing that Dan or Erin or Ken passed on to us. Lucinda and I began to take my SUV out with increasing abandon. It might have been wiser to use my old Hewes flats boat for excursions away from the cottage, but the thought of being exposed in an open boat made me think of Ander Eckstrum's murder on my drift boat several years ago. Our flats boat meandering through the channels surrounded by low marsh grass was an easy target for someone in the woods to the west. I deluded myself into believing that we were safer in the SUV.

We first went no further than successive visits to St. Augustine—to walk the old streets of the historic area and have a meal sitting on the outside balcony at A1A. Our first meal there was during January, when the Christmas lights remained on beyond the holiday. The tiny white lights were ubiquitous, draped on trees, buildings, and the railings of the Bridge of Lions that crosses the Intracoastal Waterway. Soon we ventured a few miles further to Camachee Cove, where we dined outside under the pergola at the Kingfish Grill. Another trip took us across the Intracoastal to Vilano and Aunt Kate's.

More adventurous outings followed, including to Amelia Island and old Fernandina, where we spent our first overnight away from the cottage at the elegant Fairbanks house, years ago converted to a B&B. Having breakfast on the first morning at the Fairbanks, I pleaded with Lucinda for us go to Gainesville.

"I'm not suggesting we go anywhere in Gainesville where we might be recognized," I promised. "Not to Golf View where I lived with El. Not to a sports event. We can go on a Sunday when there are far fewer students around. Even over spring break, when they're all gone."

"Why do you need Gainesville? You suffered a terrible loss there. You left Gainesville on a trip west with El and came home alone a widower. Ten years later you left Gainesville on another trip—to Washington—flew on to Guatemala, and came back to the U.S. on a stretcher. It ended your life as Professor Maxwell Hunt. Why do you have to go back to Gainesville as Macduff Brooks?"

"I lived there for twenty years. Comforting years with El, and anticipating many more after our child was to be born. With their deaths, the next decade was lonely, but I worked hard."

"Is it your reputation you miss?"

"More than reputation. I was thrilled to become a lawyer and doubly so when I began to teach law. Being part of the academic community was a dream come true. I miss that."

"If Herzog and Isfahani were out of the way, would you want to teach again? . . . Buy your old house? Is Montana important to you? Would I be part of Professor Maxwell Hunt's life if you went back?"

"I won't teach again. It's nearly eight years that I've been away from the law. I haven't read a single case or one page of a law book. My books have long had new authors added to replace me. I haven't been in a classroom or presented a lecture. The legal world has moved on without me, and I don't want to try to catch up with it. . . . But if I had any desire to teach again or even practice law, I'd want you part of it."

"Would I be 'Mrs. Maxwell Hunt'?"

"I've never thought of that. I guess so. But it's Macduff Brooks who's engaged to you, not Maxwell Hunt. Would I have to buy another ring and propose again?"

"No to both. I love my battered ring . . . and my battered fiancée. And don't assume for a minute that you have a way out of our engagement by becoming Maxwell Hunt."

"I know better than to argue that point anymore."

"Are you frustrated with your choice of being a fishing guide and spending seasons in Montana?"

"No. I love floating the rivers and wading the streams, all the more so when you're along. But I can't understand why I've been involved with so much violence. Eight years and seven people dead, beginning with Ander Eckstrum and now Tansley. Eight dead if we count Park Salisbury—Ander's killer. That's one a year. And it's not over. The spring equinox is soon. I'm convinced something will happen then."

"But you haven't done one thing or said one word that's *caused* any innocent person's death. And if something does happen on the 21st, it won't be because of you."

"I haven't done anything to provoke the killings, but they did lead to some of my own. I tried to kill Isfahani in Guatemala. And I killed Herzog's niece, María-Martinez Herzog—posing as Belinda Stamer. Plus Park Salisbury."

"You didn't kill Salisbury. It was a joint effort: Ken's swat team from the shore, you and me from the boat, and the pointed tree limb that you ran Park into to end it. But he was likely dead by that time. I shot Jimbo Shaw, after he killed Pam Snyder. I destroyed his hand, but I didn't kill him. It's a pretty thorny past, but it's mine as well as yours."

"There's more, Lucinda. When I was practicing or teaching I never took time to appreciate the world around me. I never had time for friends. Or time to take care of a dog. If I counted the hours, I'm certain I spent much less time with El than I have with you since we met. I was always gone when I was practicing, doing depositions or dealing with trials and giving lectures. When I was home, I spent long hours in the evening writing. . . . I don't want to go back to that."

"What do you want?"

"Mostly . . . spend the rest of my life with you. Not only living in a house with you; *being* with you. Sitting together in the car, on a swing, having breakfast with you the way we are here in Fernandina. And I want to see that Wuff is well cared for in her twilight years. She's nine. That's a little more than 60 in human terms."

"Wuff's a happy dog. And I'm not leaving. After all, we *are* engaged."

"I concede that. I must have caught your amnesia because I don't seem to remember much about asking you to marry me. Or about you saying 'yes.'"

"You'll have to take my word."

"I'm past the point of no return?"

"Way past."

Lucinda compromised on going to Gainesville. She insisted that it be on a Sunday. And that we wouldn't go inside the law buildings and certainly not near where Herzog's niece was shot. No retracing of the Paz shooting. No events like a baseball game or tennis match. Especially a tennis match which would take place within a couple of hundred feet from where Martín Paz shot Richard Potter and was, in turn, killed by a still unidentified party. Lucinda has—from that evening on—insisted it was Juan Santander; I was adamant that it was one of Dan's CIA agents, but I'm coming around to Lucinda's side.

When we arrived in Gainesville, I wasn't sure what we would do—probably drive through without stopping and maybe head west for a seafood meal at Cedar Key. The visit to Gainesville might be my last.

I did turn into Golf View, abruptly as we were passing and to Lucinda's chagrin. We went slowly past both my old house and Roy Palladio's. I looked hard because I won't go there again. It's difficult to believe it's been four years since Roy was killed by a baggage cart in the Gainesville airport on his long-planned trip to Mali.

After Golf View I started past the law building but impulsively turned into the faculty parking lot, grabbed Lucinda's hand, and pulled her to a bench outside the entrance where I could sit and see the full law college complex for one last time. There had been several additions, all a tribute to some generous alums and Dean Perry.

I'd only seen Dean Perry once before, at the dedication of the Catarina Paris Center, the day Herzog's niece nearly shot Perry, but did hit UF President Killingsworth.

I was looking down while reminiscing, holding tightly to Lucinda, when I heard a voice. I looked up to see a couple had stopped by us.

"Are you folks waiting to see someone in the building? If you're the Booths, I'm sorry we're late. I'm Dean Hobart Perry. This is my wife Asil."

"I . . . I . . . I," was all I could get out, stammering until I regained my composure. "We're not the Booths. We were just out for a Sunday walk and stopped to rest."

"Do you know anything about the law college?"

"Very little," I replied. "I know some people who went to law school here."

"Are you a lawyer?"

"I was a law professor. But an injury forced me to retire." That was certainly the truth. But I was trespassing on dangerous territory and immediately sorry I mentioned being a law professor.

"What's your name? Where did you teach?"

"I'm Macduff Br . . . Macduff Brown. This is my friend. . . . I taught law at Minnesota, a couple of decades ago."

"What a coincidence. I was at Minnesota for twenty-five years before I came here as dean. When were you there?"

"Early seventies, after practicing in Idaho Falls for two years," I answered, hoping he wouldn't inquire further.

"I was on leave for three years around that time to work in D.C. I guess we missed each other."

"I guess we did. . . . It's good to meet you. We had best be starting on to Tampa for a dinner engagement with friends."

Sweat was beginning to stain my shirt as we walked away. I was certain I had once more made a fool of myself, if not worse—jeopardized my life and Lucinda's. I glanced back as we cut between rows of cars in the faculty parking area. Dean Perry and his wife were talking. The dean said something, held his hands up with palms raised, and shrugged. He appeared perplexed.

"Asil," Dean Perry said to his wife. "That was a very strange meeting."

"Why do you say that, Hobart? I thought they were an attractive couple."

"I never heard of Minnesota having a visiting professor by the name of Brown when we were in D.C. He hesitated giving us his last name. And he didn't give us the name of his companion."

"It's not important. You have other things to worry about. Especially talking to the Booths about their proposed gift. I think I see them coming."

28

LATE THE FOLLOWING MORNING Dean Perry was sipping coffee in his office between meetings with a student complaining of unfair treatment by a professor and an unproductive faculty member who once again was asking for extra funds to travel to a estate law meeting—this time in Vancouver—where he was not scheduled to participate and likely would spend his time in the bars.

Perry's secretary Donna brought in some papers.

"Dean Perry, I've gone on line and found that no one named Brown, and more particularly, Macduff Brown, ever taught at Minnesota. I checked West's law teachers directory and no one by that name was listed from the mid-60s to the mid-80s as being a law teacher anywhere in the U.S. or Canada, much less Minnesota. . . . I also checked with both the Idaho state bar association in Boise and the local lawyers association in Idaho Falls. No record of a Macduff Brown ever practicing."

"I thought that's what you might find."

"Do we have a problem?"

"I don't think so. Donna, you were here when Maxwell Hunt was a professor?"

"Yes. I knew him pretty well, considering how reclusive he became after his wife died in Wyoming. He spent more time with students, especially foreign ones enrolled in our LL.M., than he spent with other faculty. He was productive and often away lecturing."

"What did he look like?"

"Tall, maybe six-three. Couple of hundred pounds. Brown hair. No glasses. No facial hair. Unlike most of the faculty, he always wore a suit and tie to work and to class. In his last years here, he didn't participate in many law college activities, even faculty meetings he was supposed to attend."

"Thanks," Perry said, with obvious satisfaction that he had filled in some gaps in recent activities.

After Donna left, Perry tilted back in his chair and thought, "Could it have been *him*? He had a moustache which he could have grown. And his glasses could be something new or even non-prescription. I've never fully agreed with those who thought he survived the beating in Guatemala. Herzog's actions regarding his proposed funding for a chair assumed Hunt was alive. I never believed Richard Potter was Professor Hunt. . . . But why would Hunt come here? Does he live in Florida?"

Perry got up and went to a filing cabinet in his small storeroom. Unlocking the drawer, he took out a file marked *Professor Maxwell Hunt's death.* It was the report former Associate Dean Gloria Martinez compiled three years ago when Herzog met with Perry and announced his proposed gift. Perry wasn't certain he wanted to delve into the matter again. There were so many unanswered questions. But he read through the report anyway, and thought, "It reads very differently to me now. Probably because I was so hopeful that we would receive Herzog's gift. Added to the circumstances of Martín Paz's death, I think I was wrong in being so doubtful that Hunt survived."

One thing that surprised Perry—there was no photograph of Hunt in the file. When he checked the personnel files, he found no file for Hunt. Only when he asked Donna to help did he see a photo.

"Dean Perry, I went through our law college magazine—the *Florida Lawyer*—starting with the year Hunt allegedly died and going back year by year. I finally found one edition—eleven years earlier—with a photo of six faculty at a conference here that included Hunt standing in the back. It's not a good photo. It was taken the year before his wife died. I recall my predecessor saying Hunt never wanted his photo taken after that tragedy. But, anyway, here it is," she said, handing the photo to Perry who looked at it carefully and set it down on his desk.

Perry looked up at Donna, and said, "I talked to Maxwell Hunt yesterday!"

29

ON THE DRIVE home to St. Augustine after meeting Dean Perry, I was unusually quiet. I was afraid Lucinda would begin an I-told-you-so lecture.

"Mac, I told you so," she started. "We always get into some kind of embarrassing situation when we go to Gainesville. I understand how you feel about the town and the university. But. . . . "

She didn't say another word about Gainesville, but it had opened a Pandora's box of issues I didn't want or know how to face. At the cottage I busied myself with annual maintenance, starting with spraying rust deterrent on steel bolts that attach the log columns to the floor beams. The protection against corrosive salt by the massed pines on my property was deceiving—the frequent winds off the ocean a mile away brought salt spray to my SUV, my tools, and every metal fastening on the cottage.

Filtering through the trees that were swaying to a January southeast breeze, the winter sun was low in the afternoon sky. Shadows danced along the wall of the cottage. Daylight became sparse. But the temperature hovered close to seventy, twice what it was at my Montana cabin.

Lucinda walked down the stairs with a bottle of wine and two glasses, looking translucent in a shapely, long, white tuxedo shirt that had knot buttons on the front placket and covered to an inch above her knees.

"Walk with me to the pier," she asked, more as a statement than a question.

"You look beautiful. . . . Something important?"

"Yes."

When we sat on the swing, she poured the wine, and we shifted our bodies to touch from shoulder to calf. She turned and asked, "Macduff, do you love me?"

"Yes, very much."

"Do you still love El?"

"Yes, . . . very much."

"Can a person truly love two people at the same time?"

"If they're both alive, perhaps not. But you're alive. El is not."

"Am I El's reincarnation?"

"Not at all."

"Do you think of El often?"

"Nearly every day."

"Do you think of me often?"

"Nearly every moment."

"Do you compare us?"

"I try not to."

"But you do."

"Sometimes."

"Do I come out OK?"

"Yes."

"Where don't I?"

"Cooking."

"Cooking? What do you mean?"

"Well, what are we having tonight?"

"Red snapper a la Sichuan."

"Case closed."

"You don't even know what it is."

"It's red snapper fish, probably freshly caught off St. Augustine, which you're subjecting to Chinese water torture."

"That's not fair."

"Then what's with the 'a la Sichuan' on perfectly good fish?"

"Sichuan is a classic Chinese food preparation."

"What's in it?"

"Sake and . . . , " she started.

I interrupted, "That's fine. Fish cooked in sake sounds delicious, but it would taste better cooked in Gentleman Jack."

"Wait! There's more."

"I was afraid of that."

"I also use grapeseed oil, chicken stock, white peppercorns, cabbage, pickled chilies, vinegar, soy sauce, and sriracha. It's served on rice with a cilantro garnish."

"Sriracha! Is that fish eyes or snake bile?"

"For you I should include both. . . . sriracha is a sweet and tangy Thai sauce used on seafood. It's made of chili peppers, distilled vinegar, garlic, sugar, and salt."

"You already said the fish has chili and vinegar on it. Srirachi sounds like an overdose."

"What would you like me to make?"

"Peanut butter and jelly sandwiches, just like my mother used to make for me." I knew the punch was coming, and my upper arm would be sore for days.

"The next time we're in Palatka, we'll stop at McDonald's," she threatened. "The treat's on me. Anything you want."

"McDonald's! Palatka! Oh my God! Let's stay home . . . and have Red snapper a la Sichuan."

And we did.

30

LUCINDA AND I, sometimes joined on the phone by Dan, talked endlessly about *where* a next killing might take place. We had little doubt that it *would* occur, and we knew the day. Tuesday, March 21st—the spring equinox.

Two weeks before the 21st, we closed the Florida cottage for the season and left for Montana. It was a little early; we would encounter snow occasionally as we drove through the Rockies, but thoughts of floating Montana's Yellowstone or Wyoming's Snake and walking the trails following high-country creeks convinced us it wasn't too early to go. Our housekeeper, Jen, promised to take good care of the St. Augustine cottage.

I was curious how the snow melt would be this year since we were a month earlier than usual in making the trip. Sometime in early-to-mid-April the temperature elevates enough to start the mountain snowpack melting and trout stirring in the spring creeks. The higher temperature also signals some decent fishing on the Yellowstone River.

But in a matter of days, no more than two weeks, the river effectively closes down to good fishing as the snowmelt cascades down the mountains, carrying the summer's supply of water and enough silt to keep the water brown for weeks. The flow in the Yellowstone can reach 15,000 cubic feet per second, too fast to comfortably drift the river. In a good year the river slows down and clears up in June; in a bad year clearing may not occur until late July or early August. That's hard on guides trying to make a living during an already short season.

Our only reluctance to start west was the drudgery of four to five days crossing the country. We stayed south of any serious snow, going along the lower edge of the U.S. to New Mexico and only then turning north to Durango in the southwest corner of Colorado. I wanted to pass through Jackson and spend a day at the annual meeting of the Wyoming chapter of the FFF. FFF looks like my math grades in high school, but it means Federation of Fly Fishers.

Based in Livingston, Montana, the organization has opened a must-visit museum of fly fishing, including the beginnings of an outstanding library. The organization is the U.S. standard-bearer for training and certifying fly casting instruction. A lot of guides have achieved CCI—Certified Casting Instructor—and a few the more demanding MCI—Master Casting Instructor. I'm neither, but I've promised myself that someday I'll earn the CCI.

The Jackson FFF program proved helpful to my casting skills, but as March 21st approached, my mind was increasingly focused on the expectancy of another explosion on a drift boat.

We knew the trip was long when, while grilling some Bison steaks our first night in Jackson, Lucinda asked me, "What was that awful wine we had in that town—the name of which escapes me the town was so nondescript— in, I think, Oklahoma, but maybe Kansas, at that restaurant called . . . I don't remember that either."

"Was that a question? Or maybe four questions? I don't remember either—to all of the above. . . . Lucinda, I want to call Erin and have you on the line. I saw someone today I was shocked to see. You've never seen her. Erin has." I dialed her number in Livingston.

"Erin, Macduff. I'm in Jackson Hole."

"Chasing Jackson girls? Does Lucinda know you're there?"

"Not a chance."

"Not a chance you're chasing girls? Or not a chance Lucinda knows about it?"

"Take your pick. Lucinda knows I'm here. She's here, too. Came out of Coldwater Creek with a big bag ten minutes ago. . . . And I haven't been chasing girls. I'm working."

"Hard to believe. What's up, Macduffy? Another body in your boat?"

"Not yet. My boats are at Mill Creek, and it's a month before I plan to launch either for the season. . . . I'm worried about the 21st. I need to tell you something since you're the one—along with Ken—who investigated Helga Markel after she killed Olga."

"Helga Markel? Macduffy, she and Professor Plaxler are dead. You know that."

The now deceased Helga Markel and Montana law professor Henry Plaxler IV were an unlikely pair. Markel wore black leather clothing and had a couple of dozen metal variations on her ears, lips, nose, chin, and tongue. Plaxler wore tweed jackets, pleated corduroy trousers, tasseled loafers, and one of a couple of dozen variations of conservative neckties. He wanted to look like a professor even though his career had proven that such title was undeserved.

Two years ago Plaxler was dismissed from the UM law faculty. Soon thereafter, Markel and he committed the murder of one of the Shuttle Gals, Olga Smits. She was strangled, her breasts were cut off, and she was left nailed and tied to a large cross on my drift boat trailer at the Pine Creek Bridge takeout on the Yellowstone River. Helga did most of the dirty work; Plaxler was involved in the planning.

"Helga was a tragic case. Plaxler and she both died when her car collided with a fire engine in Los Angeles. But drinking and driving, enhanced by drugs, is a prelude to a fatal accident."

"Who gave you the information about her death in the car with Plaxler?" I asked.

"We obtained the accident report and a copy of her death certificate from the LAPD. Why the interest in Markel?"

"I'm not sure she died."

"*What?*"

"It's not a long story. I told Lucinda about it this morning. Yesterday, I was sitting on a bench here in Jackson's Town Square; Lucinda was off searching for something to wear to dinner with the Kirbys. I was 'people watching.' Some really show-off their Western outfits to an extreme. The ones I call 'Jackson girls.' But it was cool enough for jackets and coats, so most of them were covered up. . . . Anyway, a couple walked into the square at the opposite corner from where I was sitting. I couldn't see them clearly until they were half-way across heading straight toward me. . . . I couldn't believe what I saw. The woman was Helga Markel!"

"Can't be Macduffy. Absolutely no way! Her body and Plaxler's were cremated and sent to us. Neither had any next of kin we knew about. I thought they deserved a decent burial. Her ashes were mixed with Plaxler's and then placed in a grave in Missoula. I was there a month ago and checked the marker, to make sure it had been inscribed properly. It's unusual to have two people buried in the same plot—both were named on the marker."

"That's strange. I was sure I saw. . . ."

"Did the person you *think* was Markel recognize you?" Erin asked, interrupting me as she often does when she's exasperated with me.

"That's the funny thing about it. I'm sure it *was* Markel, but she didn't react at all when she looked at me. I wasn't wearing a hat or sunglasses; she could see my face clearly. She glanced at me a couple of times for several seconds. I must have been staring at her enough to concern her. But she never acted as though she knew me."

"Was she wearing her trademark black and a lot of metal? Plus her dyed-green lock of hair in the front?"

"No. She was dressed conservatively. No metal. No dyed hair. . . .Another thing differed from Helga. I could hear her speaking. Helga wasn't a person of many words, and most of those were swearing. I didn't hear one such word from this gal. Plus, her voice sounded different, a Kennedy-like Boston accent."

"But you couldn't have heard very much from someone passing you."

"I followed them, without drawing their attention. The man and she went into a small restaurant and sat in a booth. I sat down at the booth next to them; I'd put on my hat and sunglasses. Her back was toward me. I could hear her clearly. The guy facing me paid no attention to me; he didn't bat an eye when he occasionally looked my way."

"Was Merkel talking much?"

"My gosh, *yes!* She had some of the same speech inflections as Helga, but this gal talked faster. Not just fast, a veritable diarrhea of words tumbled from her mouth."

"What were the two talking about?"

"Almost all their conversation was about each other's backgrounds. The kind of conversation people have when they don't know each other very well. Markel—I'll call her that regardless of who she really was—began to tell the man how much she wanted to visit somewhere in the Orkney Islands. I think they're off Scotland. She mentioned some strange sounding places in the Orkneys I'd never heard of. Something about big stones that she said were older than Stonehenge and the Egyptian pyramids. And I heard her mention the winter solstice and something about the murder in Missoula last December.

"The guy, when he had a chance to talk, had a British accent. Not East End. Very upper-class—Oxbridge. . . . Unfortunately, after they had coffee, they left. I followed them, but near the square I saw Lucinda. She waved to get my attention. It distracted me, and when I turned back, the two were gone."

"Macduffy, I'm going to do some checking. The only possibility, other than you're being mistaken, is that Helga had a sister. I'll get back to you."

31

ERIN DID GET BACK to me, while Lucinda and I were driving north to Montana after leaving Jackson Hole by crossing Teton Pass to Idaho. The south entrance and many roads in Yellowstone Park were closed until late April or May. There were rewards to choosing the longer route; we stopped for Huckleberry milkshakes at the Emporium in Victor.

Having finished one shake and tempted to go back for another, Lucinda looked at me, rolled her eyes in frustration, took my cell phone from my shirt pocket, flipped open the phone, saw the call was from Erin, and set the phone between us. My mind was on March 21st, and I wasn't responding to my phone ringing within a foot of my ear.

"Hi, you two. . . . I've checked on Helga Markel. She died and she's still dead, Macduffy. You didn't see Helga, but you may have seen *Hannah*. Helga had a sister as I suggested. A *twin* sister. They were from Massachusetts—the small town of Salem northeast of Boston. Known for its witches."

"Helga fit that bill," I said, "but not Hannah. What did you learn about Hannah—other than her name's a palindrome?"

"I knew you'd see that, Macduffy. You can't hear the phone ring, but you can spell 'Hannah' forwards or backwards, and it comes out the same. You're so perceptive that what I was going to tell you must seem trivial."

"Sorry. Keep talking."

"After high school Hannah chose a different path than Helga, although friends in Salem told me they were inseparable growing up. I gather they thought it best to be more independent, so they went off to different colleges. Helga to California and Berkeley. Hannah to New Hampshire and Dartmouth. Helga lost her Boston accent and adopted a new image in California that Hannah hated. They stayed apart over the next dozen years; Hannah was embarrassed to be seen with Helga. Occasionally they wrote to each other; I've seen some correspondence from just before Helga died. Hannah wanted to make amends. Hannah was devastated by Helga's death. She moved West to different places. Then to New Orleans. Nowhere for long. Waited on tables. She was somewhere in the West before Pajioli's murder. We have no evidence she was anywhere near Ennis and the Madison River."

"Erin, from what I could tell from her appearance and manner, Hannah seemed normal. Except for the habit of never giving her friend a moment to speak. . . . Nothing you've said sounds worrying, but I don't like the fact she may be seeing a Brit who is a little strange. Your description of him fits Ellsworth-Kent. Do you know where *he* is?"

"No. New Orleans is the last place we know he visited. But that was months ago."

"Erin, an old friend from my high school days in Connecticut works at Dartmouth. I think she's in admissions. She may have retired. I'll call her. It's unlikely she'll know Hannah Markel, but it's worth a try."

"Call me if you learn anything useful."

32

Margaret Jones had recently been promoted to Vice-Dean of Students at Dartmouth. When she answered my call, I said it was Maxwell Hunt. She wouldn't know me or likely give me any information about students had I said it was Macduff Brooks. Aware of the risk in using my old name, I was admitting that Maxwell Hunt was alive to one more person and relying on no one else ever talking to Jones and her mentioning this conversation.

Surprisingly, she was familiar with the name Hannah Markel.

"Maxwell, I must be losing my mind. I thought I heard from someone or read in a newspaper article that you died nearly a decade ago. I recall it was while you were lecturing somewhere. Good to hear you're alive! . . . About Hannah—as adminstrators we tend to know the best and the worst of our students. She started out brilliantly, but after she became involved with writing for the student newspaper, something happened. Her articles began to focus on cults and then even more so on sacrifices. Some of her writings were scary.

"Then the campus police discovered she had stolen an expensive Apple Mac from a fellow student, Liz Spencer. Hannah dropped out in her final term, after Spencer told me that when confronted, Markel threatened her. Said she'd kill Spencer. Markel went to Spencer's dorm one evening and beat Spencer pretty badly before some other students intervened. Dropping out was our suggestion. It was that or she'd face criminal charges. She's all through at Dartmouth. I don't know where she is, and I don't want to know. She threw away a great education. . . . Maxwell, before I get off the line, what are you doing these days? What on earth brought Hannah into your life?"

"Marg . . . I . . . ah . . . I retired early from teaching. . . . Parkinson's. I'm living in San Francisco. I do some pro bono work for a non-governmental organization that helps people in trouble who don't have funds to hire a lawyer. I can't do it full time, but I like being useful until . . . well . . . just being useful. It passes the time. . . . I really appreciate your help, Marg." I hung up before she had time to ask any further embarrassing questions.

Dean Jones set her phone down, went a few steps to the window, and watched some students walking across the campus. She loved Dartmouth. . . . And she certainly remembered Maxwell Hunt. They never dated, but Jones had a crush on him in high school. She was troubled by their conversation, and thought, "I'm *sure* I read that he died. And I recall a classmate mentioning his death at our last high school class reunion a half-dozen years ago. I remember now. He had a stroke and died. . . . But what's also confusing is that my phone says the call wasn't from San Francisco but from an area code that covers Wyoming. Oh well, Maxwell's probably traveling. Maybe he likes to ski."

I never should have called Margaret. Now she's added to the list of those few people—Lucinda, Dan and a dozen of his colleagues, and probably Herzog and Isfahani—who know that

Maxwell Hunt is alive. I didn't tell her who I am now, but the damage may have been done. The chances of it going any further are slim, but it's one more risk I realize I shouldn't have taken. On the other hand, I know more about Hannah Markel. Erin will be interested.

Lucinda, who had listened to my conversation with Margaret Jones, already looks upset with me.

33

IT WAS A little further than Lucinda and I wanted to drive in one day to go from Jackson to Mill Creek by way of Idaho. We had called our friends at Big Sky and gave our apologies for not making the Ides of March celebration. There were no complaints from Wuff about our detours. She was enjoying the ride and the walks we made with her in nearly a dozen states.

Driggs looked like a good town to stop in, and we discovered a small, quiet motel called the Pines where Wuff was welcome. After an early supper, we relaxed with an Elsa Bianchi *Malbec* from the Mendoza region of Argentina. The label said it "impresses, with pleasing fruit that mimics the aromas" of "ripe plum and violets, . . . with hints of vanilla." Violets! The one who wrote the label had been drinking something, and it wasn't the *Malbec*. Both Argentina and Chile have been producing some excellent *Malbecs*, including Miss Bianchi's.

We reclined on lawn chairs with our wine and watched the sun set shining against the "back" side of the Tetons. They are magical mountains from wherever they are viewed. But the disappearance of the sun behind us brought the end of its warming effects as the temperature dropped dramatically and chased us into our room.

I was having difficulty relaxing despite the view, and in our room I called Dan, not remembering the two-hour difference with D.C. I wanted to bring him up-to-date about Hannah. He was preoccupied with the forthcoming spring equinox. I wondered if the two—Hannah and the 21st—were somehow intertwined. I had tried to forget that the equinox would occur in a couple of days.

"Macduff, it's after eleven here. Do you keep business hours? I went to bed at ten. Thanks."

"Thought you were always on duty, serving your country. Lucinda and I have been talking about the 21st. She's on the line with me. It's only a couple of days away. Is the equinox part of the mix?"

"I think so. But I know someone's going to die," Dan ventured categorically.

"Sorry I woke you," I responded, "but you don't have to react that dramatically."

"Although I contemplate it some days, I didn't mean killing *you*. I mean someone you know."

"No vacillation with you. Who's going to die? Where? Why? Do you know more you don't plan to tell us?"

"Of course not! We've been trying to put together a pattern with common links and work from there."

"Any luck?"

"Not sure. Three killings so far—near Ennis, Saratoga, and Missoula. Each occurred on an equinox or solstice. All must have some connection with one or both of you. The first had the sign with *your* name—'Lucinda'—and resulted in killing Mac's Montana CIA contact agent. The second was the murder of a St. Augustine friend of yours. I know he wasn't a close friend, but it's a link. The third was another law professor. Not someone I even had heard of, but he had been a visiting professor at UF when you were there as Maxwell Hunt."

"We know all that, Dan. What else?"

"The only suspects are Herzog and maybe Isfahani, plus Ellsworth-Kent, and a long shot is Hannah Markel. I would add our former agent Whitman, but he's dead."

"What about Wu?"

"We've dropped him. His advances on Lucinda were part of his general conduct; nothing linked to you, Mac. Plus, he's not in the U.S. as far as we can tell."

"Ellsworth-Kent has no quarrel with me. He was married to Lucinda years ago!"

"But now Lucinda's with you. She's rejected him. Perfect for a case of jealousy. He may want revenge. He sat in a jail cell on the Isle of Wight in England for fifteen years. That's more than enough time to become paranoid and fantasize about your relationship."

"Hannah Markel doesn't know me."

"But she made up with her sister before Helga died. Helga likely told Hannah about the confrontation with you. Helga didn't like you, and I suspect Hannah feels the same. Maybe she blames you for her sister's death."

"I'm not so sure. We know all this, Dan. Isn't there anything new?"

"One idea. Maybe farfetched. I put pins on a map that includes Montana, Wyoming, and Idaho. One pin at Emigrant represents you. One pin is at each murder location. I placed strings from Emigrant outward to each of the other three pins."

"And it probably looked like a map some family in Emigrant added pins and string to, showing where they vacationed."

"It shows more, Mac. I noticed that the Saratoga location is almost exactly 300 miles from Emigrant. Missoula is almost exactly 200 miles."

"Interesting coincidence. But what about the murder of Paula? Near Ennis."

"I don't know, Mac, unless that was special and unrelated in distance because it was the summer solstice. Symbolic and a prelude to the murders to come."

"What are your thoughts about the day after tomorrow?"

"If the distance was halved from the Saratoga killing to that in Missoula, maybe the killer plans to halve it again. That means fifty miles from Emigrant. I drew a circle fifty miles around Emigrant."

"And?"

"It crosses several rivers. Mainly three. The upper part of the Snake between Yellowstone and Grand Teton parks. The Yellowstone east of Livingston. And the Henry's Fork in Idaho."

"That's it, Dan! The Henry's Fork."

"Why?"

"Not counting the summer solstice killing on the Madison, the murders were first 200 miles away from Emigrant in one state—Wyoming. Then 100 miles away in a second state—Montana. The third will be fifty miles away in a third state—Idaho. The Henry's Fork is my guess."

"Macduff, that's a lot of speculation. Interesting—you may be right. But the Pajioli murder has to be related, and I don't know how."

"The sign on Escher at Saratoga said, 'The circle will close.' What circle? Are there several? Will the circle close from Ennis? Or from Saratoga? And what about Missoula? The locations mean something. As you suggest, set aside Ennis—for the sake of discussion—as a separate warning, although it established the *method* of killing. Your circles from Emigrant beginning with Saratoga are getting closer to Emigrant with each murder. Closing the circle must mean ending with some act in June on the summer solstice. The Henry's Fork in two days is the final step before they go after one or both of you on the summer solstice —the *coup de grâce* after a year of terror."

"Mac, do you think the June murder attempt will be on the Yellowstone?" asked Dan.

"Yes, and near Emigrant."

"But the first killing last June was on the Madison; the Yellowstone was unsafe—too fast and too dirty. Won't it be the same problem this June?"

"It would but for one thing. There was little snow this winter. The snow pack this year is below normal. The Yellowstone will be pretty clear by June. By the 21st it should have slowed and cleared to allow floats. But there won't be as many floats as later in the summer. That's good. Fewer obstacles to our stopping any final solstice murder attempt."

"That makes sense. So you assume an explosion might take place on the Yellowstone about where Mill Creek joins the river a quarter-mile downstream from Emigrant."

"Exactly."

"To what do you attribute your Sherlock Holmes deductive reasoning?" asked Dan.

"To Elsa Bianchi."

"Who the hell is she?"

"She's a pretty good *Malbec*." I set down my glass. Lucinda and I had finished our second bottle.

"Mac, I know there've been lots of writers who turned out literary masterpieces allegedly writing under the influence, like Sinclair Lewis and Hemingway. I don't know any detectives who've done the same solving murders. I hope you don't mind if I don't pass this idea around here for discussion. . . . But, and that's a big but, I think you may have something. We'll know more in a couple of days."

"I hope we learn about it because if you succeed in catching the killer on the Henry's Fork, we all avoid the *coup de grâce* in June."

"We don't know where on the Henry's Fork the murder might take place. You want to drink another bottle of Elsa Bianchi and call me back and tell me?"

"I haven't thought about where on the Henry's Fork. When you drew the third circle, where did it cross the Henry's Fork?"

"Around Ashton, Idaho. Not far south of Last Chance. An appropriate name for the last killing before the final climax. Meaning it's *our* last chance to stop the killer."

"You covering the Henry's Fork tomorrow?" Lucinda asked.

"You bet. You two stay in Emigrant."

"We can't. We're still on the road from Florida," she added.

"Where are you two?"

"We're staying tonight in a very small place," I answered.

"Where is that?"

"Last Chance, Idaho!"

34

WE WERE PLANNING to depart Island Park on the morning of the 20th. As we tucked in for the night, Lucinda commented, "This is where we fished the Box Canyon!"

"It's where *I* fished and *you* fell in."

"But I caught a fish, and it was bigger."

"But weighed less."

"Mine was prettier. . . . I could have drowned in the Box Canyon when we fished there."

"No."

"Just no?"

"I saved you. If you'd drowned, I'd never have known whether your fish was a rainbow or a brown."

"You pushed me in."

"I was fifty feet upstream from you. You were being pulled by a tiny trout and fell in. I *saved* you."

"I don't remember that at all."

"I think your amnesia's back. . . ."

"Well, Mr. Guide, would you like to stay here tomorrow and let me teach you how to fish?"

"We don't have a boat."

"We can rent one. Or get a real guide."

"After talking to Dan, do you want to be on the Henry's Fork on the 21st?"

"Tomorrow's the 20th. We can leave early on the 21st."

"OK. I don't think there's a chance the killer will strike here *tomorrow*. The pieces of the puzzle are coming together.

"Where's the section we'll fish?"

"Not far south of here. There's a spectacular float from a little downstream of the Box Canyon that runs through Harriman's Ranch, now part of Harriman's State Park. It was once the playground of the wealthy Harriman and Guggenheim clans. The section we'll fish is about nine miles long, and five of those miles wander peacefully through the Harriman's Railroad Ranch. There are still some cows on the ranch."

"So we have to avoid cows in the river?"

"Not a one. They're kept away by solar-powered electric fences."

"If PARA hears about this, they'll be here the next day to protest."

PARA, or People Against Recreational Angling, was started by some disgruntled members of the better known PETA . . . People for the Equitable Treatment of Animals, known in the Mountain West as People Eating Tasty Animals.

"Members of PARA haven't been very active in Montana lately. They're focusing on the San Juan River in New Mexico. They want the Navaho Dam removed. Not because it never should have been built in the first place, but to destroy the recreational trout fishing in the tailwater below the dam."

"I thought the dam was intended to help the Navahos develop farming."

"The group apparently thinks it more important to end angling. . . . Let's talk about our fishing. My blood pressure goes up at the mention of PARA. After floating the ranch, we'll take out where the river comes back and crosses Highway 191. There's another takeout near Riverside, but if we go much further, we face a deep gorge—Cardiac Canyon, Lower Sheep Falls, and then a hundred-plus-foot drop over Upper and a sixty-five foot drop over Lower Mesa Falls. I don't do falls."

"What a learned guide you are. Now I know there're fish and cows as well as potatoes in Idaho?"

"There's much more to Idaho than potatoes," I guessed.

"I know. Huckleberry milkshakes!"

"We're not driving back to Victor for another."

"Spoil sport," she moaned.

We launched after breakfast and had a quiet float . . . only one other drift boat came into view behind us. It made me turn the boat sideways and watch to see if there was a single person tied to the guide seat and surrounded by wicker. I was relieved when I saw three people in the boat, two actively casting and the guide leisurely rowing. We fished one bank slowly and let them pass.

"What flies are we using?" Lucinda queried.

"We'll both use the same. An emerging mayfly imitation. It's called a Transition Dun, designed by a guy named Rene Harrop who's spent his life on the Henry's Fork. It's smooth water through the state park. That means a thick surface film. Fine tippets and long leaders."

"What does the fly look like?"

"Something edible to a trout, we hope. It has an olive and tan body and a similar color wing of CDC feathers. Fluffy stuff—not much color. You try a #18, and I'll try a #16."

"Unfair. Your #16 is bigger than my #18."

"How did you know the hook size gets smaller as the number of the size gets larger?"

"I was practicing tying an Adams on your fly tying bench at your cabin on a day you were guiding. I went through your hooks and stuff."

"Pretty soon you're going to want to sit in the guide seat and row."

"You betcha!"

The fly floated low as intended; I hooked two in the first half-hour, but lost them both, keeping up my practice of *very* early release.

Lucinda landed a nice rainbow on her #18.

"Lucinda, that's a cute, chubby rainbow."

"Chubby? It's beautiful. Well-proportioned."

"Actually, it looks obese."

"What would you call it if *you* had caught it?"

"Beautiful. And well-proportioned."

The best moment of the day occurred when we rounded a bend and heading toward us twenty feet above the water was the wide wingspread of a large, female bald eagle, her white head-feathers tousling in the breeze, her head bent downward, turning left and then right and then left again, oblivious to us while she searched the depths of the river. Her wings moved too slowly to call it flapping—more like incremental adjustments to propel her in a slow motion barely sufficient to maintain altitude. When she saw us, she stopped her wing movement and glided, caught a wind updraft that gave her lift, keeping her aloft as we passed directly beneath. As we slid through her shadow, she climbed and curved off to the West.

We didn't catch another fish. We didn't need to.

35

WE HAD BEEN on the road for almost two weeks and had yet to reach Montana; one more float in a great fishing location had easily justified delaying one more day. This drive west from Florida was the best yet, compared to my long days driving solo before I met Lucinda, when I stopped only after the sun set at any lodging that would accept Wuff.

Over a summer solstice breakfast on the 21st, I asked Lucinda, who seemed solemn and preoccupied, "Were you worried yesterday on the float when the other drift boat approached?"

"I was shaking. Dan thinks that this section of the Henry's Fork is where there'll be another explosion on a drift boat. Today! Looking out the window, I see more police cars than I can count. I'm not sure we were smart to stay until today."

"If the killers were after us intending to murder one or both of us here, we would have been abducted already."

"I don't want us to be stopped and identified. I'm not sure we're welcome along some of the rivers we like to fish. . . . We might want to get away from here in the next half-hour, but drive slowly and not arrive at Mill Creek until evening. Dan wouldn't want you around here if the Henry's Fork is the target. Leaving is for your protection, Mac. You have enough links to drift boat murders as it is. Another and your guide career could be over."

"But remember that *your* name was on the first sign on Paula Pajioli's wicker. We should be all right going home, but I agree about being stopped. You don't get to drive. You have more tickets in the time we've spent together than I've had since I began driving at sixteen."

"They didn't give tickets to horse and buggy drivers when you began driving. I'm a good driver; other people keep getting in my way."

"Case closed."

"I think we're perfectly safe, Mac. It's the 21st, and we're OK," she said, returning our conversation to the summer solstice, three months away—a day we both wished to avoid. "It's unlikely that anything will happen before June, except for today; the killings have been *precisely* on the solstice or equinox. In June, at least it should be closer to home, maybe very close. If anything happens today, I bet on the fifty-mile circle from Emigrant theory. That's a pattern we have to solve, especially because we've almost come full circle and the next will be the summer solstice. I'm convinced that will be the day something happens close to home.

"I wanted you to be away from Mill Creek today, but without anyone knowing you were gone. I could still drop you at the Bozeman airport in a few hours. You could fly to New York and stay until after the summer solstice."

"Three months! Not a chance, Mac. And don't argue; you'll lose."

With Lucinda alongside me, as she promised to be, we reached Mill Creek with twenty minutes to spare before Wuff's dinner was due, fully prepared, and centered on her small Oriental dining rug that we carried with us traveling.

"You don't treat me the way you do Wuff," Lucinda muttered. "I don't have an Oriental dining rug. And I don't get my meals served to me promptly."

"It took Wuff years of obedient service before she earned it; you have a few years to go."

After I unlocked the gate, I checked the mailbox. Mavis had been taking care of my cabin since last fall and picking up the mail every few days. There was only one envelope in the box. As I pulled it out, I noticed it was a plain envelope without any addresses or postage. I opened it and a single photograph dropped out. Leaning over to pick it up, I froze; it was a photo of the two of us with a black circle drawn around Lucinda. Below were the words: "You have three months to get your affairs in order."

Lucinda had been pushing the gate open and didn't see me slip the photo and envelope into my pocket."

"Lots of bills?" she asked.

"Not a one, Mavis must have picked up the mail today."

When she got back in the car, she leaned over against me and murmured, "It's good to be home safe and sound. I feel better with you around."

"That may be a very false sense of security," I thought, feeling deceitful in not showing her or telling her about the photo. I thought it best to divert her attention for the evening. Dan will call us if there's any news.

36

WHEN WE RETURNED from breakfast the next morning, avoiding even glancing at the Bozeman and Livingston newspapers' headlines at the general store, not a word was mentioned between us about whether there had been an incident the previous day. I could tell Lucinda was unsettled. Her conversation at breakfast had run the gauntlet from redoing my St. Augustine cottage kitchen and adding a better oven, to our spending a week at Cape Cod so she could photograph the undulations of sand dunes. When we got out of the SUV at the cabin, she started again on anything other than the Henry's Fork.

"Mavis must have left the door open to your boat garage, Mac. I've never been inside. Show me where you built *Osprey.*"

I played along. If it would keep her mind off the murders, it was worth the distraction.

"I built *Osprey* at Jason Cajune's Montana Boatbuilders place in Pine Creek; he rented me some space."

As we entered the garage, she looked at one wall and exclaimed, "Pollock! That looks like a Jackson Pollock."

"I wish it were. It was my floor covering at Jason's. I started the boat by laying down plywood to protect his concrete floor. Building *Osprey* consumed a lot of resin. It was mostly clear, but some was tinged with various shades of brown from filler I added to the resin and black from making the trout inlays. The last color I used on the outside of the hull was a sea green polyurethane. I dripped a lot and left every drip untouched on the plywood. The resin sometimes built up little bumps. Sawdust fell into the resin and paint. But not a drop of any of this fell on the plywood directly under the boat.

"The end result was a ten-by-sixteen-foot piece of plywood that had a perfect boat shape in the middle, framed by a Jackson Pollock—Jack the Dripper—knockoff outline of spilled resin and paint that extended from the outline of the boat to the edges of the plywood. When I was cleaning up after we pulled the boat out and placed it on the trailer, I brought the plywood home and fastened it to the garage wall. You're about the only one who's seen it. It does look like a Pollock, but it's worth a lot less."

When we went into the cabin, I wondered whether I should bring up the subject of the Henry's Fork. I decided to let her raise it when she was ready.

37

WE COULDN'T LONG AVOID learning about the previous day's events in Idaho, assuming we were correct in thinking the Henry's Fork was the next stage of a series of murders. If so, we'd have to quickly focus on the coming fifth act.

I would like to have flown east to some hideaway on Cape Cod or to the cottage at St. Augustine. But we had barely arrived in Paradise Valley and had to confront our future. We had fudged a bit yesterday by turning off our cell phones and, when we arrived at Mill Creek, unplugging the radio and TV. It was a false attempt to blot out the spring equinox.

At some exact moment during the day, the innocent sun would have passed directly over the equator, lurching north to its summer solstice destination. Then, on June 21st, it would momentarily come to a halt, reverse its direction and begin its trek south. I had been convinced someone would be murdered yesterday on the spring equinox, but was more confused about who and why than about when and where. While the sun plunged ahead north, the victim—whoever it was, if indeed there was a victim—wouldn't move at all. The sun wouldn't know if on this small place on earth a life was taken.

At four in the afternoon on the 22nd, we were both so tense we decided to face the final hours of the day knowing whether anything had happened. I turned on my phone and found seventeen calls, mostly from Dan but also a few from newspapers, TV stations, the Freemont County Sheriff's office, and the police chief at Ashton. I answered only one: Dan's.

"Tell me about the day at the Henry's Fork."

"I wondered if you'd ever call. I'm in Idaho. The local police botched it," Dan began solemnly. "They refused to cooperate with us. As recently as a week ago, they totally rejected any theory that led to a murder on their turf. They did have a dozen police cars along the highway that follows the river. When we threatened to take over, they finally came around and added a dozen drift boats on the Henry's Fork, carrying various law enforcement officials. One might have expected them to be wearing fishing garb. But they were in uniforms and each carried an automatic weapon. Frankly, they looked pretty silly. There were also swat team members every hundred yards along the banks, only partly hidden, and four helicopters patrolling up and down the river."

"Sounds like enough to scare away any self-respecting serial killer."

"It was, but except for the noise, the police made certain *nothing* happened on the Henry's Fork."

"Thank God, Dan. Maybe there won't be an attempt on June 21st."

"I'm not through, Macduff. There was no incident on the Henry's Fork, but there was on a smaller river—the Buffalo—that runs into the Henry's Fork near Island Park. The Buffalo isn't as well known, but where today's wicker man and mistletoe explosion occurred was close to the fifty-mile circle from Emigrant, at least close to a major river, and it was in Idaho."

"Am I right in assuming we lost another person in a drift boat?"

"You are. His name was D.J. Ricky. We don't know much about him yet, but he guides in the area, we think out of World Cast Anglers in Victor or Island Park. There doesn't seem to be any link to you. Or *is* there?"

"I'm afraid there is. D.J. was one of a dozen participants in my guide school about eight years ago. He was a good guy, fine caster, wide knowledge of the area, and my roommate for the guide school. I believe he grew up in Ashton and graduated from Brigham Young in Provo. Was he killed?"

"He was. Same explosives as with the others. Same wicker and mistletoe. Want to hear about the sign?"

"I guess so."

"Part of it was a little cruder than the other signs. A black marking pen was used to scribble something below the main part of the sign."

"How do we know anything at all about the sign? It would have been blown up."

"It was. But the boat had passed an upscale fishing lodge on the river's bank where a couple was having breakfast in a gazebo. The lady had binoculars. When the boat got closer, they called the lodge manager. The couple had never read of the previous murders, but they were dumbfounded by the wicker man and mistletoe. They live on a farm in rural New Zealand. The lodge wasn't about to tell them and maybe lose a week's reservation. When the guests told the lodge manager about the boat, he called the police. While he was calling, the boat exploded."

"Did the couple remember the sign on Ricky?"

"Yes, the lady with the binoculars wrote it down. It said, 'The circle is nearly closed,' and some scribbling below said, 'You're watching the wrong river, Macduff.'"

"Any idea what set off the explosive?"

"Not yet. Probably the killer from somewhere on the far bank using a remote detonator."

"What's next?" Lucinda asked.

"Sit tight. The next worry is the summer solstice. We have planning to do, including some damage control. This area is filled with TV vans and reporters, and it's only been a day and a half since it happened."

"Think it'll make the national news?"

"No question. I expect it will be in papers abroad, especially where there's fishing from drift boats. Argentina. Maybe Russia. And of course where the couple were from—New Zealand."

"I'm in for trouble, Dan. Enough guides have complained to outfitters about me. I may never have another client."

"Don't be too sure. You'll be in the news. People may want to book you just to talk about the killings, going back to Ander Eckstrum five years ago. The late night shows will compete for you."

"I already get enough people who want all the grisly details about the Shuttle Gals murders. I don't need any more. Certainly not talk shows. I want to be a guide. Nothing more. The last thing Lucinda and I need is national and international publicity. Can you imagine Herzog reading about this in the Guatemalan papers? What if my photo's printed?"

"Herzog has no idea you're using the name Macduff Brooks and no idea you live in Montana."

"Dan, we don't know what Herzog was told before Whitman was shot."

"I'll bet you my pension that Herzog's not involved. Same for Isfahani."

"Don't say that. If I win your pension, you'll have to live with us."

"I feel like I have for the past eight years."

"If you can stop by tomorrow before you head back to D.C., we'll treat you to lunch."

"Who'll cook? You or Lucinda."

"I don't do meals."

"I'll be there."

38

DAN ARRIVED AT NOON bearing a bottle of Domaine de Bernier *Chardonny*. The three of us had no trouble consuming the bottle, with no debate over our glasses being half-full or half-empty. There wasn't a drop left in anyone's glass. Another murder, and we may stop drinking in moderation.

"Mac, let's put the killings aside except to understand how they're preludes to what seems to be the grand finale—an attempt on either or both of you—and probably near here."

"I agree, but for now can you get the Fremont County Sheriff's office people off our backs? Since I talked to you on the phone, I've been summoned by the chief, Felicity Jelico. I told her in no uncertain terms I didn't intend to set foot on her turf or anywhere in her state, but I would meet with her and my attorney Wanda Groves in Bozeman. I haven't heard from her. Why do the police think Lucinda and I are involved?"

"Fremont County has elections this year. We checked on Jelico. She's in pretty shaky standing in the county and in danger of losing the election. She's been in office for fourteen years and needs fifteen for her pension to vest. She's scared and needs some scapegoat to make her look good. You're apparently it. Forget her. Assume she's a non-player.

"The people you need to worry about are the two FBI agents who gave you trouble here six months ago after the Saratoga killing. They're on the case and staying close by at Chico Hot Spring Resort. Chester Stern is an ambitious nephew of the current top dog in the FBI—Director Frank Stern. They've got a hell of a big file on you, but not close to anything that could result in charges. Well, maybe enough for charges, but not an indictment. Well, maybe enough for an indictment, but not a conviction."

"Dan," Lucinda asked, "can we put our concerns about Herzog and Isfahani on the shelf as far as the wicker man murders are concerned?"

"Absolutely. We have more recent knowledge about where they've been the past year. Herzog's apparently satisfied with putting the search on hold while Isfahani has his plastic surgery finished in Switzerland. It's taking longer than expected."

"That leaves only my ex—Ellsworth-Kent," noted Lucinda.

"And Hannah Markel," added Dan.

"That means we've solved the four murders!" I concluded.

"And a fifth may soon happen. But you're right. It has to be Markel and Ellsworth-Kent. I'd give a month's salary to know where they are."

"You may have given up your pension; now you're betting your salary! What's the latest?"

"We haven't been able to locate them. We assume they're be together. Elsworth-Kent's been off our radar for nearly a year, before the Pajioli murder. We've only been interested in Hannah Markel since we learned she was with him. They're apparently using different names. We think they might be living in Jackson, but we've searched the records of every Jackson Hole lodging, including B&Bs. No one named Hannah Markel or Robert Ellsworth-Kent has registered at any lodging. So far the same is true of lodging in the towns along the Henry's Fork. They might be in Bozeman. Or Emigrant!"

"That's unpleasant to imagine. I can't believe they would stay in Jackson Hole. If we're their main target and the previous murder locations have been measured from here, don't you think they've relocated to this area?"

"Yes. We've begun a search for them in Paradise Valley and Livingston. Nothing yet. There are some small rentals that aren't registered because the owners don't want to pay taxes on the income or be subject to Gallatin County regulations."

"Dan, were you searching Jackson Hole because of my sighting them?" I asked.

"Mainly. We didn't have anything else better as a starter."

"Have you identified the guy with Hannah?"

"Yes, it's Ellsworth-Kent."

"How do you know?"

"There's a web-camera facing the Jackson Town Square that's on the *JH News and Guide* website. It's useful for checking the current weather conditions in town. We knew what Hannah looked like. When we found her on the web-camera storage, the date matched the time you were there. We saw you sitting as you said, Mac, and we got a fair picture of her companion. The British government's MI6 analyzed the photos and said without question it was Ellsworth-Kent. They're pleased to know he's no longer in England."

"Have the Brits helped on anything else?"

"Yes. One important matter. I didn't want to alarm you. But I will in view of yesterday. Ellsworth-Kent's military experience was in ordinance. He's an explosives expert. And he's very good."

"I don't believe it! Dan, we've got to find them."

"We hardly know where to start."

39

AS THE INCREASINGLY LONGER days of June passed and spring prepared to yield to summer, Markel and Ellsworth-Kent argued about their need to find a rental closer to the Yellowstone River, but remote even from the sparse population of Emigrant, near where they would carry out their final act.

Markel wanted Macduff to suffer and die. Nothing more. She no longer cared how or where he died. But he had to die a slow death infused with suffering.

Ellsworth-Kent, on the other hand, wanted another dramatic, public sacrifice to finish the circle from summer solstice to summer solstice. While he thought Lucinda was an appropriate victim, the ceremony had become paramount, and the identity of the victim played only a marginal role in that ceremony.

What had caused such a change? Ellsworth-Kent was tired. He wanted to return to Scotland, buy a small place in the Orkney Islands, and live quietly on his pension using a different name. His pension was being deposited in his London Barclays account. How he would avoid the authorities and withdraw his funds hadn't crossed his mind.

Ellsworth-Kent knew Lucinda would never return to him. Moreover, they couldn't live together; the police were surely on his trail. Montana, Idaho, and Wyoming were all committed to preserving an enforceable death penalty.

He did agree with Markel on one matter. Paradise Valley would be ideal for the final ceremonial sacrifice. He knew she would be satisfied with Macduff's death alone, with or without ceremony, and he decided that he would be content with the grief that death bestowed upon Lucinda, if she did not die with Macduff.

The twosome was no longer the carefree bedmates they had been in New Orleans. While they shared the only bed at their Jackson lodging, each fell asleep facing away from the other, thankful they had a king-size bed and could avoid the slightest contact. They shared breakfast; or rather their proclivities to arise at the same hour brought them to the tiny breakfast room at the same time. Separately, they took most of their lunches and dinners in town, and whenever one entered a restaurant and the other was present, by unexpressed understanding the second to arrive would leave.

What caused their spilt was twofold. First, they discovered that while they shared an attraction to Druidism and the mysteries of the Orkney Islands, they disagreed about many aspects of the lives and particularly the philosophies of the ancient people. Ellsworth-Kent thought that they should follow the fundamental tenets of Druidism and undertake any sacrificial act they agreed upon, but only in a manner which would please the ancients. Hannah was determined to kill Macduff without concern for the formalities Ellsworth-Kent valued. Macduff, however, must suffer before his last breath. She increasingly thought it silly to use the wicker man and mistletoe and wished to apply the most certain means available to achieve her goal.

The second reason for their division was that they came to understand that they were simply two very different people. Ellsworth-Kent was raised in Dorset in an imposing manor house on an immense estate. He was denied succeeding to the earldom of his father only because he had one sibling who unfortunately was an older male. Fifteen years in prison left little blemish on a façade of good breeding, proper manners, and respect for those few he considered his equal.

From the lower middle class, Hannah was never comfortable with her more privileged classmates at Dartmouth. She thought she was entitled to attend an Ivy League school regardless of her ability to pay. But she never fit in. Both Helga and she had attended university only because of the largess of an industrialist from their town who left his fortune for the education of the townspeople.

What kept the duo together was the vengeance with which both addressed their actions.

"I want Macduff to suffer *horribly*," Markel exclaimed one morning. "He killed my sister. An explosion that ends his life instantly is not enough."

"But he will suffer, Hannah," declared Ellsworth-Kent. "He will be in the wicker basket with the explosives attached for some time before the timer reaches the end of its ticking. Macduff knows he has no chance of escape; no one has come close yet. There's no way he can get out of the wicker, much less out of the boat. And the explosives are *strapped* to the wicker. We've followed that pattern for four deaths. It's not time to change. . . . He will know he's going to die from the moment we abduct him because each person we have placed in a wicker man has died."

"*If* we can make his death come more slowly, we *must,*" asserted Markel.

"I want Lucinda dead," declared Ellsworth-Kent, "but I don't require her to suffer beyond the trauma of knowing this past year that she will join Macduff in death. The magnificence of the ceremony of the sacrifice is more essential than the pain."

"Aren't you too focused on the ceremony and not on killing the two?" asked Markel.

"The ceremony is essential. The ancients were ridiculed when Christianity began. We are older, dating to 200 or even 300 B.C. The Christians called us sorcerers for opposing their new religion. They rejected our belief that a sacrifice does not destroy the soul, which is immortal, but gives that soul continued life in a new body. The sacrifices must be performed in consort with the movement of the earth, the cosmos, and the stars. The most important time is the summer solstice, when the sun stops and stands still; the seasonal movement comes to a halt and then reverses direction. We must follow these beliefs."

"OK. But Robert, I don't give a damn about Lucinda," Hannah said emphatically. "I let you have your way when we killed Paula Pajioli and brought Lucinda into the picture by the sign that said 'You're Next, Lucinda.' You can shoot her or drown her or strangle her. Do what you wish. But she *will not* interfere or threaten my plans for Macduff. . . . First, we need to leave Jackson and find a place in Paradise Valley."

"I understand, but there are benefits to staying here," Robert suggested. "We've managed to remain out of view. People we see every day have gotten accustomed to us and think nothing of our presence. If we were to go to Paradise Valley, we would be walking into the very location where local, county, and state police, plus the FBI, will be searching for us."

"Searching for us! Do you think they know we're together?" asked Hannah.

"Of course. Our landlady here told us about the visit she had with a local deputy who was looking for a couple about our ages. We bought her off; we're paying much more than other tenants. If we leave, she will lose the rent and call the police."

"That means when we go we must do so quickly, without telling her."

"Or do something to her," Robert offered. "Do you feel strongly about leaving soon?"

"I can leave tomorrow. Let's talk about what to do about our landlady."

"I'm willing to go, Hannah, if you agree we'll kill Macduff and Lucinda following the ancient practices we used successfully on the four others."

"Then we must go tomorrow, after attending to our landlady."

They drove north through Grand Teton and Yellowstone parks. Both were intrigued by the natural features that hissed, erupted, gurgled, and spewed forth scalding water from the bowels of the earth. The mysteries of Yellowstone reinforced Ellsworth-Kent's view that the American Mountain West was a perfect place to engage in the ancient practices, however different the two believed those practices should be. Markel did not disagree with the rituals that had intrigued her for much of her life, but she was determined not to allow ritual to minimize suffering or avoid death.

At Mammoth, standing before the Minerva Terraces that ascend in steps up the slope and are sometimes covered with travertine deposits, Ellsworth-Kent said, expressing his awe, "I've seen nothing until today that has stirred me more since entering the Stone Age tombs of Maes Howe and walking among the standing stones of Stenness in the Orkneys."

"Don't I wish I could entomb Macduff alive in Maes Howe?" Markel reflected. "Even Egypt's pyramids are nothing in comparison to the Maes Howe burial chambers. One has only to enter the long stone passageway and enter the central chamber to feel trapped forever. . . . But Robert, we're half a world away from Scotland and must work with what we have. If we had known about the scalding pools of Yellowstone, we might have done *all* the sacrifices here."

In an outdoor wilderness supplies shop in Gardiner, a stone's throw north of Yellowstone Park, Markel purchased a Bureau of Land Management map covering most of Paradise Valley, and for the first time Ellsworth-Kent and she saw the location of Mill Creek, flowing down from the Absaroka Range to the east to mix with the Yellowstone River on its long passage to the great Missouri River. Somewhere along the Mill Creek road were Lucinda Lang's ranch and Macduff Brooks' log cabin. They would scout them out the next day.

Looking on the map along the west side of the river beyond Yankee Jim Canyon, Ellsworth-Kent noticed that the Tom Miner Road wound southwest off the main Route 89, tracing the contours of the foothills of the Gallatin Range. They drove slowly along its full reach high into the wilderness and soon rented a 19th-century farmhouse with a large barn, sitting on a knoll alongside the upper portion of the road close to where it entered national forest land. If trapped, as a last resort, they might escape using the trails taking them west through the Gallatins.

Settled in the farmhouse, sitting alone outside on the edge of a well-used wooden water trough, Ellsworth-Kent finally comprehended that he had long been delusional about reuniting with Lucinda. He forced himself to believe that he no longer even wanted Lucinda. He *knew* that he no longer wanted Hannah Markel. They could have been a good pair and were for the first few months.

Reconciled to the fact that neither woman was part of his future, he would try to set aside his disagreements with Markel and concentrate on his intention to fulfill his desire for a summer solstice sacrifice of Lucinda. He was not sure he wanted to see Macduff die; he wanted Macduff mainly to suffer the loss of Lucinda. But Markel would have no part of that. In her view, Macduff had to die regardless of what happened to Lucinda.

If Ellsworth-Kent interceded to keep Macduff alive, Markel would have no hesitation to kill Ellsworth-Kent as well. He also had issues with Markel that often made him want to kill her, but he wanted to keep her on track to complete the circle. They had done an effective job thus far.

When Markel and Ellsworth-Kent walked to the car, the next morning, he said, "Hannah, we must put aside our differences. The sacrifice near the Henry's Fork was successful. There were so many police covering the Henry's Fork we were left with not even one deputy watching the Buffalo River."

"Robert, I once wanted to do the killings where there were people present to view the wicker man and mistletoe, like at Missoula last December. When we explode the boat with Macduff, I want it to be in the middle of the Yellowstone River where it passes Mill Creek. I don't care if there are no witnesses. There's no way the police can figure out where we'll strike on the summer solstice. They may think it will be on the Madison again. Perhaps they don't even expect another killing."

"But they know the day," he offered. "We certainly have told them more is coming."

"Do you think the Yellowstone will be teaming with police?" asked Merkel.

"On some sections, yes. But the location is not predictable," Ellsworth-Kent noted. "The police don't know where or if. It might not be on the Yellowstone.

"They might even focus on the Deadman's Bar to Moose section of the Snake in Jackson Hole," offered Markel. "That's where the first person was shot in Brooks' drift boat."

"Last year's murders of the Shuttle Gals were on the Yellowstone. The Snake doesn't make sense. I'll stick with the Yellowstone; that's my choice. It's a little late to change. There are more than fifty miles of river in Paradise Valley. . . . Few if any people will be there to see the end, like they were at Missoula. That was my favorite. But I don't care if no one is there, as long as we have a sacrifice that hopefully will include both of them."

"We have enough time to plan it," she reminded Robert. "But we must take care not to be seen together. Tomorrow, I'll go alone to Gardiner to do grocery shopping. We have a laundry machine here. We don't need much else."

"We have enough explosives to blow up a fleet of drift boats," said Ellsworth-Kent, with his first smile in weeks.

"In Jackson you said Lucinda and Macduff would be sacrificed in separate boats. Did you mean that?"

"At first I did, but I have reservations about taking on too much. A single boat may be better. . . . I think I have a different use for the second boat."

"Whatever. We're very close to the end, Robert. Then we will go our own ways."

"It can't come too soon," Robert thought.

40

WHILE HANNAH AND ROBERT were debating the forthcoming solstices, not more than two dozen miles away Lucinda and I were conversing quietly at her ranch, sitting on the stone wall on the terrace of one of her guest houses shadowed by the surrounding Absaroka Range. For the past year or two, after Lucinda's amnesia ended, most of our time was spent at my cabin. Lucinda went to her ranch occasionally to advise the ranch manager. But now, at Dan Wilson's suggestion, most of our time was spent at one of the guest cabins at Lucinda's ranch.

Dan had repeatedly asked Lucinda and me to alter our patterns of living to avoid becoming easier targets. We were all convinced that the wicker man and mistletoe killers—as they had become known in the increasingly caustic media—were now planning their final act, which Dan was convinced was intended to end the lives of both Lucinda and me. We tried to divert our tension to more pleasant thoughts.

"You've never talked about the death of your expected daughter when El lost her life," Lucinda said in little more than a whisper. "She would be a young woman by now."

"She would be eighteen, graduating from high school and possibly heading off to college."

"Have you ever thought of adopting?"

"Yes, but when I have, my mind wanders to what might have been with our own daughter. . . . I never told you that when you and I met eight years ago I thought of having a child with you. Maybe I should have acted faster."

"You mean asking me the evening we met if I'd like to have your child?"

"That would have been awkward, but, I guess, yes. You're stunningly beautiful, like El. There's softness to your manner and a sense of reality that I thought would make you a wonderful mother. I've come to know my judgment was right. Now your clock is ticking past the time it's safe for you to bear children."

"My clock stopped long ago."

"What do you mean?"

"Robert Ellsworth-Kent did things to me I can't talk about. The end result was that I could never have a child. . . . I've often thought over the past eight years that you'd be a special father."

"With a price on my head for eight years and murders in my boat and all around me? I wouldn't want to risk a child's life."

"I'm still alive. Wuff's still alive. I'm sure your daughter would be, too. Oh! Maybe with a scar or two."

"It would be nice to be sitting here with three beautiful women—you, Wuff, *and* a daughter."

"What were you going to name her?"

"We hadn't decided. El's mother and grandmother were Elsbeth. It's the Norwegian form of Elizabeth. El's grandmother was called Betty; her mother, Liz. I like the name Elsbeth and thought I'd like to call her that. El and I didn't talk much about a name; we were so excited about having a child."

"Do you have visions of what she would look like and be doing?"

"Every day. She would complete my circle."

"Am I part of that circle?"

"The very center of my universe."

"I so wish Elsbeth could have known her father."

41

TWENTY-FIVE HUNDRED miles east on a similar latitude, a young woman who looked to be in her late teens sat on the porch swing of her family's Adirondack inspired cabin about twelve miles north of Greenville, Maine. She could see part of Moosehead Lake to the west. The attractive, restored 1914 wooden steamship *Katahdin* was moving slowly north on an afternoon cruise. Little snow had fallen since mid-April, each day was a few degrees warmer, and the young woman was thinking about her future.

She would graduate from Greenville High at the end of the month, and while accepted at the state university at Orono, she wondered if there were other choices she might prefer. But she didn't know her country; she had never been outside Maine. She was unaware the latter was not true.

For some reason she didn't comprehend, she read extensively about the American West. Not the popular Western cowboy and Indian novels, but books like those of her favorite author—Willa Cather. Books like *My Ántonia* and *Death Comes for the Archbishop*. On her lap was her latest book, which she hated to see end—Diane Smith's *Letters From Yellowstone*. Maybe these books captured her attention because the settings were so far away; it was almost like reading about life on other planets. At times she felt an urge to go to college in the West. She thought a place like Missoula in Montana would be similar to Maine but also would place her in a different culture. But when her thoughts turned to Missoula and the West, she realized she had a strong obligation to her mother to stay relatively close to home. Especially because of her mother's age and depressions.

The young woman's name was Elsbeth . . . Elsbeth Hunt Carson. Her mother had told her that she saw the name Elsbeth in a newspaper and liked its sound.

Two years ago her father, Gregory Carson, died of a heart attack at fifty-seven. He was using a chain saw to clear fallen trees from around their cabin when he looked up at his daughter, who was sitting on the porch steps not thirty feet away. His face turned quickly from his usual smile to a look of agony. He couldn't call out as he collapsed face down in the woods he so loved. By the time his daughter had rushed to his side, he was gone. Elsbeth's mother, trained as a physician, could not accept her husband's death.

Elsbeth didn't know that her mother had recently planned her own demise, despondent over Gregory's death and knowing her depressions would soon absorb her health. As part of her planning, she asked Elsbeth to sit down on the porch and listen to her story. A true story that very much involved Elsbeth.

"I can no longer keep a secret from you, Elsbeth. If something happened to me, you would never know the truth about your background. You have been the daughter that Gregory and I always dreamed of having. . . . But I could not give birth to another child."

"You mean I was adopted?"

"In a way, yes. But perhaps more likely stolen."

"Stolen? You and Dad would never steal anything!"

"Let me tell you, and you may decide. Your father and I wanted to have a child so desperately that it clouded our judgment. . . .

"You have no reason to know that nearly eighteen years ago, there was a terrible accident on the Snake River that flows through Jackson, Wyoming.

"A young man and his wife, on vacation from Florida where he was a professor, were being guided on a section of the river called Deadman's Bar to Moose. They were fly fishing. The guide was inexperienced at best. Their drift boat crashed into a huge pile of trees deposited during the spring runoff. The guide was found dead: the current sucked him under the tree where he lodged in branches and drowned.

"We believed the husband of the couple drowned along with the guide. The man's wife floated free, and the rapid current quickly carried her downriver. Your father and I were in our own boat fishing about a mile from the accident. We were anchored. We knew nothing about the crash until we saw a figure bobbing in the water and floating with the current. We rowed to where she would pass and lifted her trembling body into our boat. She was unable to speak. Pregnant about seven months, from my estimation. As we rowed downstream seeking help, the woman died in my arms. I was mortified about the child.

"Our RV was parked near the river's west bank a little north of the takeout at Moose. We rowed ashore before we reached the takeout and carried the woman to our RV. I had delivered many children, and by a Caesarian birth I was able to save the child. It was a girl. However foolish your father and I might have been . . . we badly wanted to keep her. We had lost our son, as you know, an Army lieutenant killed in combat. We had been bitter about that ever since. We loved him dearly. . . . As we've loved you.

"The local radio station in Jackson, Wyoming, soon affirmed that both the husband and the guide were dead, but that the woman—also presumed dead—was missing. We left Wyoming with the child and her mother's body and quickly headed east to our home here in Maine, feeling very guilty. That guilt diminished as we learned from the papers that the couple had no other children, nor any living relatives. The child would have been placed for adoption, and we believed we could be more loving than any other adoptive parents.

"We lived here in this cabin on our small pond. Your father was a professional book editor for several New England companies; I was a physician at the Greenville hospital. But of course you know that."

"This is hard to believe, Mother," said Elsbeth, incredulously. "Did no one ever suspect that I was taken after my birth mother died? Were no bodies found?"

"No. That is partly due to another terrible thing we did. We buried your mother in a wilderness area of Wyoming in the mountains near the Wind River. I know exactly where; we built a cairn of stones above her grave. Three years later we went back with a small marker that honored but did not identify her. I have a map for you. Her grave is in a beautiful and private location with mesmerizing views of the Western mountains that she loved."

"Where was my father buried?"

"That's more difficult. We learned nothing about him until more than a decade later. Remember that Northern Maine is quite inaccessible. But about two years ago, we read of the death of a Professor Maxwell Hunt in Gainesville, Florida. He was living near the university under an assumed name—Robert Potter—and was shot by a law student from Guatemala. I didn't understand what had happened but the article said Professor Hunt had purportedly died of a stroke six years before the shooting, almost exactly a decade after he lost his wife and expected child. You were that child. While it was thought that your mother and you died in the boat accident in Wyoming and your father died a decade later from a stroke, you were quite clearly alive, and your father may have been as well. I'm not sure how the shooting fits into this. If your father didn't die of a stroke, did he die at the shooting in Gainesville?

"Gregory and I were saddened to have learned that although your father actually survived the Wyoming accident and lived alone for a decade without remarrying, he died either from the stroke in D.C. or the shooting in Gainesville. That means he died without ever knowing about you for the last years of his life, which were the first years of yours. He was apparently cremated and his ashes spread on the place on the Snake River where he had lost his wife and expected daughter.

"We named you Elsbeth Hunt Carson. A small pack around your mother's waist had a name tag that said 'Elsbeth Hunt.' That was your mother's name. You have grown to be the most wonderful daughter that anyone could have. You brought so much love to a lonely, childless family."

"You're saying that both my birth mother and father are dead."

"Your mother certainly. Gregory and I saw it happen and we buried her. But your father? That remains a strange mystery."

"What is the mystery? He died of a stroke. Or he was shot."

"Gregory and I weren't happy with the way Maxwell Hunt's death from the stroke was announced, especially in view of the later shooting. I don't know why, perhaps intuition, but I suspected that there was more to his death than was made public."

"What caused your suspicion?"

"Oh, at first just the absence of a body. And no record of a burial in D.C. or Florida."

"But he was cremated and his ashes scattered."

"Do we really know that? Cremation and scattering ashes destroy the ability to prove the death."

"You've always been stubborn, Mother. Where did it lead you this time?"

"First to the archives of the Gainesville newspaper. I found one article written at the time of Maxwell Hunt's announced death by a stroke, describing how he was in Washington, D.C., attending a law meeting, but unexpectedly flew to Guatemala. He was apparently injured in Guatemala and was flown back to D.C., where he died of the stroke.

"About six years later several more articles described an intended $4 million gift to the law college at the University of Florida for a chair to honor Professor Hunt. The gift was proposed by a Guatemalan alumnus who was a former student of Hunt. The alumnus apparently believed that Hunt might not have died. An investigative reporter from the Tampa paper also raised doubt about Hunt's death from a stroke.

"A year later, only a short time ago, there was a shooting at the law school during the dedication of a new building. It was never solved. But the following year another shooting occurred near the tennis courts next to the law school. A nephew of the Guatemalan who had offered the gift, which was ultimately rejected, shot a man who the police said was actually Professor

Hunt: obviously Hunt had not died of a stroke a few years earlier. One newspaper article suggested that after he was nearly killed in Guatemala and flown to Washington, he did not die of a stroke but was placed in some kind of protection program by the CIA. The Guatemalan man and another former student, a Sudanese, had vowed to find and kill Hunt."

"Mother, this is incredible!"

"There's more. . . . Despite the danger, Hunt was said to have insisted on living in Gainesville. I didn't believe a word of it. I was convinced that Hunt didn't die and was in a protection program with a new name and new residence. Later, I learned that the man who was killed may have looked like and been mistaken for your father, but he was a New Jersey mafia figure, not your father. That means the real Professor Hunt was living somewhere under a new name."

"My God, Mother! What's his name? Where does he live?"

"Patience, Elsbeth. My search became difficult at this point. It told me that the CIA was involved. The newspapers had all but confirmed that Hunt had occasionally worked for CIA missions in several countries during his last decade as a law professor. He was distraught over your mother's death on the river. I don't know what is true. It's not easy to walk into the CIA building in Langley and be told anything about anyone."

"So that's as much as you know?"

"No, I learned that Hunt had a close friend in the CIA. His name is Dan Wilson. He was . . ."

Her eyes opened widely, she gagged, gasped for another breath that did not come, and fell forward. The talk had been too much for her heart, weakened by the earlier death of Gregory. She lay in her hospital bed staring at Elsbeth, but could not tell her more about her father. She died several hours later unable to speak another word.

Margaret Carson was buried next to her late-husband Gregory in a small cemetery in Greenville, Maine. The gravesite crested a slight knoll overlooking the southern portion of Moosehead Lake. The marker placed by Elsbeth said "She died peacefully in the company of her beloved daughter."

42

A FEW DAYS after Dan returned to D.C., Juan Santander arrived at my cabin on Mill Creek to visit and fish. We gave him no time to relax before we were driving up the Mill Creek Road to the uppermost campsite, where the creek is a fraction of its size when it passes my cabin.

"Maduff," exclaimed Juan, "this part of the creek is ridiculous; it's too small to fish. Shouldn't we be floating on the Yellowstone?"

"No and no. You'll soon see it's not too small to fish and we'll be on the Yellowstone tomorrow morning at daybreak for a long, tiring day. We won't have time to get out and wade."

"So what lives in this part of Mill Creek, guppies like Aunt Cassie has in her aquarium?"

"Be quiet and put a fly on your tippet. And use nothing larger than a #6 tippet. Number 7 is better. Number 6 tests at about three-and-a-half pounds, #7 at about two-and-a-half. You could use #8, which is good for a fraction under two pounds, bigger than what we'll find here."

"At that rate a #14 tippet, if they make them, would be about right. . . . What fly pattern?"

"My doubtful friend, try this small #18 Adams Trude. The all-purpose fly when you don't have the faintest idea what the fish would prefer."

I knew better than to help Juan tie on the fly. He held the fly in his right prosthesis and with his left hand slid the tippet through the eye, wrapped the tag end five times around the main body of the tippet, and slipped the end through the hole made by the eye of the hook and the beginning of the tippet windings. It's a clinch knot, a favorite of both beginning fly fishers and experienced guides. You can go one loop further if you wish. Take the tag end after completing the basic knot, but before pulling it tight, and run it through the new hole made by the last clinch knot loop. Then you have an "improved" clinch knot, really a *more secure* clinch knot. But if you did the first part properly to begin with, the improved addition is more for the fisherman's comfort than the tippet's strength.

"Ready," Juan stated with a grin, "let's go after those illusionary trout you talk about. How far a walk?"

"About forty feet," I answered. "Directly to the stream's bank, a little downstream of that pile of brush along the edge to your left."

"You're telling me there're trout hidden under that small pile of branches."

"That's right. It may only be a small bush, but a few roots are still stuck along the bank and the brush diverts some of the current, forming some calmer water under the overhanging brush."

Twenty feet upstream from a straight line to the creek, the brush formed an umbrella above a dark, quiet pool. The brush was too small to merit the name *strainer,* which is reserved for piles of trees and branches on the larger rivers, the kind of unruly tree-remains that took the life of my wife El on the Snake

River in Jackson Hole nearly two decades ago and then five years ago that became the setting for the final act that ended the life of Park Salisbury, posing as an overweight Oregon fly fisherman. Salisbury had shot and killed former ambassador Ander Eckstrum and then shot and killed his ex-wife and her new fiancée. He later nearly added three more bodies to his list: Lucinda, me, and Wuff.

"Juan," Lucinda offered, "Toss your fly upstream under the overhanging branches or at least to their edge. . . . And prepare to eat your words!"

"There is nothing alive under those branches, but I'll humor you both."

Juan let out nearly twenty feet of line, made one backcast and a good low sidearm cast that carried the fly a dozen inches above and across the surface, landing the fly perfectly ten inches in and under the branches.

"Wow!' Juan exclaimed as a trout slammed the fly the moment it hit the surface. "*I've got one on.* First cast. It was waiting. You must have stocked this place this morning. Damn, you're right, you two! It's a beauty, must be nine or ten inches and has the red slash throat of a cutthroat."

There was a chill from air tumbling down the Absaroka mountain range that from north-to-south towered above us. After a half-hour fishing that produced a half-dozen trout among us, we built a fire at the campsite and sat on ten foot sections of a lodgepole pine sawn at least a decade ago.

"If we were in the woods near our Florida cottage," Lucinda commented, "the downed slash pines would be rotting, and we would've looked carefully under them for a coral snake or a pygmy rattler before we sat."

"Here, we don't have to look *down* as much," said Juan, "but the rocky cliff wall near the top of the rise to our right is good cat habitat."

"Mountain lions are pretty reclusive," said Lucinda. "Mac and I thought we saw one last summer, but we're doubtful. It would be scary to be sitting here and suddenly spot one sitting on that ledge, wondering if we look like Meow Mix."

"There are too many of us," I added. But I worry when I'm here alone. I worry more about mountain lions than I do about grizzlies. A grizzly's like a B-52; a mountain lion's like a Stealth bomber."

"Seen any grizzlies along Mill Creek?" Juan asked, looking behind and along the upper part of the creek.

"Yes," answered Lucinda, shivering at the recollection.

"Mac and I saw a huge mother grizzly and her single cub, not more than forty feet away. But we were on the opposite side of Mill Creek when it was deep with fast water at the height of a spring run-off. The mother stood up on her hind feet, glared at us, and roared her disapproval. It worked; we backed off into the woods and then walked quickly and quietly to my cabin. I'm glad Wuff wasn't with us."

"Mac, let me change the subject. Have you solved any of the murders on the drift boats?"

"Not really. It appears we'll have one more chance." I told him about the photo in the mailbox. Lucinda looked at me askance to show her concern that I had waited two days to mention the photo.

Juan knew nothing about Lucinda's brief marriage and the apparent intentions of Ellsworth-Kent or about Hannah Markel. His role had been exclusively related to the attempts by Herzog and Isfahani to find me.

"Does your friend in D.C.—Don something—have any more knowledge about the Herzog guy?"

"His name's Dan Wilson. About Herzog's whereabouts? No. . . . His friend Isfahani has been undergoing more reconstructive plastic surgery on his face in Switzerland. Dan believes Isfahani and Herzog have deferred their search, but by no means abandoned it."

"Any more information about who might have shot Whitman in the back room at the place in D.C?" Juan asked.

The question surprised me. Did we ever talk about it? I wasn't certain how much I should tell him. If he's protected us from Herzog and Isfahani, he knows more about my dual life than I thought.

"Whitman's a dead issue," I replied. "Nothing in the way of useful evidence has been found. He worked for the CIA for quite a few years. Being involved with clandestine activities, he became somewhat of a non-person. Dan hasn't given any information about him to the D.C. police. They have enough crime in the District that's in need of attention. When something isn't solved right away, it tends to get lost in the police files. Unless someone comes forward and admits to the killing, we've probably seen the last of that."

"Was the CIA behind the killing?" Juan persisted. "You told me that they were furious about the prospect of Whitman's manuscript being published. . . . I'm glad he's gone for your sake, Mac."

"I still wonder about the manuscript. But we're inclined to think it's over."

"Did they find the hard drive that was missing from Whitman's computer? That may have held the manuscript."

"They found it. They didn't find any other copies or computer storage of the manuscript. We entered Whitman's condo after the shooting and did a very thorough search."

"Well . . . Whitman had it coming," Juan added.

43

WE FLOATED the Yellowstone the next day as promised, ending at dusk with three exhausted people back at the cabin, moving irregularly with painful expressions, as though all our joints had been repeatedly tested. I was two hours tardy preparing Wuff's dinner. If a dog can sulk, she was doing it to perfection.

We were on the river for a dozen hours, floating fourteen miles from Loch Leven to Carter Bridge. I hadn't planned on fishing, but Juan asked me to let him share the rowing. He's made a device to attach to his right prosthesis that helps him hold the oar handle. He's coming along well; I expect to hear soon that he's guiding.

When we crossed the cabin's threshold we were ready to face two chilled bottles of a white burgundy from one of the many small wineries in the French Mâson region, where vineyard land sells for more than a million euros per hectare—about two and a half acres and thus about a half-million in dollars per acre. The price of the wine reflects that cost.

Not one of us was especially hungry, but each could have consumed a full bottle of wine. We pretended to be *reasonably* gracious in sharing. Without dissent, but some regret, we decided to forego our reserved table and the Beef Wellington at the Chico Hot Springs Resort and pick away at left-overs. Our lights were out by nine.

Juan started the drive to Jackson early the next morning. As soon as his car disappeared down the drive, Lucinda, Wuff, and I walked down to lock the gate and check the mailbox, hoping to prove to Lucinda that I can walk and talk at the same time.

"Do you have any opinions about our conversation with Juan last evening at the campsite after we fished?" I asked.

"Like what?"

"Oh, anything he said when Whitman's name was mentioned?"

"Any time I hear the name Whitman I think 'Thank God he's dead.' I don't think clearly when his name comes up. He could have caused your death."

"And yours. Juan said two things that surprised me. He mentioned that the killing took place in a back room of that bar, Lounge Suite 14. The newspaper never mentioned anything about a back room; it referred only to the bar."

"What's the other matter?"

"He asked about the missing hard drive from Whitman's computer. He couldn't have known about that."

"Unless he's the one who took the hard drive! . . . Do you believe he was involved?"

"He must have been," I answered with embarrassing uncertainty.

"I'm not surprised; ever since you two met, he's viewed you as someone he'll protect at any cost. I think he's respected you since you took him on outside the Gun Barrel in Jackson, pretending the cap of your Sharpie felt pen was a pistol. . . .

That makes me feel good. You need a guardian angel or maybe two big, tough bodyguards. Like a rock star."

"I have you and Wuff. . . . If you're right about Juan, that makes two people he's killed protecting us, assuming he shot Martín Paz in Florida as he was about to shoot us, and then shot Whitman, who may have been about to give Herzog your name and location."

"Maybe he did give Herzog my name and location."

"No," she replied, "If he had, we'd have heard from Herzog by now. Our ashes would be floating somewhere on the Yellowstone."

"That means my ashes would have been scattered on two different rivers, some on the Snake nearly a decade ago and some here on the Yellowstone this year."

"Only here they'd be scattered with mine. You know what was scattered on the Snake was not your ashes but the ashes of the *New York Times* the CIA agent read on the plane flying to Wyoming from D.C."

This is not a pleasant discussion. . . . Are you paying Juan to protect me?"

"No. but I would if he asked. . . . At any price!"

"Any?"

"Don't press me."

Wuff had run ahead of us to the mailbox and was sitting and waiting. I like to think she was waiting for us because she loves us. But she was waiting because she knows I carry treats in my right front pocket. . . .

"This walk has exhausted me," I offered, hoping for some sympathy. "I didn't sleep well last night."

"You drank too much wine. I'm sure you took some of my share. Serves you right."

"And you drank some of Juan's. What goes around comes around."

When we had stopped and opened the gate coming home at dusk from fishing yesterday, I'd left the mail untouched.

"Mac, open the mailbox. My arm is so tired I don't think I'll ever be able to lift it and cast again."

"Complain, complain. You caught more trout than Juan and me together. . . . Who taught you to cast like that?"

"I read books and watched DVDs by Lefty Kreh, Joan Wulff, and Mel Krieger. Then John Kirby helped me correct some mistakes. He said they were all things you'd taught me. . . . And I practice in front of the cabin when you're not around."

I pouted all the way back from the mailbox.

At the cabin I went through the stack of mail. Sales brochures for hearing aids; three more notices from the car dealer informing me that my SUV was overdue for service and suggesting I might be wise to trade it in for a new vehicle; two solicitations offering credit cards from two of our "too big to fail" banks that the newspapers and TV have repeatedly identified and documented their mismanagement by officers who are under indictment, being tried, or serving sentences; and an offer to trace my genealogy at a special reduced price.

Hearing aids are not yet part of my life, though Lucinda often says I need them. I hear every word she says, but I only admit to hearing the words I want to hear.

My SUV is old; bought the day I arrived in Montana close to a decade ago. Starting two months after I took delivery of the vehicle, the dealer began to overwhelm me with urgings to trade it in. I routinely toss them out.

I'll send the credit card applications back to the banks in the prepaid envelopes, with a big "Thanks but no thanks" written on all the junk they sent me and that I stuffed back into the return envelopes. I avoid doing business with all banks that are based in New York or Charlotte, preferring more service-oriented local banks and credit unions.

As far as my genealogy goes, which isn't very far, I tossed out the "special one-time only" offer. I was tempted to accept and see what kind of family history they could discover for Macduff Brooks.

After setting all the junk mail aside, I noticed I'd passed over one plain envelope that bore no return address, marked only that it was to Macduff Brooks. I opened it and another photo dropped out. I picked it up, looked at it, and gasped. It was of Lucinda and me floating on the Yellowstone a few days ago. A circle had been drawn around Lucinda's head. Not a full circle, one missing the last quarter section. Below was written "The circle will soon close."

I stuffed the photo into my pocket. Lucinda had enough to worry about without adding this. But I felt deceptive. Perhaps love trumps deception. But it doesn't make me feel any the less abusive for having drawn her into this mess. I guess it's those green eyes. And the grin.

44

APRIL CAME and disappeared quietly. I completed without incident a few floats for a local outfitter who doesn't seem ruffled by my recent history. By the first of May the snowmelt was strong enough to send torrents of silted water down every tributary into the Yellowstone, ending floats until mid-June.

With May opening as placid as April I wondered if we had overreacted and nothing would happen on the summer solstice. Or was it the "calm before the storm?" It was the latter if Wuff's unexplainable conduct was any warning. She remained at Lucinda's side, never leaving her in a different room by herself and whining as soon as Lucinda left on an errand. Wuff never came to me as second fiddle; she lay by the door until Lucinda returned, taking up where she left off and following Lucinda about the cabin. At night Wuff normally hopped onto our bed as we read, and then jumped down and slept in various places in the cabin, directly related to the temperature. On cool nights she sought out warm rugs; on summer nights she lay on the tiled kitchen floor. But since the photos arrived, Wuff has slept on the hard wooden floor on Lucinda's side of the bed, always facing the door.

"Why do you suppose Wuff's acting the way she is?" I asked Lucinda one early May morning when she returned with food from Albertsons, "You didn't bring any dog food or treats in your packages."

"She's come to her senses. She knows who feeds her and who lets her out. . . . Remember, Macduff, I blocked some bullets on the Snake River that might have killed her."

"You mean *she* thinks I was too slow to get my Glock out?"

"You said it—I didn't."

"Would you have blocked those shots if it had been me behind you?"

"How much time do I have to answer that?"

"But I rescued Wuff six years ago from terrible owners. A year before you seduced me at your ranch."

"I didn't touch you at my ranch. I was very well behaved. When I first saw you sitting on the ice in front of my door, I wanted to shut the door and dine alone."

"But you didn't; you let me in."

"We all make mistakes."

"And you've been sorry ever since?"

"A few times, mainly when I've been recuperating from gunshot wounds. . . . Now that I think of it, living with you makes having amnesia seem not to have been so bad."

"How did we get here? All I asked about was Wuff?"

"Wuff and I have become best friends."

"But I pay for her food and lodging."

"Those are her entitlements. I protect her life so she can enjoy them."

As usual, I broke off the conversation, feeling like I had lost a twelve-round fight in the first minute of the first round. But I knew how lucky my life had been since my two gals had joined me. First Wuff, after Judge Amy Becker "approved" me as Wuff's *guardian ad litem.* And a year later, when I got up off that icy walk in front of Lucinda's ranch on a cold Thanksgiving evening, and was instantly overwhelmed by her. I don't remember, but I must have hit my head on the door stoop.

Truthfully, being with Lucinda confuses me. I still feel attached to El nearly two decades after her death. As I've become more attached to Lucinda, my feelings about El haven't diminished. Nor about the daughter I might have had.

45

IN THE FARMHOUSE on Tom Miner Road, Markel and Ellsworth-Kent were focused on June 21st, the day Lucinda and Macduff would end their lives, allowing Markel and Ellsworth-Kent to go their separate ways. Their deteriorating feelings towards each other were not helpful in planning a double murder. With each death the police learned more, which they would use to catch them before they killed again. It was frustrating for the police to know who was responsible, but not know where they were.

"There are some certainties, Hannah, starting with the date. It must be on the summer solstice. And we must continue the wicker man and mistletoe."

"We want the two dead; we can forego the wicker man and mistletoe."

"No, we must not. Our ancestors would not welcome our casting aside ancient traditions. I cannot do that as a high priest."

"Mail-order high priest," she added disdainfully.

"Will you make the wicker man?" Ellsworth-Kent said, ignoring her comment.

"If I must. Do I have to make only one?"

"You must make two, but only one for Lucinda and Macduff. They will be together."

"Then why a second?" she asked suspiciously, hoping the second was not for her!

"I have an idea. The police expect the killing to be on the 21st. But this year's summer solstice date is actually the 20th. It's a technical irrelevancy, but we need to think about it.

"So what?"

"The police will have the Yellowstone River covered for miles each side of where Mill Creek empties into the river."

"You don't think we can succeed?"

"We can. If we create a diversion. And if we sacrifice *someone* on the 20th. The police will say it was a copycat sacrifice of another of Macduff's friends. And they'll think the killings are over or at least won't occur again until the fall equinox."

"Meaning what?"

"If the police don't patrol in full until late on the 20th, we have time to strike at midnight at the end of the 19th. Then we'll deal with Lucinda and Macduff on the 21st, the day most people consider the summer solstice. And be gone before the police know what happened."

"Who will we kill on the 20th?"

"Possibly a guide friend from Emigrant—Matson what's-his-name. But we've already sacrificed a guide. Maybe one of Macduff's friends in the Gallatin County Sheriff's Office in Livingston. That deputy who helped them two years ago with the Shuttle Gals murders."

"Who?"

"I think her name's Erin Giffin, one of Lucinda's and Macduff's closest friends, or so I'm told by people in Emigrant and Livingston."

"Do we have to abduct Giffin and hold her hostage?"

"Yes, and when she's missing the focus will be on her as the natural target for this summer solstice."

"Will she be in a wicker man and have mistletoe?"

"Yes, as in the first four. The wicker man and mistletoe sacrifice is our trademark—we *must* use it."

"So you'll have your way?"

"Yes. It must be that way."

"But will no one see Lucinda and Macduff die?"

"Macduff will die a horrible death, sitting under the wicker next to the person he loves. Hearing the timer tick but not seeing it and not knowing which is the last tick. . . . We could kill him by shooting him, more certain but providing insufficient suffering. The wicker man and mistletoe sacrifice is much more likely to bring him pain, even if there is no grandstand along the Yellowstone on which to sit and watch."

"And how do we deal with our sacrificial Erin Giffin?"

"We sacrifice Giffin on the 20th. She will die downriver more than fifteen miles from Mill Creek. Everyone will soon be told that the 20th was the true summer solstice and think we planned the summer solstice sacrifice to follow the pattern with earlier ones—sacrificing *friends* of Macduff—and *not* sacrificing Lucinda or Macduff. They'll believe the signs on the wicker men were deceptions and diversions."

"It might work—I have to give you credit. The police will disperse on the 20th after the Giffin murder, except for those investigating her death. There won't be many around Mill Creek on the 21st. They'll be around the place downriver where Giffin died. . . . Do you think the police will believe Lucinda and Macduff are in Florida at the time?"

"We'll have both place phone calls—after we abduct them—to people in this area, indicating that they're enjoying Florida."

"Macduff won't make those calls. Nor will Lucinda."

"He will when we start cutting off Lucinda's fingers."

"Yes . . . he will."

"And on the 21st we strike?"

"Exactly the same as planned, a single drift boat with a single large wicker man—Lucinda and Macduff inside together—topped with mistletoe and floating the Yellowstone with very few police about. Those who are on the scene will be around the location where Giffin died. After the explosion kills Lucinda and Macduff, we'll get away easily."

"You're evil."

"It is my duty as a high priest to perform ritual sacrifices. I'm carrying out that duty."

"Rubbish! But I will fulfill my goal. Macduff will be dead. . . . I'm a little confused about the 20th and 21st."

"As I thought I explained, the date of the summer solstice varies between the 20th and 21st. It's a very complex matter to determine. This year it's the 20th, but according to the misinformed papers, it's the 21st. Most people don't think of that or care; they just assume that every year it will be on the 21st. Most of the celebrations by believers will come on the 21st."

"Meaning Giffin will die on the day that actually is the summer solstice this year, and Lucinda and Macduff will die the day after, the day most people associate with the solstice."

"Yes, and most important, Giffin will die with no one around because the police will be assuming the death will occur on the 21st near Mill Creek, and Lucinda and Macduff will die with no one around because the police will assume their deaths are not part of the scheme because Giffin was the target and the summer solstice is over. Also, most everyone will believe Lucinda and Macduff are in Florida."

"Before you tell me how Deputy Giffin will be abducted, are we going to tow the stolen drift boat we'll use for Lucinda and Macduff from here on Tom Miner Road to the river on the morning of the 21st?"

"We'd never make it. The Tom Miner Road should be OK, but Route 89 north will still have police, although most will be around Carter Bridge."

"We could hide the boat somewhere closer to Emigrant."

"That's exactly what we'll do. I rented that old barn we looked at along the river. The property is full of trees all the way to the river's edge. Once at the barn, a person in any vehicle, boat or car can't see the barn from any road or from the river. We can back the boat and trailer through the trees and slide the boat into the water. It only will have a hundred yards to float to the Mill Creek Bridge, just after where Mill Creek joins the Yellowstone. That's where the explosion must take place. I'll calculate how long that drift will take; when we set the boat adrift I'll set the timer. It's perfect."

"Are you worried the barn owner might find our things in the barn? After all, we'll have the wicker man there a few days before the 21st. And the explosives. Use of a wicker man has been in the papers, and the owner might become suspicious."

"The barn's owned by a man from California. He's working in Central America for six months. I paid him for the full time. The barn has room for the boat, the trailer, and our car. Plus it has a small bathroom. We can sleep on the floor on air mattresses for the last day or so if we need to."

"What do we do with Lucinda and Macduff when we've abducted them?"

"There's room in the barn for them as well. I want them both there a day or two before the 21st. They will suffer. They will be able to see the wicker man, the mistletoe, and the explosives and timer. They will know their fate. We should plan to be there directly after sacrificing Giffin and not leave the barn until we take care of Lucinda and Macduff."

"If we abduct them much before the 21st, won't there be a wide search of the area?"

"No, because everyone else will think they're in Florida, safely ensconced at Macduff's place."

"If that's what people will believe, won't there be fewer police around here? . . . Robert, when will we abduct Macduff and Lucinda?"

"On the day people assume they've flown to Florida."

"When we have them at the barn, their friends may call to see if they've arrived safely in Florida."

"I expect they will. Lucinda and Macduff will use their cell phones only in our presence. We will even have them phone people in Livingston and Paradise Valley, including their housekeeper, Mavis, and Deputy Sheriff Rangley. Maybe others, the woman who ran Howlin' Hounds or Matson Rogers at Angler's West. We'll listen in on the conversation and instruct them what to say. Like how wonderful it is to be in sunny Florida."

"Since they have cell phones, no one will know where they are."

"Except us."

"Now tell me about abducting Deputy Giffin."

46

"MACDUFF, WHEN do I get you to sit down and talk a minute," Lucinda asked while washing the final dish from a light supper and handing it to me to dry.

"Talk about what?"

"Some ideas I have about next week. To be more exact next week on the 21st—the summer solstice."

"I'm enjoying my wine."

"You're supposed to be drying the dishes. I know you can't shoot and talk at the same time, but is the same true about drying dishes, drinking wine, and talking at the same time?"

"Now I'm *not* enjoying my wine. Hand me another dish."

"I'll talk anyway. I think any attempt made on us by Markel and Ellsworth-Kent will *not* take place here on the Yellowstone. What do you think about that?"

"That you have more to add, which will have to be very good to make up for disturbing my wine tasting."

"I don't think they intend to kill you."

"That's good to know. Pour me another glass."

"In your lap! *Listen to me.*"

"As they say 'I'm all ears.'"

"Do you think Markel and Ellsworth-Kent have learned much about us?"

"Yes, probably more about you than me because I only go back eight years. And you have a *long* history."

"*Long* history? I don't think I like the way that sounded. . . . I'm assuming that Hannah Markel has found out all about you from the time you moved here, back before Helga Markel came into your life two years ago. Back before we met."

"Don't remind me. I'll have nightmares."

"That's not nice. I'm about to be murdered."

"So melodramatic! You have at least a few days. Go outside and practice with your Glock."

"You don't want to hear my opinion about Markel and Ellsworth-Kent?"

"I might as well. My wine glass is empty. I finished drying the last dish. The service here is temperamental. So entertain me."

"Hannah knows about the murders on the Snake as well as those here on the Yellowstone. You agree?"

"Fine. Does that make much difference in where they try to kill us?"

"Don't distract me. . . . Hannah knows about El's death a decade before you moved here. Agree?" she asked, ignoring my answer.

I sat up abruptly. "Now you're scaring me. What do you mean?"

"Markel and Ellsworth-Kent have surely been to the Jackson Hole Historical Society and Museum to search newspaper microfilm about crashes and significant incidents—such as murder—involving drift boats on the Snake. Agree?"

"Why don't I simply agree with all your 'agrees?' Those killings were, in fact, mentioned in newspaper records in Saratoga and Missoula long before the murders on the North Platte and Clark. The same may be true about the deaths on the Madison and the Henry's Fork."

"You've done thorough research in the past when you wrote law books. If Markel or Ellsworth-Kent did search Jackson Hole records, might they not have seen an article about your accident when El was killed?"

"I never wanted to read about it. I never did."

"I'm sorry to take you back, Macduff. It's because I want to spend the next decades growing old with you."

"Talking to you, I'm growing old at an accelerated rate."

"So it's possible Markel and Ellsworth-Kent *have* talked about the accident that killed El?"

"Yes," I answered in barely a whisper. I didn't like where she was taking me.

"Do you think it's possible that they wondered about any link between you as Maxwell Hunt and El's death, and you as Macduff Brooks and the others' deaths?"

"I don't think so, but I suspect you're about to tell me they did."

"Any history they have on you living in Montana begins when you arrived in Montana. They could learn the specific date. They don't know a single detail about your life before that date. . . . If they were curious, they might have gone online searching accidents on the local rivers. If they found any, could there be a link? The Jackson Hole paper said Maxwell Hunt was a law professor at the University of Florida. Markel and Ellsworth-Kent might have looked at Hunt's life *after* the accident. If they did, all the reports of Herzog and the deaths of his nephew and niece are certain to set them thinking that if Maxwell Hunt didn't die from the stroke, could he be Macduff Brooks?"

"Could Markel and Ellsworth-Kent have contacted Herzog?" I asked, worrying about her answer.

"Of course. But like Whitman, they would want to sell the information. And unlike Whitman, Markel and Ellsworth-Kent are after you to kill you, not to publish or sell information about you."

"But Markel and Ellsworth-Kent would have discovered the information well after Herzog's niece and nephew were shot and killed, and unlike Whitman's information, the knowledge Markel and Ellsworth-Kent may have is speculation."

"I don't think they've contacted Herzog—yet. They're focused on killing us by themselves. But what if they fail, as we certainly expect them to do? If they got away their next move might be to contact Herzog, give him our information, and let him do the killing. Or help him."

"We need to discuss this with Dan. But no one else."

"Thanks for listening to me."

"Pour me some more wine."

"I'm not finished. Any other places where you think Markel and Ellsworth-Kent might strike?"

"You're the one with the ideas."

"A crazy suggestion—what about on the salt water flats at your St. Augustine cottage?"

"Not so crazy, . . . but unlikely. I'm not sure how much they know about our life in Florida. There'd be logistics to deal with. Getting onto the flats, stealing a flats boat, avoiding friends of ours who live there—though we don't have many."

"You're probably right, Macduff. I'm trying to think of alternatives we need to discuss, if I can divert your attention from the wine. . . . Since we've told people we'll be in Florida on the summer solstice, if that word gets to Markel or Ellsworth-Kent they'll have to change their plans. They couldn't easily abduct us in Florida and bring us back out here."

"If they're convinced we'll be in Florida, they do have to change their plans."

"I'd like to know their thinking."

"So would I. *Now* pour some more wine."

47

HANNAH MARKEL AND ROBERT ELLSWORTH-KENT were sitting in the old barn he had rented close to the Yellowstone and upriver a couple of hundred yards from the Mill Creek juncture. The barn was weathered and looked ready to tumble in the next strong wind blowing down Paradise Valley. They had towed the second stolen drift boat after dark from the Tom Miner Road to the barn and then walked the path to the river to make sure the trailer could be backed close enough to the river to easily slide the boat off and into the water. They didn't try it with the car and trailer because they were afraid of leaving fresh tire tracks that police might see by walking the banks.

The final launch should be easy. Lucinda and Macduff would be tied in the guide seat, covered with the wicker man, draped with mistletoe, wrapped with explosives, and bearing a sign. From the time they opened the barn door to the launch in the river should take no more than ten minutes.

"Hannah, what should the signs say on the two?"

"Something that suggests the finality of the two sacrifices."

"I want it to refer to my sister Helga," demanded Hannah. "He caused her death. Maybe 'Retribution Fulfilled.' Macduff will understand what it means, if we show it to him. . . . What do *you* want on the sign?"

"Souls are immortal—they will live in new bodies."

"Meaning what?"

"A fundamental belief of the ancients. The soul of Macduff will survive to enter a new body at a later time. The soul never perishes."

"That's creepy, Robert."

"Do not disparage the ancients."

Hannah was concerned with Robert's increasing disdain for humanity. She thought it might be the ridicule he received when he claimed to be a high priest. She would be much relieved to put some distance between herself and Robert, but first she must finish her task of seeing to the end of Macduff Brooks.

"Robert, you have only one set of explosives for Giffin, and one for Lucinda and Macduff. Is that enough?"

One will blow both of them into the same unidentifiable pieces as the earlier sacrifices. . . . We are doing a great and glorious act by these sacrifices. The traditions call for sacrifice by drowning, hanging, or burning. We are adding to the tradition of our ancestors: sacrifices by obliteration in a huge fireball. A second explosive would unnecessarily add to the carnage."

"What about Deputy Giffin. Will we bring her here?"

"No. I had an idea last night when I couldn't sleep. We've both been concerned that the police undoubtedly know both who we are and that we will strike on the 21st. Plus, they may know where we will strike. But I think we can distract their attention."

"How?"

48

IN GAINESVILLE, FLORIDA, on June 17th, Elsbeth Carson parked her rental car by the UF law college. She had left Greenville at dawn the day before and driven to the airport at Bangor for the first leg of her flight to Gainesville. She arrived in mid-afternoon and, after checking into her motel, bought a street map and began her introduction to the university, the town, and the neighborhood where her birth father and mother had lived nearly twenty years ago.

Elsbeth had intentionally scheduled the meeting with Dean Hobart Perry for the following morning, leaving her time to become acquainted with the area. Three months earlier Gainesville meant nothing to her. She looked forward to many years with her mother in Maine after she finished college at Orono, where she was soon to be a freshman. She expected that she would return to Greenville after receiving her baccalaureate.

But her life had been altered with the sudden death of her mother. Three days after her mother died, Elsbeth was told by the estate executor that a considerable sum had been left to her, more than enough to pay for college and graduate school. In addition, she inherited the Carson home and all its belongings.

Dean Perry personally had contacted Elsbeth after receiving a call from Dan Wilson at the CIA headquarters in Langley, Virginia. The call shocked him. While Professor Maxwell Hunt's unclear history had taken considerable time for Dean Perry's attention, there had never been any indication that Maxwell's daughter survived the accident on the Snake.

The dean was as curious to meet Elsbeth as he was interested in helping her find her father, although Perry tended to accept the accuracy of the information released by the university that Hunt was shot and killed near the tennis courts by Hertzog's nephew, law student Martín Paz. That assumed Hunt had not succumbed to the alleged stroke a decade and a half prior to the tennis court incident.

Elsbeth left the motel and drove directly to Golf View to see the house where her mother and father lived for ten years before the accident. For ten minutes she sat outside the house with its cylindrical entry tower. Next, she went to the law school, parked in the visitors lot, and walked to the far side of the law complex adjacent to the tennis courts where her father may have been killed. Sitting on a small brick wall thinking of what might have been, suddenly she realized that she was exhausted from the travel, had a light meal, and returned to her motel.

She was due in the dean's office at nine the following morning. To Elsbeth, the law school was a confusing mix of buildings; she tried to imagine how different it would appear were the students in session. Only a small summer session brought a few score of students to the campus in June.

The dean's secretary Donna took Elsbeth into his office a few minutes early, where Dean Perry rose from his chair, shook her hand enthusiastically, and offered her coffee.

After some general conversation, Dean Perry shifted his weight in the chair and looked at Elsbeth with an intensity that showed he wanted to get to the purpose of her visit. "Ms. Carson, or if you prefer Ms. Hunt, I never knew your father. I became dean a few years after he was thought to have died of a stroke in Washington. I believe you know that background."

"I do. What I don't know is whether my father is dead and, if he is not, where he lives."

"You know I've talked to a man at the CIA named Dan Wilson. That is probably not his real name. Without telling me anything specific, I think he'll talk to you after our conversation. Talking to Wilson made me realize how much he was involved with Professor Hunt. I think that was after the alleged stroke, and I suspect Wilson was behind telling the public Professor Hunt died from a stroke. Without disclosing what might have happened, Wilson conveyed to me the idea that your father was alive after he returned from Guatemala, recovered, and then disappeared. The CIA has ways of making people disappear. I don't mean by killing them. I think in this case by hiding Professor Hunt to make him safe."

"What do you mean, Dean Perry?" Elsbeth inquired.

"CIA agents occasionally become compromised. Unless something is done, they are subject to assassination by foreign agents. What I believe is that your father was working for the CIA, was compromised, and was placed in some kind of program similar to the federal witness protection plan.

"That means he moved away from Gainesville?"

"Logically, yes. And that is why I have always had some doubt about the man called Richard Potter who the CIA identified as Professor Maxwell Hunt less than two years ago."

"Could my father be teaching law somewhere else?"

"I very much doubt that. At least not under the name Maxwell Hunt. And he couldn't teach law under an assumed name because, prior to hiring, any law school would want to have parts of his background certified, such as law degrees and bar admissions."

"So he has a new name? What does he do?"

"As to both of those questions I have no idea. But I do know he has been trying to evade two men, both former law students here."

Dean Perry outlined to Elsbeth all that he knew about the relationship between Maxwell Hunt and both Juan Pablo Herzog and Abdul Khaliq Isfahani, including giving her a copy of the report prepared several years ago by then Assistant Dean Gloria Martinez, at the time Herzog was offering to fund a chair in Professor Hunt's name.

"Is there anything more you know, Dean Perry; you've been very gracious to share with me your information."

"Normally, I wouldn't do this. But Professor Hunt has been declared dead by the university, and he had no family. Until now. As his daughter, I think you're entitled to share what we know."

Donna, the dean's secretary, knocked on his door and after a few seconds, opened it slightly.

"Dean Perry, Professor Rowgoff's here and wants to leave a present."

"It must be special. Let him in."

"Hello, Charles. How's retirement?"

"*Wonderful.* I should have retired much earlier." As he turned and looked at Elsbeth, his expression changed from ebullience to astonishment. He looked as though he was seeing a ghost. Who *are* you, young lady?"

"This is Ms. Elsbeth Carson, Charles. Ms. Carson, Professor Rowgoff taught here for many years. He retired a year ago."

"Ms. Carson, I didn't mean to surprise you, but you look so much like a former colleague's wife, Elsbeth Hunt. Maxwell Hunt taught here for two decades. During the first decade, I saw El and Maxwell quite often. Then she died in a tragic accident out West. Maxwell stayed another decade but became very reclusive. . . . What is so very coincidental is that his wife's name was Elsbeth, the same as yours."

"It's the Norwegian form of Elizabeth, Professor Rowgoff."

"It is very unusual. . . . Dean, I have a lunch I should get to. I'll leave you this present and drop in again. . . . Ms. Hunt, I mean Ms. Carson, it was nice to meet you."

Rowgoff rose and, clearly flustered by the conversation, left the office.

"I guess any doubt I might have had was settled by Professor Rowgoff. You must talk to Dan Wilson at the CIA and see how much he'll tell you."

"Thank you, Dean Perry. You've been very kind. It has meant much to me. I do want to meet Mr. Wilson."

"I'll arrange it right now," said Perry, reaching for the telephone.

49

AT THEIR RENTED FARMHOUSE Ellsworth-Kent monitored the police radio frequency of the the Gallatin County Sheriff's Office, while Markel constructed a second wicker man. He listened to the movements of Deputy Giffin to understand her work pattern and learned that she would be on a job in Gardiner at the northern edge of Yellowstone Park late on the afternoon of June 19th, the day before they planned to kill her.

Markel and Ellsworth-Kent were determined to hold off abducting Giffin, if possible, until the evening of June 19th, expecting that she would not be reported missing until sometime in the morning of the 20th. By then it would be too late to save her. When her colleagues at the sheriff's office began worrying about her on the 20th, she would be floating in a stolen drift boat on the Yellowstone River, about to be blown into more pieces than a complex puzzle.

On the morning of the 19th, Ellsworth-Kent, dressed in used clothing bought in the Jackson Goodwill store, including Western boots, jeans, a checkered shirt, and a well-worn Stetson hat. He looked like any other ranch hand in his mid-fifties. He spoke as little as possible, and when he did, he hid his English accent by changing his speech to be passed off as an Australian outback jackaroo.

With Markel lying uncomfortably on the folded-down rear seat, at 3:30 p.m. Ellsworth-Kent drove to Gardiner. On the outskirts of town, he pulled into the far end of a kayak outfitters' parking lot, stopping his vehicle so it allowed him to see cars coming from the north. The two waited impatiently, until 5:45 when he saw a police car approach and pass, the driver a woman, perhaps in her late thirties.

Ellsworth-Kent assumed her to be Deputy Erin Giffin. On the side of the car, in large letters, was written "Gallatin County Sheriff's Office." He pulled out behind Giffin and followed her up the hill. She turned left at the top and parked next to an overloaded dumpster by an aged commercial building that appeared to have rented offices on the second floor. After Giffin stepped out of the car, wearing her immaculately pressed uniform, she entered the building. The door she entered had some flaking gold letters, which from the distance Ellsworth-Kent thought said "Gallatin County Sheriff's Office—Gardiner."

He stepped out of his vehicle, stood next to the dumpster, and when there was no one in the area, spoke quietly toward the open rear window of his vehicle.

"Hannah, it's clear. I'll call when I can."

Walking to the sheriff's car, he found to his surprise the door unlocked, put aside tools that would have allowed him to break in, and climbed into the rear seat and slid down, leaving him a line of sight to see Deputy Giffin when she returned. It was two hours before she reappeared; the sun had set, and darkness was enveloping the placid Gardiner sky.

When Giffin sat in the driver's seat, Ellsworth-Kent was waiting. He placed the edge of his hunting knife alongside her carotid artery and, abandoning his Australian accent, whispered,

"Deputy, if you move one inch, your throat will be laid open, and you'll be dead in seconds. I have a gun with a silencer in my other hand. Slowly reach for your pistol, lift it with your thumb and index finger, and pass it back to me."

When the deputy complied, he made her empty the shotgun clipped in a bracket next to her seat.

"You're foolish to do this," she said quietly but firmly. "I'm expected back at the office in an hour."

"Turn your communications on with the sheriff's office in Livingston. Tell them you're finished here and going home and will see them in the morning."

She complied. Fortunately for Ellsworth-Kent the person at the sheriff's office said it was slow and they had no need for her this evening, but she should leave her radio on until she reached home. "See you in the morning," said the despatcher, hanging up the phone.

The drive north was uneventful. No melodramatics. Ellsworth-Kent sat next to Giffin; Markel drove their pickup truck a few car lengths behind. When they reached a sign-less, narrow dirt road a mile before Carter Bridge, both vehicles turned and drove the hundred yards to a small storage shed rented for the stated purpose of storing a drift boat and fishing gear until spring. Ellsworth-Kent had paid the rental fee through next May, assured that the payment bought him uninterrupted privacy.

They drove the sheriff's office car into the shed and parked it next to the drift boat they had stolen from behind a house in Livingston where accumulated mail on the porch told them the occupants were away. They would only need the boat for another twenty-four hours.

Markel stayed close to Deputy Giffin and walked her to a corner of the shed where several air mattresses were inflated and covered with blankets. Even June nights can be bitterly cold in Paradise Valley. When they were next to the mattresses, Markel plunged a needle containing a nonlethal, incapacitating chemical into Giffin's arm. Giffin winced, began to speak but uttered only two incomprehensible words before she collapsed onto a mattress. She would be out deeply into the next day, the day on which she would die without ever regaining consciousness. Markel wasn't concerned that she wouldn't suffer; she wanted to save the suffering for Macduff.

The night passed in brief, alternating segments of rest and terror in the darkness of the windowless barn. Markel and Ellsworth-Kent took turns sitting and watching the hostage, then sleeping on one of the mattresses. When either gained some sleep, it was brief and fitful, the one guarding amused at the other's tossing and turning. Over and over both worked through their concept of the morning's plan—two disparate views that didn't always mesh.

On June 20th dawn broke over the Absaroka Range with an ominous red sky that had given birth to the familiar phrase *Red sky in the morning, sailors take warning.* Recalling those words, Ellsworth-Kent thought "Sailor could as well be one on a drift boat on the Yellowstone as one on a fishing trawler off Nova Scotia."

Markel and Ellsworth-Kent decided it wasn't necessary to feed Giffin because she had little remaining time to live. It was too late to think of her as a bargaining chip; she was the central actor in creating a diversion that would make the deaths of Lucinda and Macduff more assured.

Soon after daybreak, they lifted Giffin into the drift boat, secured her to the middle guide seat, and set the wicker man over her. Her head protruded and soon was festooned with a wreath of mistletoe. Ellsworth-Kent carefully strapped the package of explosives and timer on the front of the wicker man, followed by a sign that stated "It's over. Had you worried, Lucinda and Macduff, didn't we?" The sign was another part of the diversion. The press of one button on a hand-held transmitter would start the clock running for two minutes, red numbers flickering away the final moments of Giffin's life.

Ellsworth-Kent carefully backed the trailer and drift boat to the edge of one of the Jensen's Spring Creeks. Markel and he had painted the boat to look like an official Gallatin County Sheriff's Office vessel. They were protected from view until they were a boat-length from the creek. Sliding the boat off the trailer, the boat settled in the flowing waters. Ellsworth-Kent held the boat while Markel returned the vehicle and empty trailer to the shed. She backed the trailer inside next to the Sheriff's Office car, checked to be sure they had removed or wiped clean everything that might identify them, and locked the shed doors for the final time. When Markel walked back to the boat, it was bobbing slightly in the silently moving water of the spring creek, anxious to be free and under the control of the river.

In less than five minutes, they walked the boat along the shallow creek to where it merged with the Yellowstone River. Ellsworth-Kent waded ahead and surveyed the river. There was not a boat in sight; any police activity would be concentrated miles south along the river near Mill Creek and Emigrant.

One early fisherman was casting flies from the far bank two hundred yards downstream, ignoring the boat as he concentrated on the drift of his fly. He would be the only person to see the boat pass.

Markel and Ellsworth-Kent shoved the boat out into the river; Ellsworth-Kent pushed the button that started the two-minute timing. Hurrying back to their car, they were driving south on East River Road when they heard the explosion in the distance. No one passed them on the road, but once they could see flashing lights on a vehicle to their west across the river on Highway 89. They were back at the farmhouse on Tom Miner Road within thirty minutes.

Gallatin Country was missing a deputy. What few bits and pieces that remained of the diminutive Erin Giffin were scattered along the Yellowstone.

Now, the central focus of the summer solstice ceremonial sacrifices could begin. The next few hours would be the last in the lives of Lucinda Lang and Macduff Brooks.

50

THE FIRST CALL RECEIVED by Dan Wilson on the morning of June 19th was from Maine. His secretary said it was a youthful female voice with a Down East accent. He knew who it was. Dean Perry at the law college in Florida had called him a few days earlier and told him about the meeting with Elsbeth Carson.

Dan picked up the phone with a touch of excitement at the prospect of talking to Macduff Brooks' daughter. She had spent her first seventeen years without knowing that she was adopted and the circumstances surrounding her birth father's death. Dan didn't know how Ms. Carson would react when they met.

"Hello, this is Dan Wilson."

"Mr. Wilson, I'm Elsbeth Carson. Do you have time to talk for a few minutes?"

"I do. But I'd rather talk to you here. We'll fly you to D.C., and I'll take you to lunch at a quiet restaurant a block away. We won't have to worry that our discussion might be recorded. I'm looking forward to meeting you. Could you come here next week on Wednes . . . wait a second. I *have* to answer a call. Please hold."

Wilson picked up another phone. The call was from the Gallatin County Sheriff's Office, and the secretary had given Dan a signal it was urgent. She said the background noise sounded pretty frantic."

Dan put Elsbeth on hold, lifted the other receiver, and said, "It's Dan Wilson in D.C."

"Dan, Ken Rangley in Livingston. There's been another explosion and death. This time on the Yellowstone not far south of here at the head of Paradise Valley. I'm afraid it's another wicker man and mistletoe killing. No identification of the body yet—there isn't much to be identified—but a fisherman on the river bank out early pursuing a morning hatch said it looked like a woman. And that there was a sign on the wicker man front that said 'It's over. Had you worried Lucinda and Macduff, didn't we?'"

"Does that mean the person in the wicker man wasn't Lucinda?"

"I talked to Lucinda on her cell phone ten minutes ago. She's fine. I didn't tell her about the killing this morning. I understand Macduff and she flew to Florida a couple of days ago."

"They didn't go to Florida, Ken. Remember that they use cell phones. We told them to leave and put the word out that they did, hoping to avoid a killing. But they wouldn't leave. Only their caretaker Mavis and I know they're still in Montana and not in Florida. They're staying at a guest cabin at Lucinda's ranch. I think Erin Giffin might have known they remained here: She didn't share it with me."

"Any idea who is behind the killing? Dan, do we assume what Lucinda and Macduff have told me, which is that it has to be Hannah Markel and Robert Ellsworth-Kent? And, who was killed on the Yellowstone?"

"I have a sense about who was killed, but it's not confirmed and I don't want to accept it. What the fisherman on the Yellowstone told us and my ten-minute conversation with Lucinda aren't enough to speculate on. . . . Dan, hold a second. I have a call from another deputy who's at the river. I'm heading that way in a few minutes."

Ken listened, his mouth opening and eyes widening in utter frustration. He dropped the phone, picked it up, listened for another minute nodding several times, and without a further word hung up, turning again to Wilson's call.

"Dan, I don't want to believe this. We discovered a shed near a spring creek that feeds into the Yellowstone River a few hundred yards upstream from where the explosion occurred. Inside the shed were an empty drift boat trailer . . . and one of our sheriff's office's vehicles. It's checked out to my top deputy." Ken stuttered as he identified her. "It's Erin Giffin's vehicle!" He couldn't talk anymore and told Dan he'd call when he knew more and had calmed down.

"I know Erin, Ken," said Dan, not wanting to let Ken go without knowing more. "If Erin was murdered, it'll be a huge blow to Macduff and Lucinda. The three were close friends. Erin saved Macduff when Lucinda was in a coma after the shootout on the Snake a couple of years ago. Erin found him malnourished and near death in his cabin. I don't even want to think about this."

"Are Lucinda and Macduff in danger?" asked Ken.

"I don't think so," Dan replied. "It's unlikely there'll be another murder today; I suspect this was it for this year's solstice. But we shouldn't take a chance. We need to cover the area where today's killing took place at least through tomorrow.

. . . It's your turf, but we'd like to help. And, of course, we need to have Lucinda and Macduff stay put. . . . We won't know what Erin might have told the killers before she died. There's a chance the killers couldn't locate Lucinda and Macduff and found a substitute—someone they knew. . . . Ken, was Erin missing before she was killed?"

"No. She was scheduled to drive to our Gardiner office late yesterday afternoon for what should have been a brief meeting, something any of our deputies could handle. She planned on having dinner at the Chico Hot Springs Resort yesterday evening after the meeting. It's about halfway between Gardiner and here. Erin was to be off duty for three days. She must have been abducted somewhere in the Valley. . . . Dan, this is hard to talk about. I *will* call you back."

Elsbeth had been patiently on hold for twenty minutes. She thought it must be important and maybe it wasn't fair to expect any CIA figure to spend time with her. She wondered whether to wait longer or let Mr. Wilson call her when he had time. Before she could decide, Wilson came back on the line.

"I'm terribly sorry, Ms. Carson. I have an emergency and will be gone for a few days. Let's set two weeks from today to meet here in my office at 9:00 a.m. My secretary will help you with information about the plane and hotel reservations."

"Thank you, Mr. Wilson. I'll be there."

Dan Wilson put down the phone and thought, "Poor girl. Macduff may not be alive in two days, much less two weeks. He's never seen his daughter and doesn't even know yet that she exists. I dread the idea of calling Elsbeth and telling her that her father has been murdered in Montana."

51

DAN FLEW TO MONTANA on a CIA jet. As soon as he arrived, he met in Livingston with Ken Rangley and Paula Pajioli's replacement as CIA agent for Montana, Jack Ivonski. He was assigned the position partly because he fluently spoke and read both Spanish and Arabic. Dan thought Herzog and Isfahani might cause trouble in Montana if or when they learned of Macduff's identity and location. That would never occur if Macduff were killed by Markel and Ellsworth-Kent.

While Wilson, Rangley, and Ivonski were meeting, only two dozen miles away Lucinda and I were sequestered at her ranch secluded in the guest cabin. We had our cell phones, but no other means of communication. We'd been told not to call out and answer only when an incoming call was from a familiar number.

"*Everyone* thinks we're in Florida," Lucinda said. "After one more day—June 21st—we should be able to go out again and resume living at your cabin. You want to try the radio and see if there's any talk about tomorrow?"

"No. We promised to stay out of sight and out of touch until the day after tomorrow."

We likely would have learned about the killing of Deputy Giffin if we had listened to the radio. There was neither radio nor television in our cabin.

Lucinda said quietly, "I imagine the police are going to cover the Yellowstone River area around Emigrant tomorrow with dozens of deputies—from the county, Livingston, Gardiner, and some brought in from Bozeman and Billings. Plus state police and FBI."

"I expect so."

"Macduff, who knows where we are?"

"Only Dan and probably Ken and Erin. Plus our housekeeper, Mavis. Word has been spread that we're in Florida for a week or more."

"Is that why there're no police around here? So they don't give away that we really are here? That sounds strange—we need fewer police to protect us better!"

"I guess. I'm a little perplexed. Why would we go to Florida anyway? We have better protection here, or we should have. I don't think Ken believes he can protect us. . . . Plus, if we're not here, won't Markel and Ellsworth-Kent simply put off their attempt to kill us? Or shift the scene to Florida. The Florida cottage isn't protected at all, and the St. Johns County Sheriff's Office in St. Augustine doesn't know anything about me. I want to keep it that way."

"I suspect our best protection is what we do, not how many police are wandering around outside," Lucinda responded. "If Markel and Ellsworth-Kent have gotten word about our being in Florida, they have to cancel plans for tomorrow. Or they risk being caught for a foolish attempt to kill two people who are on the other side of the country. They might postpone the attempt. There's been no wicker man and mistletoe killing except on a solstice or equinox, and I don't think there will be. Markel and Ellsworth-Kent are apparently determined to have the killings on one of those days. It's as though we aren't as important as the timing."

"I'll feel better about the whole matter tomorrow night."

"Me, too. Can I get you a glass of wine?" she asked.

"How about a double Gentleman Jack?"

"I'll be right back. There's a new bottle on the shelf in the passageway to the garage."

52

WHEN LUCINDA STEPPED into the passageway, lined with shelves containing towels, bedding, and other supplies for the guest cabins, she pulled on the overhead light cord as she closed the door behind her. The Gentleman Jack bottle was there, next to a bottle of Lucinda's favorite Montana Roughstock Whiskey. She took the bourbon from the shelf, turned, and reached for the light cord. Not more than three feet behind her stood her former husband, Robert Ellsworth-Kent. Her heart raced, and she couldn't get a word out. His right hand held a pistol; his left hand was raised with its index finger touching his lips to signal her to remain quiet.

Lucinda's first thought was about how he had aged during his time in prison. It had been nearly two decades since she had seen him. His hair was silver splashed with a few remaining flecks of brown. He was slightly stooped. What had not changed was the angry intensity of his eyes, which caused Lucinda to shiver when she thought of the last time he beat her and his eyes had flashed the same hate.

"Be calm, my love. Don't utter a word," he whispered. "We've killed five so far to get to you and doing the final sacrifices tonight instead of tomorrow makes no difference."

He grabbed her with his free hand and squeezed tightly, causing Lucinda to wince and shut her eyes.

"You're still beautiful . . . and tempting. I could take you with me but the ancients have told me that you *must* be sacrificed tomorrow—on the summer solstice. It will be the final sacrifice and will become known throughout the world of the ancients—who commanded all the deaths—as the 'solstice of the seven sacrifices.'"

Lucinda was terrified of Ellsworth-Kent; he had never appeared so savagely visceral. He was living in another world, a world of violence and inhumanity. She dared not speak.

He turned and lightly tapped twice on the door to the garage, which opened slowly. Lucinda had never seen the woman who entered, but she knew it was Hannah Markel because she had seen photos of Hannah's sister Helga. If Hannah added the same metal in her nose, lips, ears, and eyebrows that Helga had worn, she would look exactly like the Markel who threatened Macduff two years ago in front of the Howlin' Hounds Cafe—only a few miles away but in a distant era.

"We're going into the kitchen, slowly. When we do, Lucinda *will* call Macduff and ask him to come and help remove a tight bottle cap on the bourbon."

Before they stepped into the kitchen, Ellsworth-Kent put the bourbon back on the shelf, and securely duct-taped Lucinda's hands behind her back.

I was sitting in the living room, glancing at an old *Fly Rod & Reel* magazine, wondering what was taking Lucinda so long. As I was lifting my tired body out of the chair, I heard the kitchen door open. "Find the bottle?" I called toward the kitchen.

"I found it. Be there in a minute," she answered, her voice sounding as though she shared my exhaustion from inactivity due to our self-imposed confinement. "Macduff," Lucinda called, "please come help me remove a bottle cap."

I plodded to the kitchen to help, savoring the thought of a glass of Gentleman Jack. But one step inside the door I found myself in the midst of three people. I knew Ellsworth-Kent from photographs Dan Wilson had sent us. And I knew Hannah Markel because she was a mirror image of Helga. They were the couple I had seen crossing the square in Jackson.

He held what looked like a black Beretta; she gripped a classic, silver, snub-nosed .38 Special S&W revolver.

"I'm Robert Ellsworth-Kent, Mr. Brooks, the man whose wife you stole. But for your interference, Lucinda would have been waiting for me when I was released from prison in England. I planned to take her to live on the Orkney Islands, where I would reign as the high priest of the ancients and celebrate each solstice. You are responsible for my being in the United States and for the sacrifices of the past year. Your punishment will be carried out tomorrow when you are sacrificed together with Lucinda in a ceremony of the wicker man and mistletoe. Regrettably, Luc . . ."

Hannah, bored by Ellsworth-Kent's pompous absurdity, interrupted, "You bastard, Brooks, you killed my sister. And now you're mine, until you die tomorrow. I'd kill you both now and be gone, but I promised Robert to do it his way."

There was little I could say or do. Lucinda was bound tightly, looking at me forlornly. "Mac, I'm sorry. Robert had a gun at my head."

Struggling for words of encouragement for Lucinda, at a time of few expectations, I murmured only, "You did right," when my sentence was cut off by Ellsworth-Kent placing tape across my mouth. More was wrapped around my wrists.

Lucinda's mouth wasn't taped; she could speak to answer their questions. But they had few; they knew exactly what they planned to do and how it was to be carried out.

"We're all going for a ride. Not far," said Ellsworth-Kent.

Turning to Lucinda, he asked, "Where are your guards? We saw no one coming in."

"Everyone thinks we flew to Florida yesterday. You're supposed to think that, too," she responded in a voice barely audible.

"Pretty dumb," Ellsworth-Kent replied. "We never heard anything about your leaving Montana. The FBI apparently pulled all the guards, thinking no one would be staying in Lucinda's main lodge or one of these cabins. You left a light on. It was obvious."

There was little I could say. And I was more concerned with the immediate future than the unreasoned past. Ellsworth-Kent was right about the FBI. Agents Stern and Drain had asserted jurisdiction over any activities at my cabin and Lucinda's ranch, taking the guards Lucinda employed to the Madison at Ennis, where Stern was convinced Markel and Ellsworth-Kent would strike in the same manner as exactly a year ago. The one good consequence of their folly was getting rid of the two agents. But the guards might have intercepted Markel and Ellsworth-Kent if they had remained at the ranch.

I could think of a half-dozen ways to act; the trouble was each variation ended poorly. I wasn't wearing one of the protective vests Ken Rangley had left us, and my life-saving Kevlar lined Simms jacket was hanging in a closet at my cabin. I did have my Glock, but it was on the table in the living room thirty feet away. Once again being unprepared put us at death's door.

The most we could do was to commit minor acts of disobedience, not severe enough to cause them to kill us now, but to create a distraction of which we might take advantage. But *now* was soon going to be *then;* tomorrow was but a few hours away.

"Where are you taking us?" Lucinda asked.

Hannah Markel spoke wryly, showing a smile of impending conquest. "Not far. A storage barn on the Yellowstone. For tomorrow, and your last float on the Yellowstone or any river for that matter, we have a special wicker man suit for you two to wear. And wreaths of mistletoe."

53

DAN, KEN, AND JACK IVONSKI, sitting in Ken's spacious office in Livingston, continued to discuss every possibility for the next day. Markel and Ellsworth-Kent knew what was supposed to happen; they focused on avoiding glitches that might allow Lucinda and me to survive. It was hard for the two CIA agents and the Chief Deputy to be as focused because they had to imagine every variation Markel and Ellsworth-Kent might attempt to assure that Lucinda and I did not survive.

"Why on earth did the FBI's agents—Stern and Drain—go to the Madison?" asked Ivonski.

"And worse," added Dan, "take Lucinda's guards with them on the pretext that they would be helping save Lucinda."

"But Lucinda and Macduff are usually able to work out of a bad situation, even though it may take some outside help—even from a tree branch," added Ken.

"Tree?" queried Ivonsky, unfamiliar with the shoot-out on the Snake a few years ago, when, bleeding from several bullet wounds, as were Lucinda and Wuff, I rowed my drift boat into a sharp, protruding limb on a strainer in the middle of the river, skewering Park Salisbury, thus ending his life.

"Should you send a couple of deputies to Lucinda's guest cabin tonight?" asked Dan.

"If I had any, I would," replied Ken. "Every one of mine, plus a dozen state and local police, are stationed along the river, mostly near Carter Bridge where Erin was killed. We tried to get help from the surrounding counties, but they're all worried about a killing on their turf, especially the Teton County folk in Jackson because they haven't been hit yet. Macduff certainly has a history in Jackson Hole for being around when murders are committed. To be fair, the police in Madison County, where Stern and Drain have gone to help, have reason to think of another attack on the Madison. But when the Madison County and the Ennis police meet the two agents, they'll quickly learn they're more hindrance than help."

"Ken," queried Dan, "with Erin gone, do you think Markel and Ellsworth-Kent will strike again in the morning? They've killed a person similar to the previous victims—someone Macduff and, in Erin's case, Lucinda, knew and liked."

"That depends on what Markel and Ellsworth-Kent think of Lucinda and Macduff," Ken answered, not sure of his clarity or logic. "Why haven't they tried to kill Lucinda and Macduff, instead of Erin?"

"Because they think they're are in Florida?" responded Ivonsky with another question.

"They may," responded Ken. "But first, have they heard that the two allegedly flew to Florida, and second, if they have heard about that, did they believe it? We all agree Florida wasn't a good choice for a hiding place. Almost any place in the world would be better. I prefer thinking that Markel and Ellsworth-Kent assume Lucinda and Macduff are somewhere around here. Not necessarily at either of their Mill Creek places, but possibly camping in Yellowstone or staying at some friend's home."

"I'd choose to be with Juan Santander," interjected Ken. "Former Navy Seal and still a tough guy in spite of his losses, Juan would do anything to protect Macduff or Lucinda."

Ivonsky asked, "Isn't Santander the guy who's rumored among our agents to have shot that student in Gainesville who was about to kill Lucinda and Macduff, and maybe also killed Whitman in D.C.? I worked on the Whitman case before I was transferred here."

"One and the same," thought Dan aloud. "He's a loose cannon. I'd prefer to believe he's not involved this time."

"You're in the minority among your CIA colleagues," including me, broke in Ivonsky. "Santander's a Robin Hood figure to Lucinda and Macduff."

"Then let him stay in Sherwood Forest and shoot English sheriffs and nobles," asserted Ken. "But I agree that those who know Santander like him."

"Enough about Santander," suggested Dan. "What should we be doing now? I feel like I'm not even participating. That we've left too much to Lucinda and Macduff to do on their own."

"I think they're capable of dealing with it," noted Ken, with some hesitation. "I'd be surprised if Markel and Ellsworth-Kent got the drop on those two. Macduff, maybe, but Lucinda would keep him from too much harm."

54

I WAS IN NO SHAPE to help anyone. My mouth and hands had been taped by Ellsworth-Kent within seconds of entering the kitchen when Lucinda called me to help. As soon as they pulled us out of their vehicle and shoved us into the barn, Ellsworth-Kent also taped our ankles. I was deposited on a mattress only partly filled with air; every time I tried to turn, I hit bottom: the cement floor.

We had been moved from Mill Creek a short three or four miles to the barn on the Yellowstone, and not one police car was in view during the brief ride. I knew the barn; I had anchored on the Yellowstone last year and went into the brush to relieve myself and saw what was apparently an abandoned barn with a roof in serious need of repair, topping weathered siding that was once barn red but had faded and flaked. Rot surrounded the sole window.

Ellsworth-Kent had opened one of two ten-foot high board-and-batten doors that faced toward the river. The area around the barn was too unkempt to be called a yard. The inside had a smell I couldn't associate with anything living, but wasn't so bad to call it the "stench of death." If condemned persons are given a last meal of requested favorite foods, I thought a fair substitute would be to spend my last night in more attractive surroundings.

I had never seen the barn from the East River Road. The turn-off from a gravel road that served several large homes along the river gave way to a narrow dirt driveway that led to the barn. It was gated and overgrown, two marks against frequent and unwanted admission.

Lucinda's wrists had also been taped at her guest cabin, but her mouth left free to answer questions from our captors. When we reached the barn, her mouth was taped, and she was tossed onto a similar air mattress. Neither of us had been given any opportunity to initiate any conversation with our captors. We were playing a waiting game, and I doubted it would be a long wait.

Separated from me, Lucinda lay on the far side of an old drift boat that was either stolen or abandoned. From a quick glance in the dim light of a Coleman lantern Markel carried, I could see that the barn's owner had given up hope of restoring what must have been damage from a succession of storms and flooding river water. But I couldn't see much; there was no light apart from the lantern.

In the dim light I could also see a large wicker basket-like covering that expectantly soon would encompass us both. Sprigs of mistletoe laden with waxy white berries sprouted from a half-filled bottle near the wicker. Through the single window of the barn, the moon was slowly working across the night sky.

55

MIDNIGHT WAS THE HOUR that drew from miles around white-robed disciples of various agnostic persuasion. Such massing of Bards and Druids had not been expected or prepared for by the police, who were preoccupied mainly by Erin's death, but also by avoiding a repeat performance of a wicker man and mistletoe sacrifice that would snuff-out two more lives. Many of the newly arriving gatherers were hopeful of viewing a sacrifice. They considered that successful completion of the circle of sacrifices justified the loss of another life.

The earlier wicker man and mistletoe murders, including Erin's death less than twenty-four hours past, had drawn no noticeable number of adherents to the ancient use of fire, drowning, hanging, and burning. Over the past year thanks increasingly were heaped upon whoever was responsible for the sacrifices for use of an explosion that left no identifiable parts. Ellsworth-Kent was determined to rid the land of those more traditional believers who ridiculed and suppressed the ancient practice of sacrifice.

The believers began to mass along the Yellowstone near Jensen's Spring Creek where Erin was killed. As they filled the space along the river, the increasing numbers, dressed in robes with cords tied around the waist and carrying ritual knives called athemes, plus incense, candles, and chalices, set bonfires that consumed every piece of driftwood along the river and sent flames shooting dozens of feet in the air. By daybreak there would be far more solstice observers than eight hours earlier had watched the sunrise at Stonehenge and the Standing Stones of Stenness on the Orkney Islands.

They shouted and chanted what was mostly incomprehensible, but in moments of understanding included demands for religious recognition and freedom, along with promises of more wicker man and mistletoe sacrifices. Placards derided the Christian alleged omission of any respect for the summer solstice, ignoring the Christian celebration of the feast of St. John. Many cultures, from the Japanese Setsubun to the Hindu Dakshinayana, honor the midpoint of the seasons.

At the moment that the sun rose from a notch in the Absaroka Range directly in line from the point where Jensen's Spring Creek flows into the Yellowstone, a frightening clamor arose with the massed throng waving swords and various other weapons.

The noise could be been heard for miles around.

56

LUCINDA AND I HEARD the noise a half-dozen miles upriver, where we lay fitfully dozing on the barn floor. Markel awoke from a brief but deep and comfortable sleep to join Ellsworth-Kent, who had been keeping watch and listening to the increasing noise coming from the north. When he relieved Markel soon after midnight and stepped outside, he saw a red glow to the north and was pleased something had distracted the authorities from further adding to the few police who had been positioned along the Yellowstone near Emigrant.

"Hannah, it's time to prepare the boat and the wicker man," whispered Ellsworth-Kent. "I'll open the barn doors and you back the vehicle in so we can hitch up the trailer and boat."

"Shouldn't we put the two in the boat and rig the wicker man before we move it toward the water?" asked Hannah.

"Yes, we'll put Macduff in first. I've added plywood that makes the middle seat wide enough for two. Take the tape off Macduff's ankles."

"Should we carry him and lift him into the boat so we don't have to let his legs be free of tape?"

"I can't lift him, and I don't want us both to do it. I'll untape his ankles and guide him into the boat while you hold the gun on him."

"Robert, we made one mistake. Our guns don't have silencers. If we have to shoot one or both, the shots might be heard by neighbors."

"Another reason to go slowly. You hold the gun on Macduff, and I'll take the tape off his ankles and get him into the boat."

Lucinda and I had heard most of their conversation, but neither of us had an idea that might work to gain us freedom. Ellsworth-Kent shook me and warned me against any movement that wasn't ordered. He removed the tape from my ankles, pulled me to my feet, and pushed me up into the boat. When I was seated on a widened middle seat, he re-taped my ankles.

Lucinda was subjected to the same care by the two and was soon sitting against me, her ankles re-taped and then taped to mine. Our hands also were taped to each other. If we fell out of the drift boat, by accident or design, we would surely drown together.

Our captors lifted the wicker man and placed it over us. Our heads stuck through a hole at the top. I thought of the first view I had of Paula Pajioli in a similar state on the Madison River exactly a year ago. She never had a chance. It didn't look as though we did either.

Markel stepped on the trailer side beams and placed mistletoe wreaths on our heads. At the same time Ellsworth-Kent carefully lifted from a box a breastplate of explosives. A foot high, it spread across the front of the wicker man from one side to the other, with ties that were inserted into the wicker. He then connected the explosives to a small timer set on top the explosives within six inches of our chins. The device showed no lights waiting to start the countdown. Like the timer on the other murders, once turned on, it could not be stopped or disabled.

The final act preparing us for the sacrifice was the attachment of a wide sign across the front of the wicker, covering much of the explosives. Neither of us could read it; we would meet our doom never knowing what it said.

Ellsworth-Kent backed the boat out of the barn and with Markel's help began to slowly push the trailer along the narrow path to the river. Lucinda and I couldn't see because we were facing the bow, which was pointed away from the river.

I could hear the river as we neared its edge and thought how fast the final minutes of our lives would pass. We strained to look to each side but could see no sign of activity along the banks.

Markel spoke quietly to Ellsworth-Kent. "I don't see a soul, Robert. There is still noise from downriver—a rhythmic chant. It must be the crowd waiting impatiently to watch the explosion. But they will never see more than a distant flash far from Jensen's Spring Creek."

Lucinda pushed against my side with her shoulder and as best she could nestled her head against mine. The boat shook as it was backed into the river, but everything held in place. Markel held it to the shore while Ellsworth-Kent pulled the trailer from the river, returned it to the barn, and walked back to join her.

"Set the timer for fifteen minutes," I heard him say quietly to her.

I turned to Lucinda and managed a whisper. When the duct tape had been placed on my mouth, I pushed my lips as far out as I could, giving me a little wiggle room. From behind the tape I murmured, "Our last fifteen minutes will be together. I wish it could be more."

Lucinda could respond. I had managed to loosen her mouth tape—Hannah thought we were trying a last kiss.

"Mac," Lucinda whispered, "there isn't a soul to help us. . . . It's been a good run. I wanted to have you for another thirty years. . . . It was not to be."

Markel and Ellsworth-Kent gave the drift boat a shove and the current quickly took control, moving the boat northward downstream.

Turning to him, Hannah said, "Robert, it's done! Let's sit and savor the explosion; it's only fourteen minutes."

"No. We have to leave; the police at Carter Bridge will swarm here when they hear the explosion.

They hurried to their vehicle. She glanced at him and said, "No one can save them now!"

But there was one who would try.

57

A HUNDRED FEET DOWNSTREAM from the barn, hidden within the brush along the river, a black-clad figure arrived just as Ellsworth-Kent pushed a button that started red lights flickering on the front of the wicker man and shoved the boat into the current. The figure couldn't see the red lights clearly, but from the previous murders pattern, it had to be a timer that would soon set off the explosives.

Markel and Ellsworth-Kent quickly disappeared toward the barn. The figure had a choice: follow them, confront them, and probably kill them or try to save the person in the drift boat. As it drifted out from the dimness of overhanging trees into early morning light, the figure could see two people in the boat: Lucinda and Macduff. Across the front of the wicker man was a sign the figure couldn't read.

The partners in crime reached the barn and, leaving the trailer, drove off south toward their rented farmhouse on Tom Miner Road, knowing that in twelve or thirteen minutes they would hear the explosion from nearly a dozen miles away.

It had been only six hours since the figure arrived in a Jeep Wrangler at Lucinda's ranch and discovered the houses to be deserted. Five minutes earlier a stop at Macduff's log cabin had told the same. After quickly searching Lucinda's main house, the figure began with the guest cabins. Behind the third cabin was a red SUV the figure knew to be Macduff's. Entering the open door of the cabin, the figure saw two nearly empty wine glasses on a table beside the fireplace, whose embers illuminated the masculine face with eyes blackened to reduce glare. On the floor of the kitchen a knife rested on the counter and a small piece of silver duct tape lay partly stuck on the floor.

Quickly returning to the Wrangler, the man drove as fast as allowed by loose gravel on the twisting National Forest Service road. The Wrangler backtracked down Mill Creek Road west toward the valley. If Lucinda's and Macduff's abductors intended to attempt to carry out a similar wicker man explosion on a drift boat, it would have to be on the river. But where? Upriver toward Gardiner or downriver toward Livingston?

Weeks earlier the man had departed home to drive his Wrangler through the mountains, first towing his drift boat to Island Park in Idaho. Two days later he went north to Ennis, Montana, then on to Missoula. From there he made the long drive across much of Montana and south to Saratoga in Wyoming. Staying two to three nights in each town, he floated alone but never cast a fly on four of the West's finest fly fishing rivers: the Henry's Fork in Idaho, the Madison and the Clark in Montana, and the North Platte in Wyoming.

He chose the locations because they were the four places where someone had murdered four different people on the successive summer solstice, autumnal equinox, winter solstice, and spring equinox of the previous twelve months. It would soon be the summer equinox again, and he was concerned that one or more persons might meet their death on that longest day of the year. Except for a brief introduction to Erin Giffin at a lunch at Macduff's cabin, the figure knew none of the persons who had been murdered, but he did know the two people most linked with them—Lucinda Lang and Macduff Brooks.

After floating the North Platte, he drove to Cody, through the park to Mammoth, and north into Paradise Valley. A mile south of Livingston, Montana, he rented a room at the Blue Winged Olive B&B, leaving his covered drift boat in the yard. He wasn't sure he'd use the boat again on this trip. He knew Paradise Valley, having floated nearly every section over the past couple of years from the Carbella launching area to the center of Livingston.

After the killing on the North Platte, the man had begun to study everything he could learn about the horrific deaths by explosions that left little to identify, killings that had become known in the media as the "wicker man and mistletoe murders." He accumulated a thick file on each killing, containing every item from the newspapers, records of radio and TV programs, and the few police reports and public records he could persuade the authorities to copy for him. It wasn't much, but after the similar murders on the Clark last Christmas and the Henry's Fork in March, the killers were identified as Robert Ellsworth-Kent from England and Hannah Markel from a place yet unidentified, but likely California. Their photographs were broadly distributed after the Henry's Fork murder.

As is the case with many murders, the identity of the perpetrators becomes established with certainty, but often their whereabouts remain unknown. They remain free to kill again.

The man finally had come to Livingston because it was near, but not too near, Macduff's log cabin, which was, in turn, close to Lucinda's large ranch. Although the voluminous speculation in the press had not identified the Yellowstone as the river most likely to be the next target, if indeed there was to be another, the man's own investigation narrowed the places he thought might be used to somewhere less than fifty miles from Lucinda's and Macduff's places on Mill Creek in Paradise Valley, somewhere along the Yellowstone River, and somewhere that allowed an escape for Markel and Ellsworth-Kent. No trace of them had ever been found where the first four killings occurred, which suggested to the man that they carefully planned how they would get away after each explosion.

During the next three weeks, the man floated every part of the Yellowstone, dividing the fifty-mile distance on the river from Carbella, a stone's throw from the Tom Miner Bridge, to downtown Livingston. He floated in shorter stages than would represent a full day's float for a guide. Some days were longer than others; the first from Carbella to Point of Rocks was less than five miles, but the next day to Emigrant was eleven. Where the distance between ramps was more than six miles, he repeated the float a second time.

The reason for this strange pattern of drifting on the river was that the man wanted to familiarize himself thoroughly with the river, stopping often and making notes, searching for locations where a drift boat might be launched, not at a public ramp but from some property accessible by either the East River Road along the east side of the river or the main Route 89 along the west side. He was inclined to believe that the east side offered more possibilities between the Emigrant and Mill Creek bridges. That section of the river was relatively close to 89, which didn't offer as much privacy for a launch.

The man finished this task in twelve days and then began what was even less comprehensible and perhaps had not been undertaken since the days of the fur trappers two centuries ago. He walked along the river the full sixty miles between downtown Livingston and the Tom Miner Bridge, regardless of the weather and sometimes very early in the morning before people woke up and would see a trespasser crossing their properties. When he finished, taking ten days, he repeated the journey on the opposite side of the river. He spent nearly a month following the river in this manner and accumulated considerable information. He identified seven places where he thought a drift boat might be launched without arousing suspicion by residents, fishing guides on early season floats, or others out walking or jogging.

His river observations affirmed his belief that any attempt to launch and float a drift boat with a wicker basket covering a person would occur somewhere in the six and a half miles between the Emigrant and Mill Creek bridges. His floats and walks accomplished more in the way of eliminating portions of the river from further consideration than of providing any location that beyond any doubt would be used.

During the next week he retraced his walks along the river between Emigrant and Mill Creek. He was convinced that the location where Mill Creek flowed into the Yellowstone was symbolically important to Markel and Ellsworth-Kent because both Lucinda and Macduff lived on Mill Creek. Drift boats cannot traverse Mill Creek itself, but there proved to be quite good access to the Yellowstone River by what appeared to be private gravel roads that meandered close to the Yellowstone both up- and downriver from Mill Creek. He knew he took a chance of total failure by focusing exclusively on this area, but he could not cover the full sixty miles.

By the morning of June 20th, the man was concerned that he had overlooked the location that Markel and Ellsworth-Kent planned to use. That was confirmed when he received news at noon about the wicker man and mistletoe killing that occurred near Carter Bridge. He was despondent; he had heard that a single female had been killed and was sure that would mean Lucinda.

But in mid-afternoon he heard more, including that the person was believed to be Livingston Deputy Sheriff Erin Giffin. The killers had not chosen the Emigrant to Mill Creek portion that the man had determined to be where the next wicker man and mistletoe killing would be, but some twenty miles downriver, in the mile stretch between Jensen's Spring Creek and Carter Bridge.

Lucinda and Macduff were safe for the moment. But it made no sense that Markel and Ellsworth-Kent would leave the area while their two principal targets for the past year remained alive. The 20th dragged on slowly with the man in agony over what to do. As the sun set blood-red over the Gallatin Range to the west, the man was desperate. The person killed that morning was confirmed to be Erin Giffin. The 21st was only a few hours away.

The man sat at his B&B desk and listed the three locations he judged were the most likely from which Merkel and Ellsworth-Kent would strike. One was about a mile downriver from the Emigrant Bridge on the west side of the river. A narrow gravel drive angled a few hundred feet to the river. A second was further downstream at a place with easy access called "Chicory," on the favored east side of the river. The third was at a bend in the river just before where Mill Creek joined the river and a bit short of a mile to the Mill Creek Bridge.

The first location left too far to go to reach the Mill Creek area and was visible from Route 89. Only if there were few cars on Route 89 at the time of launching would it likely be unobserved.

At least one large new home would be in view at the second location at Chicory. The man had not been able to determine whether the place was occupied or maintained by an occasional visit from a caretaker.

Close to Mill Creek was the last probable launch site. There were numerous houses along the river, but the boat could be launched upriver around a bend and out of sight of the houses. The location was reached by a half-mile gravel road that wound toward the river off the East River Road. The trailer and boat would have to pass the houses.

Importantly, the property was surrounded by woods. And there was a barn. The man had walked around the barn. His notes indicated that there was a new lock on the barn door and that it seemed strange that no spaces existed in the old structure between the vertical board-siding where one might look inside.

While the proximity to houses troubled the man, he had overlooked until now that Markel and Ellsworth-Kent did not have to move the boat to the barn during the day. Their movements to the barn could have been at any time in the past several weeks, day or night, when the houses were deserted.

The figure no longer thought identifying the location was a crap shoot. The barn was the most natural choice for storage and launching the wicker man drift boat. There was no time to vacillate if the attempted murder was to occur soon after midnight.

Sipping some water, the man noticed there were only seconds to go until midnight and the beginning of the summer solstice. Looking out the window above his small desk at the

Blue Winged Olive, as the clock reached midnight a red glow began in the southern sky. Carter Bridge was only a couple of miles away, at the beginning of Paradise Valley.

Slowly the red glow grew. The man's window was open several inches, inviting a wind from the south which brought sounds coming from the area of the red glow. Sounds that suggested a cheering, frenzied crowd.

Those gathered might have been cheering what they viewed had been a justifiable sacrifice of Erin Giffin that morning, or their noise was in anticipation of another wicker man and mistletoe sacrifice on the true summer solstice. The figure was convinced that Giffin's death had been a diversion to draw attention from an attempt on the lives of Lucinda and Macduff on this very day—the 21st.

More and more the barn became the man's focus. Mill Creek had to be part of the plan he concluded: it was the home of both Lucinda and Macduff. Emigrant made the location even more important. Having the explosion occur as the boat drifted past where Mill Creek met the Yellowstone would have the most logical connection, regardless of the number of witnesses.

The ceremony was more important to carry out than to perform before a cheering crowd. There was no chance the drift boat could be launched and float anywhere between where Jensen's Spring Creek entered the Yellowstone and Carter Bridge. Too many police were covering that area, offsetting a surprising lack of police presence in the Emigrant to Mill Creek section.

There seemed no better choice in view of the arrival of the summer solstice and Lucinda's and Macduff's abduction. It had become a race against time.

58

THE MAN PROPELLED his Wrangler south on 89 as rapidly as he thought local police would tolerate. At Carter Bridge he was forced to slow, the white robed masses had spilled onto the road, and the man had to sit and wait while the police tried to bring some order by herding the robed bodies aside. The man thought the scene replicated the chaos associated with the annual bikers' gathering at Sturgis in South Dakota. But at Sturgis the crowd disrobed rather than robed. The top of the Wrangler was down; he could smell marijuana mixed with incense in the air, as robed figures wandered in circles like Sufi Whirling Dervishes, showing the drug's effects.

What seemed like ages passed before the man was clear of the crowd and free to accelerate again. He covered the nearly twenty miles to the Mill Creek Road in fifteen minutes, where he skidded to a halt, turned left to the east and crossed the bridge—slowly—searching upriver for any sign of a drift boat. The breaking morning light—the sun yet to fully emerge over the Absarokas—disclosed nothing on the river.

He swung the Wrangler right on the East River Road and in less than a mile right again to a pot-marked gravel road he remembered when searching the area weeks ago. He didn't want to drive to the barn and confront Markel and Ellsworth-

Kent, if they were there, but he was also afraid of being too late. Stopping a hundred yards short of the barn, he ran along the road and went into the adjoining woods. From the edge of the woods as he neared the barn and river, he saw a woman standing in the water, facing but not seeing him. She was holding onto a drift boat.

Recalling photos, she had to be Hannah Markel. In the middle of the drift boat was a large wicker circling two heads crowned with mistletoe. The heads were touching—one was Lucinda, the other Macduff. The man froze as Ellsworth-Kent stepped out of the barn and hurried to join Markel. He was carrying a shotgun, and the man didn't want attempt matching his small pistol against 12-gauge buckshot or slugs or the chance that a stray shot from his pistol would hit Lucinda or Macduff.

Before the man could make any decision, Ellsworth-Kent reached out to the wicker man and a flickering red light came on. It had to be a timer. The man was too far to read the numbers, which would have told him how much time remained before the explosion. But he set the timer on his watch. He could no longer focus on capturing Markel and Ellsworth-Kent; he had to try to save Lucinda and Macduff. Although he had Markel in his pistol sight, he lowered the gun and watched the two shove the drift boat into the current. He heard some conversation, but it was mostly lost in the river. The only words he could understand were Markel's "fourteen" and "no one."

59

FOURTEEN SECONDS WAS TOO LITTLE and would elapse before Markel and Ellsworth-Kent were out of harm's way. The timer must have read fourteen *minutes.* The man reset his watch to count down from fourteen minutes. The river was moving moderately under the diminishing volume of spring runoff. He thought the boat would reach the Mill Creek Bridge with as much as two minutes to spare. He was a good swimmer but couldn't hope to overtake the boat in time. He ran to the Wrangler as the timer on his watch read thirteen minutes.

Partly airborne bouncing from pot-hole to pot-hole, he was at the East River Road in two minutes where he raced on the welcome macadam to Mill Creek Road as the time remaining dropped to ten minutes, and skidded to a stop on the bridge at eight. Leaping from the Wrangler, he looked upriver and saw the drift boat emerge from around the bend.

He climbed the bridge's railing and saw that he would have a jump of eight or nine feet to the boat's floorboards. His watch passed six minutes to the explosion, and he pleaded aloud for the boat to move faster—perhaps catch a stronger current in the middle. Four minutes remained. The boat was facing him and he could see the red light on the wicker man. As it flashed two minutes he prepared to jump and try to land beside the rear seat behind Lucinda and Macduff. He could now read the timer's red numbers on the wicker man: 1:45.

As the boat passed beneath him, he released his hand from the rail. The boat hit an eddy under the bridge, and he landed not in the boat but in the water a foot behind the transom. He grabbed the dangling anchor and pulled his body up and over the side. Stepping in front of the two he ripped the duct tape away from their mouths as the clock read 0:57. He knew they had to be able to breathe if his plan were to work.

When the explosives had been attached they were taped to the outer shell of the wicker man. The man prayed that Lucinda and Macduff were not tied either to the boat or to the wicker man. He quickly discovered they weren't, and he pulled the wicker up and off them, the clock down to 0:40, and tossed the wicker and explosives over the side. But they snagged on an oarlock and hung just above the water. The timer read 0:32. He lifted Lucinda and Macduff and pushed them both overboard, following them and grabbing Macduff's collar. Their hands and feet remained taped.

The drift boat, the snagged wicker man and explosives, and the man holding the terrified couple's heads above water were all floating at the same speed, the timer showing 0:27. The man glanced ahead; the drift boat was being pulled right in a current that divided as it approached a tree hanging over the eastern bank. Known as a sweeper and a hazard to drift boats, the tree had not come free of its roots. It hung over the water, its branches like protruding fingers waiting to grab any drift boat and its crew that came too close.

As they all passed under the tree, 0:22 showing on the clock, the man managed to grab a branch. It was all he could do to hang on the tree with one hand while holding Macduff's collar with the other. Lucinda was still tightly taped to Macduff. The boat began to gain distance from them, but the timer was down to 0:13, and the man was concerned that the amount of explosives would blow bits of the boat across the water like tiny missiles.

"Take a deep breath. NOW!" he yelled, letting go of the tree and diving under, pulling the two and hearing the muffled explosion. When they surfaced, two hundred feet in front of them debris was blazing, and pieces of the demolished drift boat were scattered across the river. The man was exhausted as he pulled the two ashore twenty feet beyond the Paradise access. For the three it *was* paradise.

Within minutes a couple from a nearby home reached them and called 911. The two ran back to their house to get blankets and some hot coffee. When they returned Lucinda and Macduff were sitting trembling, their tape removed, and the man had disappeared. Lucinda said he was there one minute and gone the next. Maybe he had run to get his vehicle. The Wrangler was gone from the bridge.

But he never came back.

60

LUCINDA AND I WERE TAKEN to the hospital in Livingston and, against our wishes, kept overnight for "observation." We shared a room and spent much of the night in our separate hospital beds, hooked up to unknown machines that sent tiny peaks and valleys moving across a screen, and sometimes scared us from welcome sleep as one machine ticked like the timer on the explosives. We lay facing each other. Little was spoken; we were content with being alive and seeing that the other was safe.

After a breakfast of eggs and sausage that I downed in a few bites and Lucinda politely set aside, Ken Rangley walked into the room, neither smiling nor speaking.

"You look tired and uninspiring," Lucinda noted to our friend.

"I'm relieved you're both safe, but concerned how we managed to totally screw up the past two days. . . . There's no excuse; we blew it. And I lost a deputy. Plus, Markel and Ellsworth-Kent haven't been caught. In fact, there doesn't seem to be one lead that will help us find them."

"Ken," broke in Lucinda, "it was a terrible thing to lose Erin. They had no reason to kill her."

"The first explosion that killed our deputy was a diversion. And it worked. It redirected our attention to the Jensen's Spring Creek to Carter Bridge area. Then yesterday they struck—unchallenged—at Mill Creek. . . . But you're wrong about Erin."

"Wrong? What do you mean?" asked Lucinda.

Standing in the doorway, her diminutive body overwhelmed by the door frame, was Erin Giffin.

"Hey, Macduffy. Hi, Lucinda. It really is me."

"It can't be," I exclaimed. She came over to my bed and gave me a hug.

"It's *me*, Macduffy."

"How . . . What happened? You were blown up on the river the day before yesterday?"

"I hope I don't look *that* bad. . . . But we did lose a deputy—tragically. Karen Larson. She's worked with us since Jimbo Shaw was imprisoned.

"I was scheduled to go to Gardiner on Friday," explained Erin. "In the morning I was in my office when my sister called from California. She's an ophthalmologist. I had cataracts. I didn't want Ken or others to know, including you two. Vanity. I'm a bit young to have cataracts. My sister said she could remove the cataracts if I could fly out immediately. After the Gardiner meeting I had three days off. It was perfect for having the procedure and keeping it secret.

"Karen was standing in my open doorway while I was talking to my sister. Karen interrupted and said, 'Let me do the Gardiner meeting. You go ahead to California. I won't say a word!' I agreed. I flew to San Diego and had the procedure the next day. There was a little problem, and I was kept for two nights for observation. I couldn't read newspapers or see TV. I couldn't see to make a phone call. Anyway, San Diego isn't too interested in what happens in Livingston, Montana; they have their own sensational stories."

"When did Ken discover you were alive and Karen was dead?"

"Not until I returned and went to the office yesterday. I hadn't learned about Karen's death."

"Wasn't Karen reported missing?"

"No, she was scheduled to attend the annual Montana County Sheriffs' Association meeting in Missoula over the weekend. There are a lot of people there. She wasn't missed because she was preregistered. They sent her everything she needed—program, name tag, and a registration receipt. As soon as she paid, they didn't check whether or not she showed up."

"On Monday morning when Karen didn't arrive," Ken interrupted, "but Erin walked in, we were overwhelmed. As Erin explained the changes to us, I immediately knew Karen must have been the victim on the 20th near Jensen's Spring Creek. That was confirmed when she never showed up."

"I can't believe this," exclaimed Lucinda. "You're alive. Macduff's alive. I'm alive. There *must* be a guardian angel!"

Ken cut in, "Before we get too excited, remember that we don't know where Markel and Ellsworth-Kent have gone. The FBI has sent word to various methods of transportation they might try to use—airplanes, trains, busses, and rental cars. U.S. Customs has them in its computers. They must be holding up somewhere, maybe even in Paradise Valley."

"They've killed five people," Lucinda commented. "They can't hide forever. Erin's announced murder has finally brought the matter to the front page of the nation's major papers." She held up the previous day's *N.Y. Times*, which had a front-page report headlined: SUMMER SOLSTICE WICKER MAN AND MISTLETOE MURDER IS FIFTH IN LAST YEAR IN THREE WESTERN STATES. "They'll be apprehended with this kind of coverage. When last night's details appear in the papers, even more so."

I hadn't said much, but it wasn't disinterest. I was overwhelmed by relief, happiness, excitement, and especially lying looking at Lucinda's lucid green eyes and seeing glimpses of her grin.

"Erin," suggested Ken, "We better let these two have some rest, or do whatever they'll do when we leave and close the door!"

"One thing before you two go," asked Lucinda, "Where do we go from here?"

"I have some ideas," replied Ken. "But they can wait."

61

A WEEK LATER Lucinda and I were back at my cabin. Ken was satisfied that Markel and Ellsworth-Kent were not an immediate threat. Markel was caught on camera four days after the solstice trying to book a flight from Los Angeles to Brazil. She fled when the ticket agent asked her to wait a minute while she checked flights and left the counter and disappeared into a back room. Ellsworth-Kent was arrested in New Orleans the same day for fighting in a bar. He was booked, kept overnight, and—incredibly—released the next morning moments before the New Orleans police read information about him they had received a week earlier. They haven't caught him.

Wuff is lying in her bed, staring at Lucinda in the kitchen, unaware that she narrowly escaped being an orphan-Sheltie in need of another rescue. I'm sitting at our small kitchen table still amazed that I'm sitting at our small kitchen table or anywhere else for that matter. Not one of us shows any scars from the killings. My drift boats remain unscathed in the boat shed, waiting for me to take either boat on the river. *Any* river.

"Is that a celebratory breakfast you're working on?" I asked.

"You can call it that. After the junk food we ate at my guest house while we were hiding, I'm responsible as your nutritionist to restore your health."

"You can restore my mental health with some sausage and bacon, plus some . . ."

Lucinda interrupted, "You're first getting a plate of fruit—a banana, a cut up orange from Florida, and melon. Then you get . . ."

One interruption deserves another, I thought, and argued my case. "I need red meat to build my strength."

"You'll grill us bison burgers for lunch. For now, I'm more concerned with your HDL, LDL, Triglycerides, and PSA.

"If you were appointed Surgeon General for the country, the fast food industry would collapse."

"True, but after a few months we'd be less obese, have lower blood pressure, and live longer."

"I'm not sure I want the last; I'm terrified of what's ahead for me being around you. . . I think I'll go out on the porch and have a cigarette."

"You don't smoke!"

"Then a double Gentleman Jack—please?"

"Not till after five. This is breakfast."

"I'll never make it to five."

62

DAN WILSON RETURNED to D.C. from Montana a few days after the summer solstice events. Elsbeth Carson was in town and expected for her meeting. She seemed like a fine young woman from what Dan knew about her and their telephone conversation, but he didn't know how Macduff Brooks would take to her. He has a new life that includes some high risk, and he has a new companion. As he pondered this information over his third cup of coffee, his secretary brought Elsbeth into his office.

Rising from his desk and sitting with her in a less formal section of his office, he said, "Miss Carson, how can I help you?"

"I think you know, Mr. Wilson, that you are the only link between my father, Maxwell Hunt, and whatever name he is using. I would like to know his name and where he lives."

"What do you plan to do if you have this information?"

"Go see him."

"And just move in with him?"

"I think that would be for us to decide. But the answer is 'no.' I'm about to start college in Maine in August and have a life ahead of me. I can get by on my own. I was raised by two exceptional and caring people whom I shall always love. Gregory Carson was my father for almost two decades."

"Then your interest in knowing about Maxwell Hunt is merely curiosity?"

"No, far more than that. Apparently, he is my biological father. I want to know him better than two brief conversations with you and Dean Perry. That doesn't mean I want to live with him. And I'm not asking for a handout. My parents—the Carsons—left me funds to go to any college anywhere in the country. In April I was awarded a full four-year academic scholarship to the University of Maine, which I've accepted. That leaves more than enough funds for any graduate school, if I'm interested. I'm *not* intending to impose myself on whoever Maxwell Hunt is now known as."

"Are you fully aware of the risk I place your father in if I tell you about him?"

"I'm not. What I know is what Dean Perry told me at the law college last month."

"And that is?"

"About the Guatemalan and Sudanese former students who were after Professor Hunt. . . . "

"*Are* after him," Dan interrupted. "They have been quiet for the past months, for reasons I won't go into. I can say they remain a very serious threat to Mac . . . Maxwell. And to anyone close to him. That includes his fiancée and would include you."

"Fiancée?" Elsbeth asked.

"Yes. He has been engaged for more or less a year. There's no wedding date set. Does that change your interest in him?"

"Not a bit. I want to know him, not to intrude upon his life. My biological mother died nearly two decades ago. My father has a right to his own life."

"I will tell you a few things. Your father was a prominent law professor. He's now a fishing guide. Does that mean anything to you?"

"That's somewhat surprising. I would have thought that having lost my mother the way it happened, he would never fish again."

"What if he chose to be a guide because he believed that his pursuers would think as you, that one thing he would never do is anything related to fishing or small boats?"

"He guides in the kind of boat that killed my mother?"

"It wasn't a boat that killed your mother. It was an incompetent guide."

"It sounds as though my father has had a hard life. I feel sorry for him. All the more reason for seeing him."

"The last thing he wants is sympathy. He is happy with his work guiding and very much loves his companion."

"I should like to attend their wedding. I do want him happy. Do you think my meeting him would not be a happy moment?"

"From the brief time we have met, I believe it would be a very happy time."

"Then will you help?"

"I will do one thing. I will talk to his fiancée. She is quite protective about him."

"Is he not very strong physically or mentally?"

"I don't mean to imply that. I think I need to tell you more. Your father has been involved in some very tragic and serious murders related to his guiding."

"Murders? What do you mean?"

Over the next hour Dan told Elsbeth about Macduff's life, aware that he was disclosing enough that Elsbeth might identify her father's name and location with an online search. The more he disclosed, the more he knew Elsbeth was entitled to meet her father.

"Miss Carson," Dan said as he finished telling Elsbeth about the incidents on the Snake, the Yellowstone, and other rivers, always referring to them by false names, "I think you can understand the risk in being around your father. There are four people whose exact locations are not known by us, but who would like to see your father dead."

"As I said, all the more reason to see him."

"Then you will. . . . Your father is known as Macduff Brooks. His fiancée is Lucinda Lang, which is not an assumed name. They live mostly in his log cabin in southwest Montana in the summer and in a small cottage in Northeast Florida in the winter. I'm going to give you his telephone number and that for Lucinda."

They talked for another hour. There was laughter and a few tears, but Elsbeth seemed to glow with the increasing knowledge of her father and Lucinda.

"Before you go," Dan said as he walked her to the front entry of the building, "I think you should also know that Macduff and Lucinda have become my personal friends. I have considerable respect for both of them and don't wish to harm our friendship or increase their risk. And I am reluctant to place you at risk."

Elsbeth thanked Dan and turned to walk away, but came back and hugged Dan tightly, whispering in his ear, "Thank you so very much. My father owes his life to you."

In her hotel room that evening, Elsbeth sat by the window, looking out at the lighted Washington Monument, and thought carefully about what she had learned about her father. Should she call him? Talk to Lucinda first? Have Dan call them? Simply show up at their door in Montana?

Although she had learned much about her father, she thought it would be good to talk to Lucinda, who obviously had come to love him, and shared difficult and dangerous times with him. She would better know whether and how to approach him.

63

THE DAY AFTER ELSBETH RETURNED to Maine, she waited until noon and called the Montana number Dan had given her for Lucinda's cell phone. She hoped her father was on a river guiding or doing something that kept him away from the cabin.

Lucinda was in the yard with Wuff. Macduff was guiding, not on the Yellowstone but on the Snake in Jackson Hole, helping John Kirby during some of the busiest days of a good fishing summer. Macduff didn't want to take on the Yellowstone just yet, nor the Madison, the Clark, the North Platte, nor the Henry's Fork. The memories of the past year lingered, wrapped tightly around wherever in his brain his memories were stored.

Lucinda saw the call was from a Maine area code, and said, "Is this Elsbeth?"

"Yes, Miss Lang."

"Call me Lucinda, please. . . . Dan Wilson called yesterday and suggested we talk before your dad is told about this. I know he is going to be happier than I've ever seen him."

"Is he an unhappy person?"

"He's different, Elsbeth. It started with your mother's death, and what he was certain was your death as well. He was very depressed. So much so that he withdrew and taught his classes, but rarely socialized. Perhaps worst of all for his health, he drank too much.

Your father kept busy writing, lecturing, and consulting abroad. He was apparently happier when he was abroad. I think he was better when he was away from the house they lived in, but he couldn't bring himself to sell it."

"But Dan said he loves you, partly because you've taught him to enjoy life."

"With the help of some friends here."

"Dan also said you two are engaged. Will you marry soon?"

"We've been together about six years. We met some eight years ago. We've been engaged for a little over a year. He doesn't need to be pushed. He has some issues he'd like to resolve that Dan may have told you about."

"Juan Pablo Herzog and Abdul Khaliq Isfahani?"

"Yes, and more. The two who killed four of Macduff's acquaintances—and Karen Larsen—over the past year haven't been caught. They spent a year killing in preparation of their goal—to murder Macduff. They weren't successful but may not be finished."

"Dan said my father was not the only target; one of the two wanted him dead, but the more dangerous of the two was after you."

"Well . . . that's mostly right. But the person after me seemed more focused on the ceremonial part of the killings."

"But he killed *five* people. Could they all have been ceremonial?" Elsbeth asked.

"Mostly. Each was someone Macduff knew. The first four were not close friends. But the attempt on Erin Giffin's life three weeks ago was directed to a very dear friend. They were all symbolic killings, intended to frighten your father and me. They succeeded. Our last year was increasingly terrifying."

"He has a lot to work out, Lucinda. So do you. And he needs you. Maybe it's better for me to back off for some months until you think he's ready for the shock of seeing me. I could complete my first term or year of college and then talk to you again."

"No. It won't be a shock when he sees you. He's been deprived of your presence for nearly two decades. It shouldn't last a day longer. . . . Dan said you look exactly like your mother did when Macduff and she married. It will be the best moment of his life after the tragic loss of El."

"I don't think you're being fair to what you've done for him. I've been told that he barely survived when he thought you were gone after the shooting on the Snake River."

"Elsbeth. . . . Will you fly here Thursday? Macduff will be back that day from Jackson. I'll have you stay with our friend Erin when you arrive, and then, at a lunch we have planned the next day, we'll have your 'coming out.' Really your 'coming back.' Seeing you will be the best possible way to get a new start after what's happened the past few years. Your father's a local celebrity. But for some here not a welcome one."

64

LUCINDA WAS VISIBLY ANXIOUS the day I arrived from Jackson. After the long but always spiritually rewarding ride through the parks, I knew something preoccupied her. In the evening she knocked over and broke a wine glass on the porch. It didn't get any better the next day. She dropped a pan containing the first bacon and eggs she's cooked in a year. Wuff got to them on the floor before I did. After lunch I grabbed Lucinda's arm and looked straight at her eyes from no more than a foot away.

"What's troubling you?" I asked quietly. "Last night you broke your wine glass. You hardly slept; you were up walking about for hours. Now this morning you dropped a milk carton, bacon, and half-dozen eggs at breakfast. The rainbow trout for lunch was burned through. You've hardly said a word since I returned from Jackson. As a matter of fact, you were pretty quiet the morning I left four days ago. . . . Anything I can help with?"

"No Macduff. . . . I guess I'm not concentrating."

"Not concentrating! Next you'll burn down the cabin. I know you well enough to realize your mind is a million miles away." If I'd known more of her thoughts, I would have said seven hundred miles—she was thinking about a young woman in Maine who was about to enter my life.

"Macduff, Erin and Ken will be here tomorrow for lunch. Plus your attorney Wanda Groves and Judge Amy Becker. Should we be celebrating? Herzog, Isfahani, Ellsworth-Kent, and Merkel are out there somewhere not thinking pleasant thoughts about us."

"This will be mostly about Erin. We all thought she was gone. It's tragic to have lost her partner, Karen Larson. But I think the wicker man and mistletoe murders are over."

"But Hannah and Ellsworth-Kent are free. They may be through with using the wicker man and mistletoe symbols, but that doesn't mean they're through with us," I offered gently, not wanting to put a damper on her positive manner.

"Maybe our relief is only momentary, but it is good to have a few pleasant moments."

"Agreed. Now what are you making for supper?"

"You don't remember? You're taking me to Chico Hot Springs for dinner."

"When did I offer that?"

"You didn't. It just came to me."

65

LUNCH THE NEXT DAY included no discussion of either the five murders over the past dozen months or the killers who were free to try again. Lucinda still seemed preoccupied, but with the help of friends prepared a feast. There were dishes I couldn't hope to identify and wouldn't try. It was a time for the folks of Livingston to stay inside—Erin's and Ken's presence, plus Karen Larsen's loss, cut in half the sheriff's force patrolling the county.

I feel certain that Merkel and Ellsworth-Kent are no immediate worry. Furthermore, as far as we know Isfahani hasn't recovered from his newest reconstructive surgery in Switzerland, and Herzog has entered the race for the Guatemalan presidency. Attempting a murder wouldn't help his campaign.

Wanda has brought two Key Lime pies for dessert. She's never been to the Florida Keys and suggested they must be just around the corner from my Florida cottage. Being around the corner from St. Augustine actually means about 400 miles and seven to eight hours on the road. But the pies make me think of Florida. Lucinda and I are three months shy of leaving for the winter, but I already have visions of the salt marshes and swaying palms.

"Why *two* pies, Wanda?" I asked, "We're finished with lunch and haven't eaten one."

"Just wait," she said. "We have a surprise for you and Lucinda." She went to the front door, opened it, and there stood Dan Wilson, John Kirby, and Juan Santander."

"We heard there was a party," said John. Juan and I dropped everything and left Jackson early this morning."

"I decided yesterday to stay a few more days," confessed Dan. "I've been helping Jason Ivonski. It's been a tough first month for him as my new agent for Montana."

"Just when I thought the second pie was all for me!" I said feigning disappointment.

I had no sooner shut the front door when I heard another knock at the back door. Opening the door, I knew Wanda had put something illegal in the pie. Standing in the doorway was a young woman who was typecast to play El in the story of my life. I was speechless. In the next half-minute I had flashing visions of many of the best days of my life.

"Can I help you?" I stammered.

"Yes, very much. My name is Elsbeth Hunt. I'm your daughter!"

EPILOGUE

Elsbeth felt strange after having read three manuscripts by her father, ending with her becoming a live participant at the very end of the third. She was, of course, several decades older than when she first met her father a few days after the end of the summer solstice murders. That was many years ago.

Reuniting with her father had begun a new part of her life. She often thought about her 'adoptive' parents, Gregory and Margaret Carson. She could not have had a more loving father and mother than the two who raised her until they died when she was a late teen and she soon thereafter met her birth father for the first time.

She made more tea and sat on the porch, looking at the three manuscripts on her table. They made a thousand letters; they were written in Macduff Brooks' words and filled in so many gaps in the life he and Lucinda had led before Elsbeth entered their lives. On many days Lucinda and Macduff were subjected to dangers they did not wish to share with Elsbeth. She was beginning her adult life when she first met her father and was about to enter college, which would keep her away from Lucinda and her father for much of the next few years.

Elsbeth assumed that there would be no further manuscripts. But she was unsure of that because her father had enjoyed writing the first three for her. There were many things yet to say. Elsbeth was not always told the full story of the different episodes Lucinda and her father lived after he and his daughter were reunited. At the close of the third manuscript, all the murders had been solved, but only half the perpetrators, Park Salisbury and Jimbo Shaw, had been killed or caught. Four remained free: two were under surveillance—Herzog and Isfahani—and two had disappeared—Markel and Ellsworth-Kent.

The day after Elsbeth had read the third manuscript, she received a letter from her father.

Ms. Elsbeth Hunt Brooks
14 Seahorse Way
Captiva Island, Florida 33924

Dearest Daughter,

In another month I will have moved to join you and likely forever left this vast open land between the mountain ranges. It has been more than forty years since I set foot in Paradise Valley as Macduff Brooks, still struggling to accept the loss of El and you. Lucinda saved me and taught me to live again, convincing me that I could love her and El without detracting anything from either.

When you entered my life, there were moments when seeing you made the pain of losing El all the more unbearable. Only with your help added to that provided by Lucinda have I been able to feel fulfilled.

I have now lost El and Lucinda. El suffered great pain; Lucinda passed peacefully in her sleep. You share so much of both El and Lucinda. For me to have some years with you is more than I could hope for.

With this letter, we end our cross-country correspondence, exchanging it for what will be many cross-table conversations.

Packed boxes stand waiting for the trek to Captiva. There is some sadness and some happiness in leaving all my fishing things to the Federation of Fly Fishers here in Livingston. I have saved one item, a bamboo fishing rod I made for Lucinda only a year after we met. I know you have the second bamboo rod I made for you not long after you arrived on my doorstep from Maine.

I must get back to packing; the moving van will be here tomorrow.

Your loving father,
Macduff

Elsbeth set aside the letter; she, too, had things to do in preparation for her father's arrival in less than a week.

AUTHOR'S NOTE

I enjoy hearing from readers. You may reach me at:

macbrooks.mwgordon@gmail.com

Or through my website:

www.mwgordonnovels.com

E-mail will be answered within the week received, unless I am on a book signing tour or towing *Osprey* to fish somewhere.

Because of viruses, I do not download attachments sent with your e-mails. And please do not add my e-mail to any lists suggesting for whom I should vote, to whom I should give money, what I should buy, what I should read, or especially what I should write next about Macduff Brooks.

My website lists coming appearances for readings, talk programs, and signings.